Tasting Temptation

ARIA GLAZKI

ANIKA PRESS

TASTING TEMPTATION Copyright © 2016
by Aria Glazki

Storytelling is an art. Copyright exists to protect the rights of storytellers and all artists, while encouraging them to create the works which enrich our lives and culture. Unauthorized copying, reproduction, or distribution of this book in any format, other than brief excerpts for review purposes, is theft of the author's intellectual property. All rights reserved.

This book is a work of fiction. Names, characters, places, and incidents are either products of the author's imagination or are used fictitiously. The author makes no claims to, but instead acknowledges the trademarked status and trademark owners of any word marks mentioned in this work of fiction.

ISBN: 978-1-943572-06-9
Copyright registration number:
TX0008359242

To the friends who won't let me shatter

One

"Zip me up?" Gina asked, coming out of the dressing room in her maid-of-honor dress.

Roger dropped his cell phone beside her purse and stepped up behind her. "Can you *believe* Sabella's getting married, and we don't even have dates to the wedding?"

She shot him a chiding look over her shoulder. "Sabella deserves her happily ever after." And being date-free suited Gina just fine.

Roger tugged the zipper up then resettled her hair. "I know! She does. But, seriously. Us? Stag at her wedding?" He plopped back onto the plush cream bench across from the angled trio of mirrors. "Unacceptable!"

"Ever the drama queen." Gina stepped onto the raised ivory platform to assess the alterations, trying not to look too hard at her reflection.

Roger actually stuck his tongue out at her.

"Weddings are supposed to be great for meeting people," she reminded, turning toward him.

"Easy for you to say, Miss 'I can pick up any man I want without even crooking a finger.'"

Gina shrugged the sudden tension from her shoulders. The last thing she wanted was to be tied to another man. "There are worse fates than a trip to Sonoma for a wedding, Rodge. Even without a date."

His lips found the impeccable pout that always made Sabella jealous. "You're grouchy today."

"That's 'cause you're extra whiny today," she shot back lightly, trying to sound normal.

He sighed, twisting open the cap to his diet iced tea. The salads they'd picked up for lunch on their way to the boutique waited patiently beside him. Gina swept her hands out, silently asking about the dress. Roger's nod of approval ended with a head tilt.

"Look," she said, checking the hemline in the mirror one more time before stepping down, "you're the one who broke up with his hottie boyfriend because he got bored."

His shoulders and eyebrows lifted with choreographed innocence. "What can I say? I'm hard to keep satisfied."

"Well, then. Good thing you work for me and not the other way around." She softened the comment with a smile. Roger's mouth still dropped into a nearly perfect "o." Rolling her eyes at his dramatics, Gina turned away and swept her hair to the side so he could undo the zipper. He obliged silently, and she walked back to the dressing room to change.

"Speaking of work," he called from the other side of the heavy brocade curtains. "You leave Saturday, right?"

"You just can't wait to get me out of the office." She paused, smoothing her palm over the dark-purple chiffon. Sabella and Kane's wedding was something *good*. And Gina couldn't wait to see her best friend outside of a computer screen again.

"I like being in charge," Roger admitted, drawing her back to the present.

"Good thing we're wrapping up the layout today," she said, slipping the dress off to change back into her knotted skirt and Rebecca Taylor top. "So you'll only be in charge of brainstorming ideas for the next issue." She was mostly kidding. Roger was a fantastic assistant, and he was really developing a good eye.

"And what have I ever done to you?" She would have bet he was pouting again. "Anyway, I was *going* to say that you could use the break."

"Well that's true." Gina tucked back a flyaway strand of hair before taking the dress and rejoining him in the main room. "But since I don't particularly want to lose this job, we better get back to work."

"Yeah, yeah. It would be nice though, snagging a hunky millionaire at the wedding. Just think of all the clothes we could buy… Oh, and fashion week!" He fixed her with a solemn stare. "Promise me, if you ever marry rich and go to fashion week in Paris or New York, you'll take me with you."

A chuckle bubbled from between her lips. Roger might be fickle with men, but he was undeniably devoted to fashion. "I'll think about it," she said. Not that she would ever date a wealthy man again.

"You're cruel," he accused, holding out her purse.

"Have to keep you motivated. The department gets strong enough, we won't need some benefactor to pay our way to fashion week."

"And meanwhile"—he sighed—"we settle for Sonoma."

"Wait 'til you see this place, Rodge. It definitely beats New York."

Two

"Okay, I am officially stealing you away," Gina declared, steering Sabella away from the bevy of cars that had somehow managed to arrive all together. Gina had driven up with the bride-to-be's sister, Trisha. They'd beaten the rest of the bridal party by a half hour, but then Gina had learned to drive in Boston.

Sabella craned her neck toward all the activity behind her. "What about my dress?"

Sighing, Gina stopped, pulled her sunglasses from her nose and into her hair, and scanned the milling crowd until her eyes landed on a curvy blonde in paint-splattered jeans. "Hey, Trisha?"

She spun toward them while everyone else continued unloading.

"Would you please make sure that no disaster befalls Sab's dress between here and our suite?"

Trisha nodded vigorously, rolling her eyes for good measure, and shooed them away.

Sabella laughed and looped her arm through Gina's. "Okay, what about your dresses?"

"We already hung them up. And anyway, you shouldn't be worrying about that." Gina led them to the terrace where various employees were setting up round tables and chairs. They skirted the bustling activity, keeping close to the wrought-iron fence that blocked off the overhang. Gently rolling vineyards splayed out beneath them in a blend of greens.

Sabella's shoulders dropped as she exhaled, leaning over the railing. "It's almost quiet here."

Gina chuckled. They'd spent five days surrounded by Sabella's and Kane's families, and Kane's bandmates, all in a lovely four-bedroom home in Mountain View. "Cramped" didn't quite cover it. The craziness of last-minute planning hadn't helped, adding to the chaos. The drive up had been the most relaxing time Gina'd had all week, until now.

She inhaled the crisp air, letting the peace envelop her. "It's so beautiful."

Ignoring the bustle behind them, they gazed out at the neatly organized rows below, glinting under the sun. Sabella'd fallen in love the second they saw a virtual tour of Cavaliere Vineyards. "Chivalry vineyards" she had not-quite-translated when they'd found it online. With the large yet secluded terrace opening onto this breathtaking view, it was an undeniably gorgeous setting for a wedding.

"You know?" Sabella turned toward her, smiling. "I'm kind of excited."

"Kind of? You're *kind of* excited for your wedding? Maybe we should call it off."

Sabella's head tilted slightly to the side, her lips pursing. "You know what I mean. Everything has been so hectic lately, but now that we're actually here... This is really going to happen."

"I can't believe we pulled this thing off in less than a year."

Sabella hummed her agreement.

A breeze wound its way around their shoulders, and Gina straightened, exhaling. "All right, I'd say it's time for a welcome to Sonoma drink. Unless there's something you need to tell me?" she half-teased.

"A glass of wine sounds lovely," Sabella answered, trying to keep a straight face at the suggestion.

Elbows linked, they strode up to the secluded balcony bar with its own magnificent view. A few of the winery's patrons surrounded them, seated at wrought-iron tables with partially filled glasses and tiny cubes of cheese.

"Riesling okay?" Sabella asked. "Or a white Zin? They have this really interesting one with a bit of a raspberry flavor."

"Shouldn't I be the one buying?" Gina offered, picking up the tasting menu.

"I think the least I owe you is a glass of wine, Gi, with all your help, and putting up with everyone."

If anything, Gina owed Sabella—everything. "Your family's a piece of cake compared to mine, as you well know," she brushed off. "Or have you blocked any memory of the trauma?"

"Oh, shush you. Your family's wonderful."

"Loud. Overbearing. Completely nuts."

Sabella crooked an eyebrow.

"And, yes, wonderful," Gina agreed. "But you didn't have to invite them, you know."

"Of course I did. And anyway, it'll save you at least one of your mother's guilt trips about visiting home."

She had a point. Maybe.

As the bartender set out a couple of glasses, efficiently filling them with Riesling, Sabella added, "You know she's cooking brunch tomorrow?"

"You're kidding." Not that Gina was all that surprised. Her mother was physically incapable of not feeding everyone around her. "How did she bully you into it?"

"Bully me into accepting her free labor and delicious food?" They moved toward a lonely table in the shade, resettling a pair of chairs to face the view before lowering into them. "Maybe we'll get lucky, and she'll even make truffles," Sabella said after tasting the wine.

Gina took a long sip rather than answer, letting the pleasantly crisp white flow over her taste buds before swallowing.

"I tried to talk her out of it, since she's our *guest*, and Kane offered to help out, of course, but she wouldn't have it." Sabella smirked. "She said it'd be good practice."

"Oh? Is Donny getting married?" Gina asked, deadpan.

Sabella chuckled. "It's too bad your brothers couldn't make it."

Gina hummed noncommittally. Annoying as he was at fifteen, Donny always made them laugh. Her older brother, Gerardo, wasn't half bad either. She did love and miss her family. She just usually loved them most in small doses or when they were on the other side of the country. But her best friend wanted them here, and the least Gina could do was ensure this weekend was all about Sabella.

"Gina, you've barely eaten. Are you sick?"

She'd had two servings of everything. "Ma, I ate plenty, I promise. And it was delicious. I've really missed your cooking." She squeezed her mom's familiar hand. "Sabella's lucky you made brunch."

"We all are," Bobby, Kane's bass guitarist, chimed in from across the table, picking up an empty bowl. "Thanks, Mrs. Sabatino."

Her mother's cheeks rounded as a blush spread over them. This wasn't that big a group by her mom's standards, but brunch really had been amazing. Gina would have bet everyone ate too much, unable to resist the tantalizing assortment. Their tables were still covered in nearly emptied dishes, which the groomsmen were slowly clearing.

Trisha broke away from the bride's and groom's families and swished over. "So everything's set for tonight, right?" She popped a lingering truffle into her mouth.

"I think so. Could you just confirm the limo one more time?" Gina asked.

"Oh, yeah. No problem."

"Beatrice, are you coming?" Sabella's mother called. She never seemed to shout, though her voice always carried as far as it needed to. It was as impressive as it was intimidating. Nothing at all like Gina's mom, who preferred to rely on guilt trips.

Trisha forced a smile. "Family bonding time." The families were heading up to Calistoga for the afternoon, though Trisha had promised to ensure they'd be back before Sabella's surprise bachelorette party. "You sure you're all set with treats and the cards and everything?" she asked.

"Treats? What treats?" Gina's mom interrupted, stacking empty plates for Kane's bandmates to take away.

"For the bachelorette party, Ma. I need to run out and pick some stuff up, but it'll be taken care of," she assured Trisha.

"Okay. Thanks again, Mrs. Sabatino. Brunch was unbelievable," Trisha said before hurrying off.

"I will come help you, with the treats, Gina," her mom declared.

"You didn't come here to work, Ma. You should take Dad, and go explore. It's beautiful out here."

"I can spend some time with you, and help you, and your papi and I can explore tonight, when you girls are out. Or do you not want to spend any time with your mother, even though you never come out and visit."

Gina didn't even pretend that was a question. "You know I'd love your help. I just don't want you to miss out on seeing

Sonoma. But I bet everyone would love it if you have some more of those truffles stashed away somewhere."

"I have extra chocolate, I'll make more for you girls, but I need sugar. We finish here, and we go to the store, okay?"

"You're leaving me?" Gina's dad chimed in with a smile, coming back to their table, drink in hand.

Gina threw her arm around his sturdy shoulders. "I'm stealing her away, just for a bit."

He chuckled, returning her embrace. "Mi passerotta. Why haven't you been home? Ci manchi."

"I know, papi, I miss you guys, too." She'd spent the December holidays with Sabella's family, to help plan the wedding. And because after last summer, she'd needed more time before facing her family's overly perceptive gazes. "I'll come visit soon, I promise."

"Ai." Her mom's hand landed on her shoulder, squeezing gently. "She was busy, planning all this. And now, I'm here to help. So, let's go."

The groomsmen had already insisted on taking care of the dishes, and there wasn't a point in arguing anyway. Gina kissed her dad's cheek then looped her arm through her mom's. Sometimes, it was more than nice having them around.

Three

Two hours later, Gina had changed her mind. Logically, she knew her mom meant well, but the poking and prodding questions about her life, and settling down, or moving home were enough to drive her up a wall. And then she'd been kicked out of the borrowed kitchen! Not that she didn't have plenty to do before tonight, and it was undeniably sweet of her mom to make all those chocolate-dipped snacks for them, but still.

Gina stalled in the vaulted entryway and debated—hallway one would take her back to the guest rooms, all filled this weekend with the bridal party, plus Gina's parents and Kane's manager; hallway two opened onto the main tasting room. It wasn't like having a glass of wine in the afternoon in the middle of wine country would be particularly notable. And she could use some time to wind down, so she didn't destroy tonight's goodies when putting them together. *Tasting room it is.*

The room was empty, but with the gorgeous weather, most visitors probably preferred the outdoor terrace. Gina chose a stool by the bar, absently tapping her fingers on the wood as she waited. Various wine-themed knickknacks covered display tables and shelves around the room. The faintest smell of wood somehow still lingered, though the construction was lacquered and far from new. Maybe they pumped it in for atmosphere.

She flattened her palm on the bar and sighed. Maybe the emptiness was a sign that a drink was a bad idea.

Before she could make her mind up to leave, a barman came out of the back room, carrying a fresh case, which he set down with a clunk. His eyes raked over her torso before his lips pulled into a crooked smile. "You look like you could use a drink."

"How extraordinarily perceptive."

His smile grew, crinkling around his eyes. "Maybe if you're nice to me, I'll pour you one."

Gina exhaled, focusing on the man before her. This was a game she'd mastered long ago, even if she was a bit out of practice. "Maybe if you're nice to me, I'll let you."

He strode closer. "What'll it be?"

"What are you offering?"

He picked up a towel and wiped off his hands before running his fingers over the bottlenecks arrayed between them. His faded tee shirt stretched slightly across his chest and shoulders as he moved. Deftly, he spun a glass from its spot out of sight and placed it silently on the bar. He uncorked a fresh bottle with a pop. A deep red gurgled into the glass.

Gina lifted it and took a long sip.

The barman's eyebrow crooked. "Glad I didn't pour you the good stuff."

She set the glass back down, half-drained, and shrugged. "I'll be paying you for it, regardless."

"Wine isn't about the money. It's about the experience." He fitted the bottle with one of those tops that control how much is poured at a time.

"Or the goal."

Friendly eyes caught her in their gaze. "There are better ways to de-stress, you know."

"Are you saying I seem stressed?"

"You're part of the bridal party, aren't you?" Another smile tugged at his lips. "Stress comes with the territory."

She leaned slightly over the bar. "And you're offering to make it all better?"

He sobered as his eyes trailed over all the skin exposed by her summery top. "How could I deny you?"

Gina traced the stem of her wineglass with her fingers, knowing exactly where his mind would go. "Is this a service you frequently provide, then?"

"Maybe I should start." He leaned onto his elbows on the bar, so their faces were almost even.

Gina's lips parted as she considered the man before her. Dark hair lay tousled, with stray locks drifting over his forehead. Symmetrical eyes demanded attention, easily holding their own with the strong line of his pronounced nose that drew her gaze to gently curving lips, set in a wash of stubble that flowed over a crisply defined jaw. De-stressing definitely didn't sound like a bad idea, if they played on her terms.

His eyebrows lifted in challenge.

She stood, picking up her wine, and scooped her purse off the stool beside her without breaking eye contact. He straightened and gestured to the far end of the bar. Her heels clicked on the stone floor as they moved toward it. The door he'd entered through was still open.

"After you," his voice sounded next to her.

"Aren't you going to get in trouble for this?"

Amusement or something like it flashed in his eyes. "I'll risk it."

Anticipation tingled through her. A short staircase led into a cellar of sorts, brightly lit by sunlight streaming through the high windows. Ignoring the footsteps that followed hers, Gina laid her purse on a stack of boxes. Glass in hand, she strode to the nearest wine rack, examining the wooden vees that separated the various vintages without really seeing them. She could handle the bartender, she reminded herself.

He came up behind her, and she casually took another sip. He brushed her hair away from her upper back, exposing the ties of her halter top and skin. His lips came to the curve of her shoulder, and the wine glass drifted down to her side. Warm fingers worked it from hers, and he stepped away to set it aside.

Gina turned to watch him as he moved back to her with an effortlessly comfortable gait. When he reached her, Gina tilted her chin up, and he obediently joined their lips. Heat from his body combined with the velvety touch, but slow surrender wasn't what she wanted. Palms splayed on his upper chest, she deepened the kiss, angling against his mouth. He followed swiftly, one hand cupping her head as the other landed over her ribs.

His tongue tangled with hers, easily finding the right balance between timid and overbearing, underscored by the light scrape of stubble. *Good kisser.* He led her backward as their tongues danced, and Gina's palms explored the muscles covered by his shirt.

His hand left her ribs, and he stopped the backward motion. A soft impact went through his shoulder as she looped her hands at his back. His lips broke from hers to tease a pattern down her neck, bristle scraping delightfully against her skin, sending shocks of sensation to replace the stress. Her head fell gently to the wall behind her, cushioned by his hand. Air chilled her skin as his mouth lifted away.

Gina opened her eyes. Had he changed his mind? He tugged her away from the wall, still bracing against it, and she lowered her arms, waiting for the explanation that didn't actually matter.

"Can't have you all scratched up for the wedding," he murmured above her.

Curving her lips with a confidence she didn't quite feel, she pressed her palm into his chest and pushed him in an arc until he bumped into the uneven wall. He smiled, settling his hands over her hips as she stepped nearer. Their mouths met again, melding together, and his fingers dipped under her top. He hesitated for the briefest moment before sliding one hand up. Her barely B-cup breasts meant she could forego bras, so his palm met skin, and his thumb brushed her nipple, sending a shiver through her.

Steeped in missed sensations, she broke their kiss to catch her breath. He brought both hands back to her ribs and lifted, pushing away from the wall so she could wrap her legs around him. Bumps in his pockets and a larger, much more intriguing lump pressed against her through the thin fabric of her skirt. He kissed the base of her neck, and she arched her back to encourage him lower. His tongue trailed circles down until he met the draped fabric of her top.

Bracing on his shoulders, she shifted her hips over him, and he groaned, the sound vibrating through her. His hands moved down to cup the back of her thighs, but he lifted his head. Gina ground her hips against him again.

"Dammit," he muttered, leaning away though his thumbs still slowly traced over her thighs.

She blew her breath out, unwrapping her legs. *So much for stress relief.* These little pauses were making her even more antsy.

Darkened brown eyes met her gaze. "No condom."

"Not a very well-thought-out plan, then, was it?"

"Guess not."

Silently, she turned away from him and walked over to her purse. Voices from the bar echoed down to them. He strode to the mini staircase and shut the door, pulling keys from his pocket. She plucked a condom from a hidden compartment, watching him. He left the keys in the lock. Mentally shaking off the intruding anxiety, she held up the tiny packet between two fingers.

He closed the distance between them, then snatched the condom and recaptured her mouth. She focused on the pleasant slip of their lips, the friction of their tongues, the delicious scrape of his stubble, the scent of him she couldn't quite place. Despite the interruptions, there was still a chance.

No strings. No commitments. No lasting connection.

Just some hopefully decent sex.

His hand played at the back of her neck, and suddenly the fabric of her top drooped, sliding to reveal her to the air and to him. He lifted her again, holding her slightly suspended as his lips closed over her breast. Gina's fingers dug into his biceps, her starved body drinking the sensation. She'd only been with a couple guys since last summer, and other than Kane's drummer, they had been utterly disappointing, further damping her faltering desire.

But the barman's gentle sucking stoked a buried blaze. He found another wall, leaning back as he wrapped an arm around her waist and slipped the other hand between her thighs, pulling the fabric of her skirt out of the way. The teasing licking shifted smoothly to her other breast. His fingers barely brushed against her as he fumbled between her legs, and then he pushed aside the wisp of almost-there fabric that was her thong and thrust inside.

Gina gasped as he stretched her, the sudden pressure bucking her against him. He recaptured her lips for a deep kiss that mimicked the rhythm of his hips. The fabric of his tee shirt rubbed her breasts as their bodies slipped together. Fingers still between her thighs flicked over her, tightening her around him. She braced one hand against the rough stone behind him, lengthening the timing of her movement, but soon his fingers threw it off in a shiver of pleasure, and his hips took over. He lessened their kiss, brushing their lips together as their breath mingled and their eyes met.

Pressure built between her thighs, but he maintained the relentless rhythm, stroking and circling until she broke their bare kiss to duck her head into the crook of his shoulder. His arm tightened around her waist, and she clenched her muscles in response, prompting a deeper groan. His rhythm faltered, and she smiled, until another flick of his fingers stole her breath and her control. He lasted through the first waves of her pleasure then stilled, spilling inside the thin barrier separating them.

She waited 'til their breath slowed and his arm slackened, then lifted away from him. His lips brushed her temple before he let her go, and Gina turned away as they both resettled their clothes. She shifted her shoulders as she retied her top, luxuriating in the electrified warmth that suffused her. It had been way too long since she'd had good sex, and almost as long since she'd wanted to, but the barman had surpassed expectations in the end, like a delightful palate cleanser. With one more deep breath, Gina gathered her purse.

He brought her wine glass over, watching her with the knowledge he'd gained and assuredness he hadn't earned. Gina took the glass and sipped the remaining wine with regained composure.

He smirked, unfazed, gesturing toward the wine with his chin. "What do you think?"

"It grows on you."

His chuckle followed her to the door.

Four

"You look beautiful," Gina murmured the following morning, pulling back from a careful hug. "Kane's the luckiest cowboy in the world."

Sabella smiled, shrugging delicately. It had taken many hours of poring over magazines and visiting bridal boutiques, but she now wore the perfect dress, with a sweetheart neckline topping a structured bodice that spilled into a loosely flowing skirt. An unobtrusive veil floated over her classic French twist and down her back, held in place by a jeweled comb they'd found last winter. She was flawless.

"Thank you so much, for everything," Sabella said.

It was Gina's turn to shrug.

"You know none of this would have happened without you." Even on her wedding day, Sabella was incapable of having everything be about her.

"It's what I'm here for." Gina stepped away so they wouldn't cross the line into horribly girly and cry. "Forcing you to enjoy bachelorette parties and push boundaries with your nail polish."

Sabella laughed, examining the lush purple that now covered her nails. The color matched Gina's dress and the accent color of the wedding. Trisha and Gina had decided on a deep-magenta polish instead.

"Last night surprised me, I admit," Sabella said. "It was unforgettable." She picked up the digital frame that had already been loaded with photos of last night's antics, smiling at a group shot in their custom tees, everyone playing with their violet feather boas. The shot changed to one of Sabella, laughing behind her hand as three guys they'd met at the wine bar knelt before her, proposing with outstretched bottles, then to one with Trisha, giggling as she read risqué trivia questions. "I still can't believe you two pulled all of this together."

"We were highly motivated."

Gina's coconspirator flounced back into the dressing room. She joined them before the antique standalone mirror and lightly stroked Sabella's shoulder. "They're almost ready for you, sweetie."

Sabella took a deep breath, blowing it out between perfectly glossed lips, and set down the frame. "Okay. This is actually happening, right? We're really doing this."

"The sixty or so people out there certainly hope so," Gina joked, bringing over their bouquets.

The three of them stood for a moment, holding hands and exchanging smiles with a faint sheen of tears in their eyes.

Someone knocked on the door, and Sabella squeezed for a second before letting go to take her bouquet.

Gina met Steve—Kane's drummer and best man—in the hallway. The slight awkwardness of seeing each other again after their little fling had all been worked out earlier in the week, and he smiled at her easily, offering her his arm, then led her outside.

The crowd was still murmuring as they waited in the sunshine. Two gorgeous paintings with abstract, swirled bodies, one reminiscent of Sabella and one of Kane, stood on easels on either side of the opening between the chairs—Trisha's gift to the bride and groom. A third painting of them joined stood on the slightly raised dais where they would soon vow undying love and devotion.

A melodic string-and-sax combo accompanied the procession. Gina and Steve made it down the aisle without incident, splitting to their respective spots. Kane smiled at her somewhat nervously, a touch out of his element in the gray tux, and Gina smiled back with a nod. At least she could be certain Sabella would be in great hands. Trisha and Bobby soon joined them, and more grins were exchanged. In the front row, Kane's mom pulled a handkerchief from her purse as her husband spoke quietly to Sabella's mother.

Gina briefly caught a bittersweet smile on her own mom's face before rustles and shushing sounded as the guests stood, and Sabella took her rightful place in the spotlight.

✧ ✧ ✧

"Just as I suspected," Roger complained, lowering into a chair beside Gina now that the structured part of the reception had ended. "Plenty of eye candy, and no one to bite into."

Gina sipped a glass of the winery's sparkling Muscat. "You do remember that that's not why we're here, right?" Though, really, she was one to talk.

"I know, but, believe it or not, I want this." His hand fluttered, gesturing vaguely around them.

"A wedding at a vineyard?"

"Well, no, though this is definitely fabulous."

The outdoor reception had come together exceptionally, with a decently sized dance floor and plenty of space for the jazz quintet. Both the sunset earlier and the unobtrusively placed lighting that was gradually taking over as the sky dimmed only added to the romance of the setting. It couldn't have gone better, and Sabella deserved no less.

"A vineyard wedding is so not me. But look at them." Roger nodded to Kane and Sabella who were turning and rocking around the dance floor, watching each other with quiet contentment. "I want that."

Gina drained her glass. Once upon a time, she'd hoped to find that solid, supportive love too, even if she wasn't quite as idealistically romantic as her best friend. Now, she knew better. Independent solitude with the occasional fling to scratch any itch suited her well enough. Fun, and flirty, and casual, and brief, like she'd kept it before, especially if the guys scratching those itches were as yummy and unassuming as that bartender. "Maybe you should stop breaking up with perfectly nice guys, then," she told Roger, refocusing on their conversation.

He sighed dramatically. "I should. But, can you really blame me for being picky? I want 'just right,' not 'good enough.'"

"Well patience is a virtue, Rodge. If you want 'just right,' you have to be willing to wait for it, and to fight for it." And to ignore the fact that not everyone could find a good match, much less a perfect one.

He scrunched his nose at her. "I'm thinking about hitting some bars when we get back."

"Yeah, that sounds like a good way to find someone for a meaningful relationship."

"Well, what do you suggest? Trolling through our building? I don't look as cute as you do accidentally tripping into a businessman."

"I have never done that!"

His eyes narrowed.

"Okay, maybe once, but that was a very long time ago." Years back, when she'd first started at the magazine and hadn't known better. "And anyway, I don't think you should date anyone from our building."

"Yes, ma'am." He mock saluted.

Gina rolled her eyes, trying not to react to the memories. This weekend wasn't about the past.

"Anyway, you should come with me," Roger rerouted. "It could be fun."

"I don't know, Rodge." She could no longer fend off over-confident, often drunk men as lightheartedly as she once had, and as Roger would expect her to. "Where would we even go?"

His lips twisted to the side as he thought. "How about Alan's bar?"

Gina's eyebrows shot up. "You want to get back together with your ex?"

He grimaced. "No, absolutely not. But it's a great bar, with guys more likely to drool over me than you."

She would probably be the only woman in the room, but then, she wasn't the one looking for a man.

"We should go," he needled, his knee bouncing.

"Okay, okay. We can go find you a new friend when we're back in Portland."

Roger grinned, straightening in his chair. Gina would have rolled her eyes again, but her papi came up, hand extended, and she laughed instead, standing to follow him onto the dance floor.

Hunter paused in his inventory count. The wedding party was pretty on track with his expectations so far. A few guests had probably trickled on home, but the celebration was still going strong. The couple seemed sweet, and the revelry genuine.

There had yet to be any drunken confessions leading to destructive fights, so it was a win in his book. Less cleanup.

Yesterday's gorgeous brunette flitted among various partners on the dance floor, sporadically stopping to chat or pull new people into the mix. Something about her made him want to smile, though the memories of yesterday stirred entirely different desires.

But occasionally, out of sight of the other guests, tinges of sadness snuck through her smile.

"Oh my gosh, you won't believe this!" Trisha exclaimed, plopping down in an empty seat at the main table. Her face scrunched apologetically. "Sorry for interrupting."

"How dare you," Gina teased.

Sabella laughed and twisted slightly toward her sister. A few wisps had escaped her previously impeccable coiffure, but the warmth or the excitement blushed her cheeks and lit her eyes. "What's going on, 'Treace?"

"Well, don't be mad," Trisha started.

Sabella's eyes grew wide.

"So, you know those paintings?" Trisha asked.

"The fabulous ones?" Gina chimed in.

Trisha ducked her head self-consciously. "Thanks. But, so, a local gallery owner was here, talking to the owner about an event or something when I was putting them up, and she saw them. So I gave her my card, with a link to my portfolio. And…" She whipped out her phone. "Well, see for yourself."

"You were checking email at my wedding?" Sabella teased. Only about half the guests remained at this point, and Sabella was far too laid-back to be offended.

She and Gina leaned curiously to see the screen, but before they could read the message, Trisha blurted, "She wants me to do a show at her gallery!"

"Oh my gosh!" Sabella echoed, putting a hand on Trisha's shoulder but continuing to read the message for herself.

"That's fantastic! Is it going to be your first show?" Gina asked.

"Well, my first one outside of my loft." She shook her head. "But it'd mean flying back out here, and shipping my paintings, all in the next couple weeks."

"But we're still going to be on our honeymoon!" Sabella exclaimed, obviously dismayed.

"Well, we know it'll be the first of many." Gina raised her glass in a toast.

The sisters eagerly bumped their glasses against hers, and everyone took a sip.

"I'm just not sure about doing it," Trisha confessed after swallowing. "What if no one shows up? I mean all of my friends will be in New York, and I know Mom and Dad will make the drive, but how pathetic would that be, if they were the only ones there?"

"Oh, stop it. Your work is amazing," Sabella said. "It's about time you got some recognition. It's so unfortunate we're going to miss it."

"Miss what?" Kane put his hands on his new wife's shoulders, and she beamed at his presence. He looked much more comfortable now that he'd discarded his bowtie and jacket.

"Trisha's going to have an art show," Sabella told him.

As the sisters filled Kane in, a glimpse of yesterday's barman drew Gina's attention. He didn't look half bad in obviously tailored slacks and a button-down shirt open at the collar. Since there was no chance she'd see him again after this weekend, there was no risk of things getting complicated. Maybe a repeat would be in order.

"She's worried the room is going to be empty," Sabella was saying when Gina tuned back in.

"I doubt that'd happen," Kane answered automatically, wholly supportive though he probably hadn't seen any of Trisha's art other than today's trio. Then again, those paintings would be enough to sell anyone on her talent.

"Well, so, I was thinking, maybe you'd be able to come down?" Trisha asked cautiously, looking at Gina. "I know, it's a horrible imposition, but the show would open Saturday night, so it wouldn't even have to be a long weekend. And I would totally treat you to a spa day or something on Sunday," she added with a falsely angelic smile.

Sabella and Kane silently exchanged glances Gina couldn't quite read.

"Of course, I'd love to see more of your work," Gina agreed. Sabella would feel better about missing the show, and coming back to Sonoma wasn't actually that big of an imposition. "Then I can say 'I knew you when.'"

"Oh, thank you!" Trisha sagged in her chair and downed the rest of her wine. "I owe you."

Sabella mouthed a silent *thank you* before adding, "You'll have to tell us all about it when we return."

"We'll save the newspaper clippings," Gina assured.

"Oh, stop!" Trisha giggled. "I'm already nervous enough."

"Wait, am I going to see you when you're back from your salacious adventure?" Gina asked.

Sabella scrunched her nose. "Salacious? Really?"

Kane chuckled.

"And yes, I mean, that's the plan," Sabella confirmed. "I'm going to spend at least a portion of the summer in Portland, while they're on tour."

"Spending endless hours trapped on a tour bus just not tempting enough for you?" Gina asked.

"You can't get rid of me that easily," Sabella answered, not rising to the bait.

Gina didn't bother to hide her relief. Sabella moving to Nashville full-time would be horrible, no matter how happy Gina was for her. Portland would feel less like home without her best friend. "Oh, admit it," she said. "Kane just isn't exciting enough for you."

Both newlyweds' lips twisted at the teasing.

"No one's as exciting as you, Gi," Sabella said wryly.

"But I'm better in bed," Kane added.

"How do you know?" all three girls asked at once, and everyone burst out laughing.

"Well I hate to break up this party," Roger said, sidling up to them, "but you, Miss Beautiful Bride, promised me another dance." He paused, tilting his head toward Kane. "Unless the cowboy wants to take your place."

Kane actually took a step back, palms out. "Suppose I could let you borrow her for one dance. But you better bring her back in one piece."

Sabella pulled Roger away before he could respond. For whatever reason, he got a kick out of baiting Kane, even though Kane had never seemed bothered by the blatantly inappropriate flirting.

"So, which one of you lovely ladies could I convince to distract me from the absence of my bride, er, my wife?" He flashed them a somewhat cheesy grin that rounded his cheeks and crinkled around his green eyes.

Trisha laughed, the pink in her cheeks darkening. Kane was quite the charmer when he wanted to be.

"I've done my fair share of babysitting," Gina said, "so I hate to break it to you, Trish, but it's your turn."

"Oh, well, if you insist. Guess I can take one for the team." She placed her hand in Kane's smoothly offered one.

Kane winked at Gina as he led Trisha away. She smiled back then also stood. Sitting alone at the bridal table wasn't particularly appealing. She skirted the mostly emptied reception, watching the circular sway of the remaining couples on the dance floor.

"How's that stress level?" a voice asked behind her.

Five

The echo of a shiver ran through her insides, and Gina twisted to the barman. "Wedding's over. So's the stress."

His eyes trailed over her with yesterday's knowledge. "Guess I should be happy for you."

She angled her body toward his, settling onto one hip. "Why wouldn't you be?"

"Figure I should get some more practice before deciding whether to start offering those services we discussed."

"Might have to find someone else to practice on." She fingered the draped chiffon at her waist. "This dress isn't particularly well suited for a quickie."

"You could try out the premium package."

She mimicked his earlier assessment, stalling in the vicinity of his crotch, and crooked an eyebrow before reclaiming eye contact.

"You're right." His full lips curved. "The basic package is pretty premium. Maybe I should call it the 'extended package.' The 'Slow Simmer.'"

"Thinking about branding already?"

"What do you think? Effective?"

Extremely, judging by the heat of remembered touches building in her body. "You have some work ahead of you."

"Might have to focus on my strengths, then."

"And what would those be?"

He didn't miss a beat. "Guess I'll have to remind you."

Gina glanced back to the reception happening beside and around them. Sabella and Kane rocked on the dance floor, murmuring to each other. All the parents had retired a little while ago. She wouldn't be missed, and she had never before been the type to turn down a night of fun, uncomplicated sex. Especially good sex.

"Guess so." She turned to walk away, leaving it up to him to follow.

He trailed her without a word. Their footsteps echoed in the empty halls outside the guest rooms, though he maintained an entirely appropriate distance until they were inside her room. The bridal suite had been well designed, with a mini seating area and two separate bedrooms, for a bride and her entourage. Of course tonight, Sabella would be joining Kane in his room.

The barman didn't seem interested in their surroundings. "Should I be asking about alcohol consumption and consent and such?" he murmured.

A curl of anxiety Gina'd been ignoring loosened slightly, and she turned away, dropping her sequined clutch onto a nightstand. "Why don't you assume various legal indemnities are taken care of."

"Well, then." He stepped up behind her and lightly placed his palms on her arms. When she didn't shrug him off, his hands sifted through her hair to the hook-and-eye closure of her dress, then easily unfastened it. The single diagonal strap on her shoulder kept her dress almost in place, until his hand brushed it off, and the chiffon fell. She stepped out of the purple pool of fabric, automatically scooping up the dress to drape it over the back of an armchair.

When she turned back around, his gaze was glued to her body. The formal gown called for more conservative under-garments, so she was actually wearing a strapless bra tonight. With his gaze trained on her, she reached behind to unhook it, then tossed it in the vicinity of the dress so all she wore above the waist was the glittering necklace Sabella's parents had given her for the wedding. She moved toward the bed, and he swiveled on the spot, smoothly keeping her in sight.

Still in her slip and heels, she lowered to the edge of the mattress then laid partially back onto her elbows, crossing her legs for a perfected casual pose. "Your turn."

He raised an eyebrow and undid his shirt, one button at a time, then the cuffs, then pulled the tails out of his slacks, before shrugging it to the floor. Tanned skin met her gaze, tautly covering a defined chest and tight biceps. His abs lacked the overdone definition of a six pack, so apparently he didn't waste time on working out just for appearance's sake. She liked him better for it, though that didn't really matter.

He unfastened his belt and the top button of his slacks, but didn't take them off. Instead, he strode to the bed and knelt on the mattress, leaning over her. Gina brought her hands up to trace over the solid warmth of his torso. He lowered into a pushup to kiss her, delving deeply right away. When her fingers tightened over his muscles, he broke the kiss, trailing his lips over her neck and lower. He'd shaved for tonight's event, so the movement lacked the soft scrape of yesterday's stubble, gliding smoothly over her.

His knees left the bed as he reached her slip, dipping a finger below the waistband as his mouth played over her stomach. She lifted her hips, and he slid the silken fabric down her legs, leaving the bed completely. The warmth of his hands around her no longer crossed ankles startled her enough to tense, but his thumbs brushed up and down her calves until she exhaled. His hands extended the motion, skimming up the back of her legs, then his mouth dipped to her inner knee.

Lips and tongue played gently at the press of her legs until they relaxed. Cupped under her knees, his hands instantly separated them. He licked up her inner thigh, tracing a flowing pattern with his tongue up to her lace panties. She waited for him to get rid of the final scrap of fabric, but he lingered in the crevice of her hip, hands gripping her thighs, until she writhed against him. She parted her legs further in pointed invitation, and he shifted his attentions to her other thigh. *Slow simmer.* The words flashed through her mind.

When she'd almost had enough of the mild teasing, he bit gently, jolting her feet off the floor. He licked over the bite and hooked her knees over his shoulders, but then shifted higher, lips and tongue teasing along the upper lace trim of her panties. One sure stroke licked up to her belly button, and her fingers clenched in the sheets. His chuckle vibrated through her. She rose back onto her elbows, meeting his gaze down the length of her body.

His head ducked to the base of her stomach, but he didn't break eye contact, watching her with that same assuredness as her hips wriggled, responding to his manipulation of their own accord. His fingers dipped under her panties but didn't move them, and she would have groaned in frustration, but the challenge in his eyes made her deliberately lick her lips instead.

He rose then, letting one of her legs fall but delightfully stretching the other as he moved to her breasts, splaying her against his torso. Sure strokes circled one nipple, arching her against the press of him, and then he sucked, catching it lightly between his teeth. Her head fell back as her lungs stilled under his ministrations. A last brush of his lips blew her breath out, and she dropped back to the bed.

Finally, his fingers snatched the panties, stripping them down her legs and somehow over her heels. He kicked his own shoes off, losing the illusion of finesse as he removed his socks.

Somewhat reassured by the sign of imperfection, Gina watched him languidly. But his trousers stayed on.

He walked to the side of the bed and plucked a pillow from beneath the covers. She started to twist toward him, but he tucked the pillow behind her head and lightly pressed her shoulders back down. Silently, he knelt back at the foot of the bed, hands covering her knees. Propped up, she parted her thighs and watched him trail kisses up over her skin again. His hands led the way, reaching her hips first. His thumbs brushed over the front of her hips as he exhaled against her, and it was enough to make her shiver.

She tangled one hand in his hair, and his eyes rolled up, crinkling slightly, before he finally tasted her. Here too, he started with long, sure strokes, holding her hips in place as he made her writhe. When her muscles clenched, her hand dropped to his shoulder, and he paused in his assault for a few heartbeats, only to torture her then with deliberate flicks of his tongue.

Her breath sped up, and he mixed his attacks, sure strokes and feathery flicks and gentle circles combining so she wriggled and shivered at once, until her toes curled, and her fingers flexed into his muscles and the bed, and warmth flooded her before she finally stilled.

Soft kisses punctuated his movement up her body, sending tiny tremors through her. He propped himself up on an elbow as he landed beside her, fingers stroking up and down her stomach. When her breath settled, she shifted to face him, mimicking his pose and reaching for his slacks.

He met her lips briefly before murmuring, "Condom."

Gina dropped her hands and pushed to an upright position. He was right—better get one now than have to stop later. Pieces of discarded clothing lay scattered around the room, but yesterday's purse was nowhere to be seen. He sat up next to her when she didn't move.

"Do you have one?"

"Somewhere." She was never unprepared—it was a habit she'd picked up back in college.

He chuckled, leaning down to nibble at her earlobe, somehow managing not to catch his lips on her dangling earrings.

Where had she put it? *Dammit.* "Oh!" She nearly jumped off the bed. She plucked the purse from inside her suitcase and pulled out a couple packets. He was smiling when she turned around, and she cocked her hip, posing.

"What do you think, should I lose the heels?"

His eyes slowed in their path over her body, and his jaw clenched, which was answer enough.

Gina strode the few steps to the bed and tossed the condoms behind him. "You should probably take those off," she told him.

He stood, brushing against her, and let the slacks fall.

She splayed her hands on his chest, skimming them up and over his shoulders. He cupped her head, angling it for a deep kiss. She leaned into it, her breasts grazing his chest, and she could feel him press against her hip, straining through the cotton still between them. Their tongues tangled, and she pushed him onto the bed, straddling him. He moaned into her mouth, sweeping his free arm out behind him to find one of the discarded squares.

She rose on her knees so he could get rid of the last bit of fabric separating them, and he tugged it down, growling low as his tip brushed against her. She smiled into the kiss, but he soon broke it, shifting to her breast. Still sensitized from his earlier ministrations, she reacted instantly, digging her fingers into his shoulders.

He pressed a kiss between her breasts, and finally she lowered onto him, drawing out a longer moan. His hands came to her ribcage, fingers idly teasing tremors from her body. She recaptured his lips, biting the lower one gently before dipping her tongue inside. He met her seamlessly as she rode him, arching her hips with the downward slide until his hands closed around her waist. In an easy motion, he twisted them so she landed on her back, hooking her legs instinctively around his hips.

He slowed his stroke until her nails bit into his back, seeking an outlet for the pressure coiling inside her. He stilled almost completely, forcing a moan from her, then he finally gave in, driving into her strong, and deep, and fast, until she soared, milking his orgasm as she fell.

✦ ✦ ✦

When he recovered, Hunter kissed the light swell of the brunette's breast.

She hummed, stretching contentedly alongside him. He lifted onto an elbow to look down at her.

"Not bad," she murmured, lips curving slightly.

A lesser man would've been cowed by the words, but Hunter just chuckled. "High standards?"

She hummed again in response. Stunning light-brown eyes smiled up at him. Shame she was only in town for the weekend.

"So you went to bed early last night. Are you okay?" Sabella asked as they watched the guys load the cars from a nearby picnic table.

Gina crooked an eyebrow at her, smiling as she sipped her coffee. They'd both opted for caffeine over more wine.

Sabella's eyes grew round. "You met someone! Wait, someone at the wedding? Was it one of the guests?"

"Slow down! And technically, no, I didn't meet anyone. I don't know his name."

Sabella's jaw actually dropped.

"Don't look so shocked." They'd been perfectly safe, and it wasn't exactly unusual behavior. Or it hadn't been, until this last year.

Still, despite their longstanding friendship, Sabella somehow retained her wholesome purity, even though Gina knew for a fact Kane had broadened her sexual horizons. "Well, you look satisfied," Sabella commented, recovering.

Gina just smiled. The barman hadn't disappointed. A few times. And he'd known exactly when to leave without making it awkward. That was definitely a plus.

"So, who was he?" Sabella asked.

"One of the bartenders. And anyway, *Mrs.* Hartridge, shouldn't we be talking about your night?"

Sabella blushed, biting her lip. Her gaze flicked over to her husband, and her lips curved into one of the private, shy smiles that knowing Kane had brought into her life.

"Tell me you did something fun."

"Being with him is always fun," Sabella countered.

"Always?"

"Well, no. Sometimes it's sensuously serious, and thoughtful, and passionate." Her lips twisted to the side. "And all that other cheesy stuff."

"Good." Gina set down her coffee. "You deserve all that cheesy stuff."

Sabella knocked a knee against hers. "You do, too, you know."

"I'm much better off being on my own. Fun flings, and none of that crazy drama." The hint of worry that appeared whenever they now discussed Gina and relationships flashed in Sabella's eyes. "Besides," Gina said, changing the topic, "I get to focus on finding Roger the most patient man on Earth, now."

"A man patient enough for Roger, and enough of an enigma to keep his attention? Talk about Sisyphean." Sabella paused, licking her lips. "But that doesn't mean you should forget yourself."

"I'm fine. You know I was never meant for that whole traditional relationship paradigm. And now that one of my best writers is going on her honeymoon, I'll have tons of work to do."

Sabella didn't smile at the jab, but she dropped the subject, which was good enough. Not everyone was meant for happily ever after, but that wasn't a topic for this weekend.

"Just don't kill Roger while I'm gone," Sabella instructed, ever the peacemaker.

"I won't. If he doesn't give me a reason to."

"*Tsk*, even if he does."

Gina took a long drag of her coffee, watching the guys squabble over how best to secure Trisha's paintings. "I was thinking about cutting my hair again," she said after a while.

Sabella's eyes trained back on her. "That short, uneven cut?"

"I know you think longer hair looks better."

"Gina, it's your hair. And that cut looked absolutely amazing on you."

"You don't think it's too…extreme?"

"It's a hairstyle that makes you look even more gorgeous, if that's possible. I'm not telling you to do it if you don't want to, but even Michel thought it was his best work on you, and that your idea was genius."

The style had been a hit with everyone. Well, almost. "So much has changed, hasn't it. You wanted to kill Kane that day, remember?" And Gina'd been excited about a first date.

"I did not! I simply didn't want to have anything to do with him anymore." Sabella shook her head at the memory of her and Kane's first fight. "And you were mostly surprised I'd met a musician." Sabella's overly expressive eyes couldn't hide that she remembered what else had happened that day, but thankfully she didn't mention it.

"Well, leave it to you to turn a hot fling with a singer into getting married," Gina teased, elbowing her.

Sabella laughed. "I know, I'm an utter disappointment."

They exchanged smiles, and Gina tipped her head back, luxuriating in the warmth of the sun.

"It's not so bad, though," Sabella said eventually, "taming a musician."

"Way better than being tamed," Gina answered without thinking.

Sabella let the comment pass without a response, but she laced their fingers together, squeezing tightly, and that was answer enough.

<h1 style="text-align:center">Six</h1>

"Y ou. Look. Amazing," Roger said almost as soon as Gina opened her door.

She stepped back without commenting, turning away to gather her keys and pull her ID and some cash from her purse.

"We're still going to *freego*, right?" Roger asked from the doorway.

"If that's where you want to go." She was only going out to keep him company, like she'd promised. "Free Go? Really?"

"It's an inside joke. You know this is a gay bar, right?"

"I had an inkling," she assured, shooing him back out the door. They walked down the private outdoor staircase that led to her apartment and headed over to her car. Gina was driving so she wouldn't be stranded if Roger found "the one." Or more likely "one for tonight." "So what's the joke?" she asked, unlocking her car.

"There's this gay bar in Paris called *freedj*. Free-d-j. Except when they pronounce it, it sounds kind of like fridge. So this place is called *freego*, because in French, the short form for refrigerator is *frigo*. So, fridge, *frigo*."

"Brilliant," she said drily. "You don't speak French."

Roger shrugged. "Alan told me, and they needed a name. It's as good a name as any for a bar, and people see all kinds of liberal, gay rights stuff in it."

"Well, I mostly care about their drinks. And maybe having a free barstool to watch the mating rituals of your people."

"Yeah, and that's why you got your hair done."

"I didn't get it done, I had it *cut*. And I had to see Michel today, because next weekend, I'm going back to Sonoma for Trisha's art show, as you well know. And anyway, I thought you liked it."

"I do, I just think you're wasting it on *freego*. Though, you know, this night is supposed to be about me, and you haven't said a word about how I look." The pout was back.

"If I was a gay man, I'd take you right here," she told him, deadpan.

"Stop!" He swatted her arm. "I'm serious. I want to meet someone fun, and exciting. Or hot."

"You look good, Rodge. We threw out anything unwearable in your closet, remember?" He was wearing a tailored gray vest over a lilac shirt, with gray slacks and a broadly striped tie in vibrant shades of orchid and turquoise. It was almost understated for him.

Gina found a spot fairly close to the club and shut off the car. "C'mon, Cinderella. Your bar awaits."

Inside, pounding music and pulsing lights assaulted them.

"I'm gonna get us drinks!" Roger yelled over the noise and left to fight his way for a bartender's attention.

Gina scanned the crowd, curious if there were any other women. A particularly self-confident guy was dancing on his own in the middle of the room, grinding occasionally on innocent bystanders. Most ignored him or shuffled uncomfortably away. It was kind of sad, but he seemed to be having a good time, or he was great at faking it.

Gina shook her head and made her way to an empty spot by the wall, which luckily included a free stool. Not one head swiveled her way or watched her walk. The relative invisibility was a relief.

It took Roger almost no time to find her, two swirly drinks in hand. He slid hers onto the protruding ledge beside her that conveniently stretched around the room.

"What is this?" she yelled in his ear. The stool was high enough that, even sitting, she was almost on a level with him.

"It's like a mudslide! But with no ice cream, and more alcohol!" He sipped it, scanning the men behind her.

Gina picked up the chilled glass and sucked on the plastic straw. A chocolaty, creamy blend with a coffee-ish kick poured into her mouth. Roger's eyebrows lifted in a silent question. Gina nodded back, pleasantly surprised by the drink.

He leaned down again. "It's Alan's specialty!"

Of course it is. Roger's ability to stay on what he considered good terms with the guys he dumped was astonishing. They all seemed perfectly content to continue almost pampering him.

"Oh! I see a cute one," Roger said in a brief lull from the pounding music.

Normally, Gina didn't mind the bar scene, but this place seemed to be even louder than usual, a relentless bass pounding through her.

"Should I go over?" he asked, eyeing the toned guy who'd caught his attention.

"Of course." She forced some perkiness into her voice. "That's why we're here, right?"

Roger's lips pinched, and the next song picked up momentum. Gina straightened his tie, and mouthed, "Go!"

He took another long drag from his straw, set down the drink, and sidled off. His target eyed him and smiled. Roger said something and palmed the guy's bicep through his tee shirt.

Gina rolled her eyes and took another sip of the chocolaty concoction. The guys chatted for less than a minute before moving away from the walls to the de facto dance floor, both jiggling and swaying their hips to the music. It was almost hypnotic, the pounding rhythm and the matching movements of those surrounding her. Even those chatting seemed to subconsciously adapt to the shifting beat until it suffused their gestures and strides. It was so easy to fade into the background, observing the complex patterns of interactions.

A brush on her shoulder jolted her on the stool. Michel's friendly face came into focus, and she smiled, relaxing again as her heart slowed.

They exchanged two air kisses—a French custom he maintained despite years spent living in Portland. When he stepped back, his eyebrows slanted inward. "*This* is where you waste my work?"

Gina laughed. He almost sounded like Roger. "I'm here for a friend." And this time she truly hadn't had him cut her hair for the sake of impressing anyone.

Michel glanced around the room.

"Are you looking for someone?" she asked.

He shrugged elegantly, slightly shifting tonight's scarf. Sabella was right, the man's neck was never bare. A green sweater had replaced his earlier tee shirt.

"Have you been here before? *Freego* is an interesting name," he commented as quietly as the music would let him.

Roger reappeared before she could respond. His shoulders rose, and he grinned before picking up his drink. It took him another second to notice Michel.

"Michel, this is my friend, Roger," Gina introduced, leaning from one to the other. "Roger, the genius Michel."

Michel smiled politely, but Roger tilted his head, giving him the once-over. He glanced back to the guy he had apparently selected for the evening.

Michel leaned toward her. "I'm going to find a drink!" He moved slightly to his left, and she repeated the kissing ritual automatically before realizing he meant it as goodbye.

She stopped him with a hand on the forearm. "I'll see you later?" He nodded, though she doubted he meant it. She'd spent a fair bit of time in the salon where he worked, but for whatever reason, they'd never transitioned to socializing outside its walls.

Roger stepped into her line of sight when Michel left. The song selection changed to one mildly quieter, giving their ears a bit of a break.

"I came over to ask what you thought, but *that's* Michel? Is he single?"

"I don't know, Rodge. But I am *not* setting you up with him."

Predictably, he pouted. "Why not?"

"Well, for one thing, I think that guy thinks you're going home with him. And for another, Michel is brilliant, and I don't want to have to find a new stylist for fear of having my hair butchered in revenge."

"I'm not all that bad!" he protested.

She raised her eyebrows rather than respond.

"I'm not. And maybe he's my happily ever after person, and you're keeping us apart."

"Or maybe the cute guy staring at you is."

"Oh, please. He's eye candy that'll hopefully be a good lay. No depth."

Well, at least he had *some* standards. Then again… "You've spent like five minutes with him!"

"I have a good sense of people," Roger claimed. "And there's something about Michel."

"The fact that he's off-limits?"

He scrunched his nose but switched seamlessly to a smile when the guy from earlier tapped him on the shoulder. The guy nodded to Gina but quickly returned his attention to Roger. Gina twisted away to give them a semblance of privacy, and they soon moved back to the dance floor.

She twirled the straw in her drink, glancing around the room again. The earlier lone dancer had either gotten tired, met a friend, or moved out of sight into the back half of the club. A couple of giggling, overdressed girls stood encouraging a bashful boy in the far corner. So she actually wasn't the only woman there tonight.

Out of the corner of her eye, she saw Roger set his emptied glass down on the ledge behind her, and she turned to face him.

"We're going to take off, go somewhere quieter. You going to be okay?"

He wasn't really asking, and they both knew it. Gina tilted her drink in their direction. Almost as soon as they were out of sight, she set it aside, slid off the stool, and walked out into the fresh night air.

She'd always enjoyed nights out, and bars, and partying, and that hadn't changed, exactly. Usually, she could still be the flirty, carefree life of the party everyone expected. But some-times, pretending last summer hadn't changed her was just too draining.

Tonight, watching movies on her couch was infinitely more appealing.

Seven

Gina plucked a glass of sparkling wine from the passing waiter's tray and surveyed the tasteful gallery with its subtly creamy walls. The room wasn't packed, but that meant people had plenty of space to move around, exploring Trisha's work. Gina wasn't any kind of expert on art, but the paintings ranged in styles and themes, and Trisha had spent all of yesterday arranging them for maximal effect.

She now stood in a far corner with her parents, nearly vibrating with excitement as people milled around the room, discussing her work. The dress she'd chosen looked amazing, highlighting her bust and loosely flowing over her curves in a wash of blues and purples, hitting just above the knee.

Gina made a mental note to plan a feature on dressing for various shapes in a world with standardized sizes.

She wandered the gallery unobtrusively, eyes skimming the clusters of admirers as much as Trisha's work. Upscale casual defined the attendees, whose hands snatched hors d'oeuvres and drinks from a passing tray with an accustomed ease. Money wasn't a stranger to this room, which could be promising for Trisha.

Those unfamiliar with the events of society's upper echelon were instantly recognizable. They had dressed more formally, though in cheaper brands, and their hands shyly remained tucked away, uncertain of the protocol for interacting with the single waiter. They had come to see the art, not to pass judgment on the artist's future or to be seen themselves. Undoubtedly there were also a few chameleons like her, self-trained to appear comfortable in this world though not really of it. Appearing naturally at ease among the wealthy was an integral part of her job, working with prominent and aspiring designers alike. She had become even more skilled at it last summer.

Gina stopped her circle near a lonely painting, idly sipping her wine. Wind blew through the hair of an obviously battle-worn woman who stood, bruised and tattered, staring at the sun rising over an untouched town. Gina blinked, shaking her head gently to shatter the illusion of life on the canvas.

"What do you think?" Trisha appeared at her side.

Gina twisted away from the captivating piece, taking a bracing gulp from her glass. "It's really amazing, Trish. And what a great turnout! You were crazy to worry."

Trisha's eyes widened, and her cheeks rounded as she tried not to grin. She exhaled, looking around at the people murmuring in small groups. "Do you think people like it? Sorry, I mean,"—she placed a hand on Gina's elbow—"I'm really glad you're here."

"No, I get it, don't worry. I don't see how they couldn't love it. I really doubt they're sticking around for the wine and cheese." Though the former definitely wasn't bad.

Trisha let out a little breathless laugh, which was a good sign. "What do you think? Of the actual paintings, I mean."

Gina nodded with affected equanimity toward the cityscape hanging beside them. "This one is really intriguing. What inspired it?"

Trisha looked at her with an unreadable expression. "What do you see?"

Gina returned her attention to the painting, only faintly registering the idyllic expanse of the village. "A woman who survived hell, seeing a town she cannot enter because it's never been touched by that kind of pain. The village wouldn't understand it, and she can't be the one to introduce it." She paused, then shrugged. "But I don't really know anything about art."

"You know," Trisha said seriously, "sometimes what we paint, what we see when we create, isn't what matters, not as much as the perspective that it opens for those who see it, or experience it. The fact that this painting speaks to you, in a way more significant than aesthetics, that's just about everything I could have hoped for."

"My opinion does matter so much more than everyone else's," Gina teased quietly.

Trisha chuckled, shaking her head indulgently. An elegant older woman gestured to get her attention, and Trisha flashed Gina an apologetic look before crossing the gallery to her side.

Hunter preferred avoiding opening nights, but the gallery's owner, Caitria, was an old family friend. He couldn't argue that the paintings at the Hartridge wedding had been exceptional, so he'd agreed to take a look at more of the artist's work, lending his body to fill the room.

Some of the pieces were nice enough, and there was one he kept coming back to, but none had truly spoken to him. Caitria was busy rubbing elbows with the wealthy attendees who may be convinced to purchase a piece, or sponsor a future show. Hunter scanned the room, seeking any familiar faces of the vineyard's local patrons.

A slender brunette stood with a blonde he recognized from the wedding—possibly the artist—discussing a notably isolated painting. He would have thought she was the same, sultry woman he'd enjoyed, but her hair was different. Not that a hairstyle couldn't be changed. The more salient point was that the brunette hadn't been local, and he should really quit thinking about her anyway. Sexy as she was, she wasn't his first weekend fling. Reasonably, she wouldn't be his last.

Hunter shook his head and crossed to a quiet part of the gallery, drawn to a vibrant depiction of a young woman, covered only by her rainbow-colored, impossibly long hair that seemed to float weightlessly around her, set off further by the grayscale background. An intriguing innocence bubbled in her expression, despite her tastefully covered nudity, but otherwise the piece didn't do much to hold his attention.

The blonde strode across the room, and the brunette turned, sending her unevenly cropped hair gently flying and catching his eye once more. Hunter smiled and moved toward her.

"And here I thought you were from out of town."

Gina turned to the unexpected voice. Deeply brown eyes smiled at her, but it was memories that tingled through her. She refocused on the painting to avoid reacting visibly. "Wouldn't expect to see you here," she said evenly, though the sight of him tasting her flashed in her mind.

"I can't be interested in art?"

"Are you?" She tilted her head to the painting. "What do you see?"

She felt it when his gaze shifted from her.

"A survivor," he eventually said softly by her ear. "A warrior who's made it through, and found her haven, waiting below."

He looked back to her as he finished talking. Gina stared a bit longer, trying to see the woman as he did, before reconstructing her composure and returning his regard.

"You look beautiful." He kept his voice low and his stance casual.

She hadn't considered seeing him again, but her body tightened of its own accord. Maybe one more time wouldn't change anything, other than giving her another rush to tide her over. Who knew when she'd next have an opportunity for risk-free but satisfying sex? "Shouldn't you be looking at the art?"

His lips pulled into a hint of a smile. "It is quite something."

"Trisha—Beatrice is really talented." Gina looked back to the painting where he'd seen strength, and sanctuary.

"Caitria, the owner, she's built her career on discovering underappreciated talents."

"Intimately acquainted with her, are you?" Thankfully, her voice didn't reflect the unwarranted twinge of jealousy at his familiarity with this other woman. She wouldn't want to interfere in whatever arrangement they had. Even if the potential of being with him once again was tempting, it wasn't why she'd come here. Though now that the option seemed to present itself, it was quite tantalizing. Still, mild disappointment was the biggest threat of it not happening, which was the wonderful thing about unattached flings. She glanced at him when he didn't respond.

He gestured toward her glass. "That's Cavaliere wine you have there."

Oh. "Of course it is."

"Best wine in Sonoma Valley." That hinting smile grew wider, crinkling lightly around his eyes.

She lifted the glass, tipping it toward her parted lips. He watched the liquid trickle into her mouth, and that humor disappeared. Her turtleneck shifted with her movement, caressing her under his gaze.

"Looks like you could use a refill," he offered when she lowered the emptied glass.

"I wouldn't object."

His fingers grazed hers, and his head inclined obligingly before he walked toward the bar beside the refreshment table the waiter occasionally visited to restock his traveling tray.

Gina looked back to the painting. She could almost see what he had, now—the sanctuary he'd glimpsed in the twinkling town; a chance to pretend what happened outside its untouched tranquility, hadn't.

"Oh, my gosh." Trisha reappeared next to her. "I don't even know why I'm surprised you were talking to Hunter," she said conspiratorially.

Hunter. She hadn't really thought about his name. "The bartender? Do you know him?" She wouldn't be surprised if charming the winery's guests was literally a part of his job description, though he had implied he didn't usually cross that particular line. Granted, it wouldn't matter much if he did.

Trisha's eyebrows furrowed slightly. "Know him? Gina, that was Hunter Cavaliere."

Gina's jaw clenched, and her throat seized around her swallow. She blinked, trying to make sense of the information.

No wonder he hadn't been worried about getting in trouble for their little trip to the cellar.

"He owns the winery where we had the wedding," Trisha finished, driving the point home. "You didn't know?"

"No," Gina forced herself to say. He was just now picking up two fresh glasses and turning to head toward her. How could she not have noticed the impeccable cut of his suit? He wore it over a simple shirt with a rounded collar, but it fit his body seamlessly, obviously tailored, or possibly even made for him. He'd dressed casually during the weekend wedding, but apparently it had been the designer kind of casual, and she hadn't paid enough attention to notice. So much for being a fashion editor. "Excuse me," she murmured to Trisha, moving to meet him halfway.

He offered her a glass, but she ignored it.

"How generous of you, Mr. Cavaliere."

An eyebrow lifted, but he didn't comment.

"So you own the winery, and what, just enjoy slumming it occasionally?" She kept her voice as low as possible, trying not to cause a scene in the middle of Trisha's show despite the adrenaline thrumming through her. "Interesting pastime for a man as wealthy as you."

He actually took a half step back, then effortlessly placed the glasses on the moving waiter's tray. The ease was unmistakable. Watching her coolly, he tucked his hands into his pockets. "Anger. Not the reaction most women have to that information."

"I'm not most women." Or she wouldn't have been such an easy target.

"Well I had noticed that." His gaze skimmed over her body, picking out the countless flaws he'd want to *polish* away, by any means necessary.

Gina resisted the urge to cross her arms. How had she wound up here again? Too stupid to have seen that his charm was nothing more than calculated manipulation, fueled by the impunity of wealth. "Sorry, but I'm not interested in entitled, rich playboys."

He didn't hesitate. "You prefer working-class playthings?"

She spun away, heading toward the calm of the street. She wouldn't ruin this night for Trisha, but that didn't mean she had to spend another second in the barman's—*Hunter Cavaliere's*—company.

He moved more quickly than her pencil skirt would elegantly allow, cutting off her path. Despite herself, Gina shrank backward, before resolutely squaring her shoulders.

"We didn't exactly share many personal details," he reminded.

A year ago, Gina would have offered him a dismissive smile. Tonight, her nails bit into her palm as she fought for calm. *We're in a public place.* The need to maintain his agreeable façade would keep him in check. And she would be leaving tomorrow, never to see him again. "No reason to change that now."

His eyes narrowed, evaluating her bravado.

Two figures joined them in the middle of the gallery, and he blinked, shifting his attention away from her. Gina forced herself not to rush away, biting back the unsteady gasps battering inside her chest.

"Mr. Cavaliere," Trisha breathed. "Thank you, so much."

He smiled at her with deceptive amiability. "Please, call me Hunter. And it is genuinely my pleasure. I consider it an investment."

"And you didn't even want to come tonight," the older woman, who had to be the gallery's owner, said with a familiar smile. "You would have missed out. I have no doubts those paintings would have been snatched up right from under you."

Trisha blushed, laughing shyly. "Mr. Cavaliere has purchased two of my paintings," she explained. "Including the one we were talking about, Gina."

Gina forced a smile. "How wonderful. Congratulations, Tr—Beatrice." Trisha used her full name professionally. "Though Mr. Cavaliere is correct, it is certainly his gain."

"One of many surprises tonight," he added smoothly.

Gina didn't look his way. Happy as she was for Trisha's success, she was so ready to leave Sonoma.

Eight

You're back!" Gina flung her door open to the anticipated knock.

"I'm back! And I come bearing gifts," Sabella announced, walking in and dropping a couple bags onto Gina's corner couch. "And you look amazing, not that I'm at all surprised."

"Why, thank you. You don't look too terrible yourself. I see being married agrees with you."

Sabella hummed as she drew back from their hug. "You're making brownies."

"Obviously." They'd perfected a sinfully chocolaty recipe in their senior year of college. The scent that now surrounded them had become one of Gina's all-time favorites. "So, Mrs. Hartridge."

Sabella grinned at the name.

Gina led the way to the couch and plopped down. "Tell me everything." She poured them both some chilled sangria from the pitcher she'd made earlier.

Sabella kicked her shoes off and curled on the couch,

accepting a glass. "I don't want to have to repeat it all for Roger. When's he coming?"

"In like an hour. So quick, tell me the things Roger isn't allowed to know."

Sabella laughed. A new, easy maturity seemed to cling to her, not that Sabella had ever been immature, exactly. She was just more comfortable in her own skin now.

"You look happy," Gina said.

She took a deep breath. "I am happy. I love him, and being around him, and knowing he'll be there, that we get to spend our lives together."

"So happily ever after's starting out okay?"

"Infinitely better than okay."

Gina nudged her with her foot. "Worth having to move to Nashville?"

Sabella groaned, head falling back to the couch. "We still haven't quite figured all of that out. Obviously, he'll have to spend quite a bit of time there, for his music. But I don't know about actually moving there, and leaving you, and Portland, especially in the summers when they'll be on tour. And we, quite successfully, didn't really discuss it while we were gone."

"Of course. I hope you didn't spend all that much time talking at all."

Sabella exhaled through a self-conscious smile, then licked her lips reflexively. "Of course we talked. And didn't talk. And both were fantastic."

"Have you done it in a shower yet?"

"Gina!"

She grinned at the shocked blush that spread over Sabella's face. "You did!"

"Kane is more than sufficiently adventurous," Sabella said circumspectly, then promptly covered her face with her hand.

"Oh, come on. You're a married lady now. You officially don't have to feel guilty about enjoying sex."

The hand dropped. "Oh, really? That's the rule?"

"Well not in the real world. But in idealistic romantic world. Isn't that what happily ever after is for?"

"I don't exactly have a basis for comparison, but I imagine there's more to it," Sabella said with a wry smile.

"Yeah? Have you guys talked about 'more'?"

"Not in any immediate sense. We both definitely want kids and all that, but we should probably figure everything else out, like where we'll live."

"On a tour bus?" Gina quipped.

Sabella started to protest then shut her mouth. "Probably, yes, at least some of the time."

The oven beeped, and Gina got up to check on the brownies. "Are you going to go out with them again?"

Sabella'd spent part of last summer touring with Kane's band. She followed to the adjoining kitchen area. "Maybe for some of the nearby shows. I'm definitely not flying out for the Southern part this year, and we're both here until Benny and Melody's wedding, so, you're stuck with me for a while."

"The horror," Gina teased, bumping the oven door closed with her hip. Benny worked security in Gina's building, and though he looked like he could kill you, and he probably could, he was actually one of the sweetest guys she'd ever known. Nothing could shake him. Gina had introduced him to his fiancée, Melody, a spitfire who'd helped draw him out of his shell. Now Gina was going to be a bridesmaid in their wedding.

"So," Sabella said, drawing out the syllable. "Tell me what's been going on with you?"

"More of the same, Sab. " In fact, a return to normal was pretty much Gina's number one goal lately. "I'm not the one who was on her honeymoon."

"Still." Sabella pulled a serving dish out of one of the cabinets as Gina sliced the gooey brownies. They both knew each other's apartments as well as their own.

"Not much is going on, besides work, but we can talk about that later. Oh, Melody's bridal shower is next weekend, you remember that, right?"

"Yep."

Gina swiped her finger over the knife, plopping the lingering goodness into her mouth. Sabella scooped a brownie out of the pan, unable to resist. Both of them moaned, laughing at each other.

"So good," Sabella said, walking back to the living room. "Are we having a real dinner at some point? I did bring these." She pulled a glass container from one of the bags.

"Ooh, what's that? And Roger's supposed to swing by and get Thai food on his way over."

"They're this cheesy, quiche-y, puff pastry delicious thing that Kane makes." She brought the box to the dining table, pulling the lid off.

"He got up this morning, bought groceries, and cooked?"

Sabella shrugged, smiling as she always did nowadays when Kane came up. "Jet lag, I guess. Or boredom. He's kind of ridiculous," she admitted.

"And you love it."

"Try one. You'll love it, too." She popped the dish into the microwave. "I have something else for you, but it should probably wait until there's no food involved."

Gina shot Sabella a gratefully reproving look. "You didn't have to get me anything."

"I know, but I thought you'd like it, so I did. Anyway, tell me about Trisha's art show."

"It was a huge success, of course. Have you seen her work lately? Some of it was incredible, and my entirely biased opinion was shared by pretty much everyone there. She sold the first two paintings in less than an hour."

"Oh, I know. I wish I could have seen them in person, but those paintings she did for us? We might have to move to Nashville, simply because we're hanging them up in Kane's house there."

Sabella's apartment admittedly didn't have the wall space for them, but Gina shrugged. "You could find a bigger place here."

"Maybe, at some point."

They brought the snacks back to the living room and resettled on the couch.

"So Trisha told me something interesting," Sabella said, leaning back with her sangria.

"Yeah?" Gina popped a cheesy puff into her mouth. A saltier set of gooey flavors filled her mouth. "Oh, wow," she moaned. "Now, I see why you married him."

Sabella didn't react to the teasing. "She said you had a fight with Hunter Cavaliere."

Gina stilled, then sighed. *Of course she did.* "It wasn't a fight. I made sure we didn't make a scene."

"I didn't realize you knew him."

"Well, technically, I hadn't been introduced to him until the art show," she evaded.

But Sabella was clever enough, and focused enough on word choice, to figure it out. "He's the bartender you slept with?!"

Gina sipped her sangria and grabbed another warm puff. She didn't really want to think about the ramifications of that decision. For that matter, since he was hundreds of miles away, there weren't supposed to *be* any ramifications.

"What happened?"

"I thought he was a bartender! And as it turns out, he's actually extremely wealthy and just, I don't know, enjoys pretending otherwise."

Sabella set down her glass. "Why does him having money affect anything? I mean, you had fun, you know, being with him."

She couldn't deny that the sex had been memorable. "Fun isn't the word I'd use. But that's just it, Sab, all it was supposed to be—a physically satisfying fling on a weekend away. Not some repeated booty call, or anything else. And especially not with another entitled rich man who thinks his money can buy anything, and excuse anything, and allow him to control anything. I don't..." She trailed off, shaking her head.

"Want to be vulnerable," Sabella finished. They didn't talk about it much. Sometimes, they even acted like it wasn't true. But Sabella knew Gina better than anyone, and she definitely noticed that some things weren't the same after last summer.

"I will *never* put myself in that kind of situation again."

Sabella took her hand, squeezing gently. "Why does that have to mean never even spending time with anyone new? I know, it's tough for you to trust someone, even a little, right now, but—"

"You don't understand, Sabella," Gina cut her off, pulling her hand from her best friend's and standing to stalk about her living room.

Sabella remained seated, still the dependable calm support.

"Every time a guy smiles at me, I think that, maybe, here's another man who sees me as a trophy he can mold. Who just wants to control me. To demean me. And then I think I'm being paranoid. But I'd sure as hell rather be paranoid than ever go through that again." Gina stopped, staring directly at her friend. "So I have to be in control, always, with everyone, because I can't trust myself to know when something's off anymore." She blinked back the prickling in her eyes.

Sabella watched her as expressionlessly as possible. "Not every man is like Alistair," she said quietly.

Gina's jaw clenched at the name.

"Not even every rich man, and I know you know that. And you should be in control, doing whatever it is you want to do. What he did doesn't have the right to define you or determine how you live your life. Hunter is off in California, so he's kind of irrelevant, but him having money..." She shook her head slowly.

"I don't belong in the world of the wealthy." She could fake it for work, but that was it. "I learned that lesson. I don't need someone else trying to add the necessary polish."

Sabella shot up from the couch. "Alistair's twisted perspective doesn't reflect reality. Yes, there are snobby, conde-scending, elitist people out there, but that's not defined by wealth, and I bet the vast majority of them would take absolutely no issue with you anyway. That man is messed up."

Gina looked away. She didn't disagree, exactly, but what the hell was so wrong with her that she hadn't known it? For too long, she hadn't seen past his generous, refined façade, wanting to believe someone like that—intelligent, cultured, successful—could want to be with her, could care for her. He'd subtly shown her she wasn't suitable for his world sooner than even Sabella knew. Then he'd stopped being subtle, and she'd been too weak to stop him, to walk away from the illusion of being chosen, almost enough. She'd thought she could become good enough.

Back then, Gina had wanted to be loved. Now she knew better.

"I just think you shouldn't give up on finding love because of it," Sabella said carefully.

Gina shrugged the statement away. "I don't need a man to be happy."

"I know. But you also don't need to be scared of them, especially of having something more with them than casual sex. You're—"

"What? Stronger than that?" Gina spat out bitterly. "Obviously not."

Sabella's lips tensed. "I was going to say 'incredible.' You're an amazing woman in your own right. Alistair was wrong. And you ultimately showed him that."

"How can you say that? I'm not the person I was a year ago. I don't even really know who I am now."

Sabella came closer. "You are an intelligent, compassionate, supportive, and determined woman. And otherwise, you have a lifetime to decide who you are, or who you want to be. It's entirely up to you. And you don't have to avoid all emotional connections in order to do that."

Gina's lips twitched, trying to find a smile. "What about adventurous, outgoing, fashionable, and all that other stuff."

Sabella shrugged, smiling outright. "Those things, if you want to, you can choose to change."

It was amazing how Sabella took all of this in stride. She didn't necessarily know what to do, but she was ready to do whatever needed doing, to find a solution to every piece of the problem that came up. That support, knowing it wasn't going anywhere, that was worth everything.

"Here," Sabella said, wiping her hands on a napkin then moving back toward the bags she'd left on the couch. "Let me show you what I brought you before Roger gets here."

The abrupt change in direction wasn't like her, but Gina followed. The paper package Sabella handed her was flexible and light, crinkling under her fingers as she opened it. A beautiful scarf in an assortment of grays lay inside. Gina unfolded it, unsure what to make of the gift. Long before they'd met, she had been known for her daring, colorful fashion choices. For that matter, Sabella had noticed something wasn't quite right partially because Gina's wardrobe lost so much of its color, and Gina had tried to reclaim the outgoing style, though in comparison her choices could still be considered somewhat subdued. She'd thought Sabella was disappointed by her inability to return to that previous vivacity.

Hazel eyes watched her silently.

Gina spread the delicate fabric out, and light played over the stitched pattern, revealing an unexpected shimmer of colors. She shook her head at the not entirely subtle metaphor, not fighting the smile that tugged at her lips. "It's beautiful. Really, thank you."

Sabella smiled too, then plopped back onto the couch, reaching for another cheese puff. "You should probably put it away before Roger gets here. You know he'll be jealous."

Gina chuckled, turning toward her bedroom just as a knock sounded at the door.

"You two are going to kill my figure," Roger moaned, polishing off the last brownie.

"Nobody's forcing you to eat with us, Rodge," Gina pointed out, relishing the incredibly satisfying feeling of fullness, even if it did threaten her waistline. Empty containers from the Thai place now joined the other dishes on her coffee table, and they were almost out of sangria.

"She's right. You should learn to resist temptation," Sabella teased, standing to help collect the trash.

Gina pulled a new garbage bag from below her sink. Sabella dumped the containers then turned to the fridge.

"Don't tell me you're still hungry!" The shock brought Roger up from the couch.

"Grab a dish, will you?" Gina asked.

"I was reaching for the water." Sabella shut the fridge, shaking the pitcher she held to emphasize her point. "But if you're still peckish, I'm sure we could find something edible."

Roger dumped the glassware in the sink, groaning.

Gina left them to their bickering, walking over to her entertainment unit. "What are we thinking for a movie?" she called to them, running her gaze over her DVD collection.

"Something cheesy," Sabella suggested.

"Don't even say the word 'cheese,'" Roger chided half-heartedly.

"Who is that, making you smile?" Sabella asked.

Gina twisted toward them as Roger tucked his phone back in his pocket. "Is it that guy from *freego*?" she asked.

Forgetting the movie, both girls resettled on the couch, watching Roger.

"What's 'free go'?" Sabella asked.

"A gay bar. What'd you call him? 'Eye candy'? Was he just really good in bed?" Gina prodded.

"He was okay. And this is someone else, and I don't want to talk about it," Roger said primly, also returning to his spot on the couch. The reticence was entirely unlike him.

"Why not?" Sabella asked.

"Just okay?" Gina asked simultaneously.

Roger scrunched his nose. Sabella swatted Gina's arm.

"Wait, is this serious? Why wouldn't you tell us?" Sabella asked seriously.

Roger looked at Gina then down to the coffee table. "It doesn't matter, and weren't we going to watch a movie?"

"Oh, my, God, Roger. You stalked Michel," Gina accused.

Sabella looked between them curiously. "Michel?"

"I didn't stalk him," Roger protested. "I went by your salon, and we hit it off, and it's none of your business anyway."

"What's wrong with him seeing Michel?" Sabella defended, the automatic peacemaker.

"Nothing's wrong with him *dating* Michel. The problem happens when he dumps Michel for no good reason."

"Okay, hold on you two." Sabella turned to Roger. "When did you even meet Michel? Did you go with Gina when she got her hair done?"

"No, he was at freego. Though she *could* have introduced us a long time ago."

"I like Michel too much."

Roger's eyebrows jerked up briefly as he looked away.

Sabella's lips twitched, but Roger didn't notice. "So, wait, do you really like him then?" she asked. "Have you guys gone out?"

"A couple times," Roger admitted. "And I think I really do like him. There's more to him than you'd think."

"No one's doubting that," Gina acceded.

Roger ignored her, talking to Sabella. "He's so strong, emotionally I mean, and funny. And he has this ability to take things in stride. He has a really clear sense of who he is, and what he wants. I watched how he is with his clients, and he's so much more serious and thoughtful outside of the salon than that act he puts on."

The girls exchanged glances.

"Sounds like you really like him," Sabella murmured, ever the romantic.

Roger smiled shyly. "He's not really what I expected, you know? But I think we might really work, if he doesn't realize how superficial I am."

"Oh, shut up," Gina said, smiling. "Everyone knows that shallow, self-centered thing is also an act."

Roger looked at her for the first time since Michel's name had come up. "So you're not mad?"

Gina sighed. "I want you to be happy, Rodge. I just don't want you to get bored, like you usually do, and hurt him."

"Don't worry. He's already said he knows you'll choose him over me," Roger said drily.

"You know it," Gina teased.

Roger pouted.

Sabella tossed a throw pillow at her.

"Stop pouting," Gina amended obediently. "You'll simply have to stay in this relationship forever for the sake of my hair."

Sabella laughed, but Roger wasn't appeased. "You keep worrying about my hurting him," he said, surprisingly serious. "What if he's the one who hurts me?"

Over my dead body. Gina shrugged. "I'll steal his scissors."

Nine

Caitria strode confidently into Hunter's tasting room, heels clacking on the floor.

He smiled, picking up a fresh glass. "Hello, gorgeous."

In one motion, she dropped her purse on the bar and swept her sunglasses back from her face. Long black hair swished around her. She ignored the wine he'd poured her. "I brought your paintings for you."

"Wonderful." He rounded the bar.

She twisted to dangle her keys out for him. Hunter shook his head, heading out to her car. Beatrice Faure was certainly talented. He liked supporting worthwhile artists, and Caitria's discerning taste made that easy.

He popped the trunk on her Subaru and reached for the two carefully wrapped canvases as the sun warmed his back. It was early enough in the summer that the winery only had a few languid visitors, most up on the outdoor terrace, taking advantage of the sunshine along with their wine. It was a morning made for enjoying the vineyard.

Careful not to stretch the canvases, Hunter balanced the wooden frames on his knee to shut the trunk, then walked back to Caitria. She still stood at the bar, paying no attention to the familiar room. She'd first come to the winery before he'd even been born, determined to establish community support for her then-fledgling gallery. She'd been coming back ever since. If Hunter had made any changes since her last visit, she would have noticed instantly, and commented without hesitation. At least she'd picked up the glass of wine.

He leaned the paintings in a safe part of the combination tasting room and souvenir shop and joined Caitria by the bar.

"Thank you," he said, offering the keys back to her.

She hummed noncommittally, taking another sip. "Since when do you fight in my gallery?"

Hunter winced. They'd been fairly circumspect, but Caitria missed nothing, and he'd known this conversation would have to happen, even if he hadn't foreseen the argument itself at all. "I'm sorry, Caitria," he said dutifully. There was a downside to her easy familiarity, though he wouldn't have traded it for the world. "It took me by surprise." He returned to his side of the bar.

"Who is she?"

"As far as I know, a friend of the artist. I think her name's Gina."

"Seems to me, you know her a bit better than that."

"She was at the wedding, where you met the artist." Hunter

frowned, remembering the spat. "Turns out, finding out her bartender actually owned the winery upset her."

"Upset isn't the word I'd use." She didn't comment on the obvious part of their association he hadn't mentioned, but he knew she hadn't missed it, either.

Hunter had gotten the same impression. The brunette had been downright distraught because of the information. Most women went after him because of it. He sighed. "It doesn't matter, does it? We've never even been officially introduced, and I sincerely doubt I'll ever see her again." Then again, he'd thought that after the wedding.

Caitria's pale-green eyes narrowed. "It's long past time for you to find a good woman, Hunter. This place isn't the only part of your grandfather's legacy he'd want you to follow."

"How can I, when the most beautiful woman in Sonoma would turn me down?" He flashed her a smile for good measure. This wasn't a conversation he wanted to have. He knew what he was missing from his life.

Caitria pursed her lips and tilted her head slightly in a gesture that hadn't changed since she'd been his babysitter, way back when. "Flattery will get you nowhere, young man." Her nails clinked against the glass. "Whoever that woman was, she broke through that unaffected shell of yours. That's not nothing. And you know what your grandfather would say about running into her out of the blue."

Everything happens for the best. Wisdom Hunter lived by, but what was the best here? Other than reminding him not to fool around with customers, not that he usually needed reminding. "I do know. But I like my life, Caitria." *Mostly.* "This place, it's enough for me, and I have plenty in store for its future."

She set down the half-full wine glass and scooped up her purse. "Don't forget your own future."

Hunter nodded, and she turned away without a goodbye. They didn't need it. He dumped her remaining wine then walked back to the paintings to take them into his office.

Maybe Caitria was right, and this brush with the high-strung brunette would finally push him to find a decent, down-to-earth woman. One who wasn't bizarrely opposed to him having money. That had thrown him for a loop. He was used to women setting their sights on him because of the family name, but running the opposite way because of it? And regardless, Hunter wanted to find someone who wouldn't care about his money either way, if such a woman existed.

He was lucky to have the money. He was grateful to have the money. But he was more than just his money. He needed a woman who would understand that; one who would love him and be open to being loved, the way it had been for his grand-parents. He wanted a woman for a lifetime.

Sexy as the brunette was, he had to stop thinking about her, piercingly beautiful eyes and plump lips be damned. If he did want to try his hand at finding the right woman, he couldn't spend his time focusing on a fling that was never meant to be more than a memory. He didn't even know where she was from.

There were plenty of sweet, intelligent, beautiful women right here in the Sonoma Valley, and more than a couple had hinted that they would welcome getting to know him better. None had really caught his eye, but if he was honest, he hadn't been looking. He hadn't been lying about having plans for the vineyard, and he had his work cut out for him to keep his grandfather's vision alive and thriving.

Still, maybe he should give one of them a call.

Ten

All right, guys." Gina glanced around at her junior editors. "What have you got for me?"

Krystiana raised her pen. "Summer essentials?"

Beside her, Roger rolled his eyes.

Gina fixed them all with a mildly disappointed look. "We can do better."

"Celebrities spotted in Portland and how to get their look?" Leila suggested.

"Horrifyingly, we've already done it. Come on, it's our midsummer special. We need to do better than beach cover-ups and bikinis."

Krystiana twisted her lips to the side, looking around at her colleagues, who were all carefully avoiding Gina's gaze.

"What is it, Krystiana?" Gina asked, but a knock at the door offered her a reprieve.

Tristan, their circulation director, poked his head in. "All employees to the conference room in five."

Gina nodded, and the door shut almost silently. She refocused on her team, all of whom had started whispering about the mystery meeting. "Krystiana," she called, and they all quieted. "Idea number two, let's hear it."

"Well, maybe, summer trends around the world? And how to give them a Portland spin."

"Maybe feature some local indie shops that are on trend?" Roger chimed in.

Gina glanced out the window at the gathering clouds. She knew everyone exchanged looks as she mulled over the idea, but they were off their game today. "Okay, I've got it." Four sets of expectant eyes trained on her. "We'll do a feature on Portland trends that made it around the world. Can we get a couple people looking into that?"

Charlie nodded, jotting down notes as her curls bounced.

"And we'll transition to eco-friendly fashions for this summer, maybe a spin with leading the world in responsible, green fashion. Actually, Rodge, we should find out if that's true."

He nodded too and looked at the others. "Okay, everyone, you're spared for now by the mercy of the mystery meeting. Progress report at three."

They all chuckled, and new murmurs started up as people headed for the door. Roger hung back. "Shall we? Will you give me a sneak peak of whatever this big news is?"

Gina stood, adjusting her open-face jacket. "You know as much as I do this time."

"How mysterious," Roger teased, eyes wide as he held the door open for her.

Gina shot him a smile and crossed to the bigger conference room. Most of their full-time staff was already gathered inside, gossiping about the various rumors of buyouts, and parties, and exceptional features that always flew about the office, wondering which might actually be announced. Roger split off to gab with a chatting group of assistants. Gina exchanged a mix of smiles, nods, and half waves with some of the magazine's other editors.

"All right, everyone, let's quiet down," their editor in chief's voice sounded, silencing the room.

Gina snuck a glance at her phone then focused on Vivian, and froze. *Just breathe, Gina.* It wasn't the first time a collaboration of some kind had been worked out with someone from the financial firm upstairs.

Her fingers tapped her phone erratically. The impeccable blond man beside their editor in chief scanned the room emotionlessly.

"We have some exciting news," Vivian announced.

Roger appeared beside Gina, hovering at her elbow.

"Some of you may have heard whispers that our magazine will be switching hands in the near future," their editor in chief continued.

A swell of murmurs greeted the comment. Gina hadn't paid any attention to the rumor mill, and she'd been a bit preoccupied with her trips to California. Should she have seen this coming?

"Though the details are still being finalized, I can now announce that we will indeed be transitioning to Mr. Talbot's care in the next few weeks."

A smattering of claps sounded. Charcoal eyes she'd never forget found her, and pale, thin lips stretched coldly.

"Though changes will be implemented, rest assured that no plans for re-staffing are in place." Vivian continued speaking, but Gina glanced at her phone and lifted it to her ear, then slipped out of the conference room. She crossed the empty office quickly, heading for the restroom. Safely inside, she locked the door and dialed Sabella.

"Hey, Gina." The easy perkiness in her voice grated.

Gina shut her eyes. "He's buying the magazine."

Silence was worse. Gina's nails dug deeper into her palm.

"What happened?" Sabella finally asked.

"They're having a meeting to announce it right now, and he's there. Here. He's literally going to be my boss."

"Where are you?"

"In the bathroom." She opened her eyes to face her reflection under the fluorescent lights, fighting the urge to find and fix the countless flaws he would have seen. When was the last time she'd stepped on a scale?

"Benny's working today, right?" She could almost hear Sabella's mind working on the other side of the line. "Go to the elevator and go downstairs. We'll figure the whole thing out later, just get out of the office."

Gina exhaled, staring at her pallid reflection. "You're right." He wouldn't go near her with Benny around. She could escape through the elevators while everyone was still in the meeting.

And the deal didn't sound like it was completely in place yet. Maybe there'd be some way to derail this. Why the hell did he want to own a women's magazine anyway?

But the answer was obvious: *her*. He was finally getting back at her for last summer, for what he saw as humiliating him. He was regaining control.

The upbeat chime of the elevator landing in the lobby should have brought relief, but that didn't come until she saw Benny. Benny, the teddy bear who looked like he could hold his own in an Ultimate Fighting Championship ring. Benny, who wouldn't ask questions she couldn't answer. His muscles bulged in the security guard uniform, but she didn't question the safety of their strength. She strode through the elegant marbled lobby as quickly as possible without drawing too much attention.

"Are you downstairs?" Sabella asked through the phone Gina'd almost forgotten about though it was still by her ear.

"Yeah. I'm going to let you go."

"Okay. Do you want me to come by?"

Despite the adrenaline zooming through her body, Gina's lips curved slightly at the offer. "No. Thanks, though. I'll give you a call later, okay?"

Mildly calmer, she lowered the phone to the counter in front of Benny.

"Hi, Gina," he greeted warmly. Whoever else was on duty today must have been on a break, which afforded a semblance of privacy. Otherwise, he wouldn't have used her first name.

"Hey, Benny. How're the wedding plans?" Small talk had to be the key to restoring normalcy.

He smiled. "You know Melody. She's pretty excited for the shower Sunday." His eyes narrowed on her. "Tough day?"

"Just thought I'd come say hi." She flashed him a tight smile and glanced back toward the elevator bank, avoiding his gaze. There was no need to worry him unnecessarily.

His solid hand landed on hers, fully claiming her attention. Benny knew she had a detrimental past relationship with one of the men in the building, even if he didn't know the details. "Do you need me to escort you upstairs?" he asked solemnly.

"No, that's okay. I'll just hang out for a little bit if you don't mind."

"Of course not."

The other guard returned, and Benny withdrew his hand.

"Careful," Hector teased good-naturedly. "Your fiancée might get jealous."

Benny shot him a look that would have been intimidating, if he hadn't had to suppress a smile at even that mention of his future bride. The reminder of her friends' happiness displaced thoughts of the disaster upstairs, if only for a few seconds. Gina took a deep breath then glanced around the lobby, using the rhythm of the mundane movement around her to piece together a composed façade.

✧ ✧ ✧

Maybe it was the boredom, but Hunter could have sworn he saw the same brunette from the wedding crossing the lobby where he waited. What were the odds of that? Way more likely, he was hallucinating in an attempt to distract himself from the inevitably wearisome business meeting that awaited him. Though he'd learned it out of necessity, the formal and financial sides to his business were only a tedious, unavoidable obligation.

He had long planned to come to Portland to explore some potential plots to expand the vineyard, but those visits weren't until tomorrow. He had extended his trip by a day out of courtesy for a meeting requested by a businessman who probably fancied himself a wine connoisseur.

He'd arrived at the office building early, as always, but the leather couches in the lobby were appropriately comfortable, so waiting shouldn't have bothered him. Still, all he could think about now was the woman he was supposed to be forgetting, and how much more fun a midday meeting with her would be, or would have been before their bizarre art gallery argument.

After talking with Caitria, he'd actually called Paige, a sweet, wholesome local girl who worked at another Sonoma winery. They had plans for next week, but fantasizing about her would be presumptuous, and he didn't have high hopes for their date anyway. His grandparents had married after three days, and ridiculous or not, he believed in the possibility of that kind of instant connection. The times he'd been with Paige, sweet as she was, had lacked that unmistakable spark. To be fair, being with the brunette had been almost entirely physical, and while they obviously had chemistry, their time together hadn't really offered a chance to feel that deep, resonant link. Their conversation at the gallery negated almost any possibility of that.

So why was he still stuck on her?

Maybe because she was standing at the security desk, looking around at the lobby. It would be their third time unintentionally running into each other. After glancing at his watch, Hunter stood and crossed the airy space to her side. "Gina?"

She twisted at her name, then straightened. An almost impeccable poker face replaced a hint of anxiety between her brows, though tension still obviously vibrated through her. "Mr. Cavaliere. What are you doing here?"

Both security guards stepped surreptitiously away.

"I have a meeting upstairs. What brings you here?"

"I work here." She lowered her voice. "Are you really going to claim you didn't know that?"

"I didn't even know you lived in Portland," he pointed out. "Though I can't say I'm not happy for the coincidence." He was probably happier than he should have been, given their last conversation.

Her eyebrows arched over skeptical eyes. "And why is that?"

"I've never been to Portland before. It's always a pleasure to see a"—he paused, smirking at the irony—"*friendly* face. Maybe this will afford me the opportunity to make amends if our previous interactions somehow offended you."

The almost emotionlessly polite expression didn't yield. "No amends necessary."

Somehow, the fact that she didn't melt at the apology further piqued his interest. Maybe he was a glutton for punishment. Or maybe some version of fate kept bringing him together with a beautiful, intriguing woman. "Well then. Perhaps you would grace me with your company later today, show me around Portland."

Her gaze skimmed over him pensively, but a third figure joined them before she had a chance to answer, drawing her attention.

"Gina. You know better than to take a call during a meeting," the other man reprimanded.

The bigger security guard moved to the outside edge of the counter that separated him from the trio, poised to intercede. Hunter looked at the blond man, trying to discern the dynamic. Perhaps he was her boss, though chastising her in public was horribly unprofessional.

Gina's chin notched up, and her shoulders lifted almost imperceptibly. "How's your nose doing?"

Hunter almost took a step back from the obvious hostility. A tick jumped in the blond man's jaw. Seething eyes shifted to Hunter.

"Mr. Cavaliere, I'm Alistair Talbot," the man said with cool politeness, butchering Hunter's last name but confirming his suspicion. "So sorry to keep you waiting. Please, let's head upstairs."

There were too many coincidences for Hunter's liking. Had this meeting been something Gina had suggested? It seemed unlikely, given her obvious dislike for the man, and apparent surprise at seeing him. "I'll join you in just a moment," Hunter said politely yet firmly.

Mr. Talbot held his gaze for an instant then tilted his head, before striding to the bank of elevators.

Hunter refocused on Gina, who had grown pale.

"That's who you're meeting with?" A blend of emotions he couldn't quite pick out added breathiness to her voice.

"You don't seem to like him." And it seemed personal, not that it was really any of his business. "A former friend of yours?" he asked anyway.

He could see her swallow. "Something like that. Enjoy your meeting."

"Have lunch with me afterward?" Hunter would bet that whatever Talbot wanted to discuss, he wasn't interested. Thankfully, he had the luxury of avoiding business with those who rubbed him the wrong way, even if he felt obliged to take the meeting.

Gina's eyes flicked to Talbot, and she took a step back, not looking at Hunter. "I don't think so."

"How about instead, then?" Something about the man had her spooked, and that wasn't a good sign, even if Hunter had been interested in whatever endeavor the man wanted to discuss.

That got her attention. "People don't skip meetings with Alistair," she said quietly, all traces of the polite half-smile gone.

"I'm not most people." Though apparently he was dumber than most, unable to walk away from what was obviously a complicated situation he should have been avoiding.

Her eyes flicked back to Talbot, waiting by the elevators. "Really, I imagine you have important business to discuss, if you truly came all the way up here for this meeting. Wouldn't want you to waste your trip."

Hunter would have protested, but the security guard moved closer. And really, she was right. It wouldn't do to offend Alistair Talbot, even if Hunter was already disinclined to enter into any kind of business arrangement with him. No sense in burning bridges unnecessarily. Eyes on the hovering guard, Hunter dipped his chin and left to join the businessman.

`Where did you go?!?`

Roger's text vibrated her phone in her palm as Gina exited the elevator.

A heightened sense of activity filled the cubicles around her as she strode to her office. Roger stood waiting outside her door. His mouth opened as she approached.

"Not now," she said before he could ask again.

He followed her inside and shut the door.

"Did I miss anything important?" She lowered into her desk chair, waking up her computer to check her email for a sense of normalcy.

"Your jackass ex-boyfriend is buying our magazine."

Gina arched an eyebrow at Roger's classification.

"And he wants to take an 'active part' in helping to shape its future, though he wouldn't want to 'interfere in its proven track record.'" Roger plopped onto one of the conference chairs. "What, am I wrong?"

Not in the least. Though Roger didn't know the details of her relationship with Alistair, apparently he'd noticed more than she'd thought. "Did they say anything else?"

"Nothing particularly interesting, except the usual fake assurances about staff retention." Roger crossed his legs, tapping his knee impatiently and waiting for her to comment. When she didn't, he asked, "Did you really not know?"

"We haven't exactly kept in touch," Gina answered. Maybe she should have seen it coming, but she was notoriously clueless when it came to Alistair.

"What are you thinking?" Roger asked.

Gina couldn't fake a platitude, so she just shook her head. "I need to not be disturbed for a bit, okay? Can you just remind them all that they still have work to do? Save the gossip for their lunch breaks."

She knew she was in trouble when Roger followed her instructions without comment. He shut her door with a little *click*. Gina ran her fingers through her hair, gently massaging her scalp as she exhaled. A few seconds later, she used the reflection in her computer screen to resettle her hair, as though her problems were that easily fixed.

She'd actually gotten complacent about him. He hadn't approached her at all since that last night in her apartment when Kane had interfered. He may have considered coming near her at first, but Roger and Benny had kept her surrounded for a while without really knowing why, probably on Sabella's orders. Still, she should have realized he wouldn't have let it go. Let her go.

She couldn't figure out his play, though. He would be able to fire her, but then she would be back out from under his thumb. He could micromanage her, but wouldn't that be too obvious to her coworkers? Maybe he was simply trying to prove that she couldn't get away from the power his money could buy.

And then there was Hunter, who kept popping up. Flashes from their time together had run through her mind since her conversation with Sabella: him kissing her temple after their first time together; him questioning her clearheadedness rather than taking advantage; him trying to balance as he took off his socks; the unabashed appreciation in his gaze as he watched her. Even the strength he had seen in the woman in Trisha's painting spoke to his character. Alistair would have seen desperation, fault. A woeful lack of suitability.

Was it coincidence, Hunter being there? Sabella would probably have claimed it was fate. Not long ago, Gina would have considered it an opportunity for a bit more fun. Now, she didn't know what to think. She didn't want to think. And what if something more nefarious was at play?

Though he really was a great kisser. And he'd called her beautiful.

Somehow, she hadn't noticed last summer that Alistair had only paid her backhanded compliments, if that.

A knock on her office door brought her out of the circular contemplation. Hunter stood on the other side of the glass, drawing looks from her coworkers. Roger was nowhere in sight.

Gina glanced at the clock, then back to the door. With few other office-appropriate options, and since their interaction would be seen if not heard, she waved him in.

Hunter shut the door once inside but didn't approach her desk. "Hi," he said simply.

"Fast meeting." He'd been up there for barely half an hour.

Eleven

onger than it needed to be, Hunter thought. The conversation had started out professionally enough, discussing the possibility of Cavaliere Vineyards' involvement in the opening of a new local wine bar. Then Talbot had not all that subtly recommended Hunter avoid association with "women of Ms. Sabatino's ilk," for the sake of maintaining their reputations if they were to go into business together. Condescension like that churned Hunter's stomach. On the plus side, Talbot had used her last name, which made her office infinitely easier to find. "What can I do for you, Mr. Cavaliere?" she asked with a slightly less cheerful version of that blank professional expression from downstairs.

"It appears I have the rest of the day free."

"As you can see," she said, gesturing to the modern office around them, "I am in the middle of my workday."

The chilled tone was worse than when she'd hissed at him in the gallery. And if he thought she'd been tense the day they met, it was nothing compared to how she looked now. Downright skittish. He really should let it go, but there was some mystery here, and running into her yet again had to be more than a random coincidence.

At the same time, he shouldn't keep pushing her. So what was he doing in her office? "If I cannot convince you to join me, then perhaps you wouldn't mind offering some suggestions for my time here."

An eyebrow crooked. "Portland has some great food trucks, if those aren't beneath a man such as yourself."

"Not at all." She clearly really took issue with wealth. Then again, if she was used to men like Talbot, she couldn't really be blamed.

"And otherwise, if you're seeking company, you should try Eighty-second Avenue."

Years of business dealings were all that kept Hunter from outwardly reacting to the suggestion. "I'm not interested in just anyone's company," he countered. *And definitely not in prostitutes.*

She watched him expressionlessly.

All he could think was to lay his cards on the table. "Look, I apologize if my presence is unwelcome, although I would hope your memories of our time together are not entirely unpleasant."

Her only reaction was a slight shift of the shoulders.

"Personally, I don't believe in coincidences," he continued. "Since we keep running into one another, perhaps we could get to know each other better?"

"Is there something you would like to know?"

She wasn't going to make this easy. Maybe she was involved with Talbot and didn't want the man finding out about their fling. It didn't seem likely. And intentional or not, she had given him an opening. Against his better judgment, Hunter asked, "Why did you make that comment about Talbot's nose?"

She froze, lips slightly parted, then dropped her gaze, blowing her breath out.

"I'm sorry, it's none of my business," Hunter backtracked immediately.

Righteousness sparked in her eyes when she looked back to him. "I'm fairly certain Kane, the groom from that wedding, broke it last year." Her gaze trained evenly on him, gauging his response.

It didn't make sense. The singer hadn't struck Hunter as particularly belligerent when visiting the winery to plan the wedding. If anything, he'd been easygoing and respectful, and Talbot clearly wasn't the type to get into random fights. The man probably detested the idea of a speck of lint on his tailored suit. Hunter's sense of people tended to be accurate, but if he was wrong about the singer, it would be good to know before the group's return to his vineyard for their summer concert. "Why would he do that?"

Her shoulders shifted again, anxiety she was trying to contain fighting its way out. "I suppose he was trying to make a point."

Hunter could feel his brows draw together as he puzzled through the information, gazing around at the bright trim and vibrant pops of decoration scattered about the office, without really paying attention. His jaw clenched as the pieces clicked, from Gina's carefully controlled tension and the security guard hovering, to the painting she had focused on, and the one thing that could prompt even an even-tempered man to fight.

"He hurt you?" Hunter asked softly, hoping he was way off.

Shock or panic sharpened her gaze and slightly pinched her lips, confirming the suspicion.

Hunter tried to breathe through his own building tension. No wonder he'd felt reluctant to enter into any kind of business deal with the man. Not even a man. "Want me to go break it again?" he half-joked. "No strings attached," he added for good measure.

What the hell could she say to that? The offer had come out of nowhere, following the too insightful guess. Kane had at least had some reason to feel protective. The delicate brush of Hunter's lips on her temple floated through Gina's mind again. "Why would you do that?" she managed to ask.

"Because apparently your friend's lesson didn't stick." He didn't look furious or impassioned, but rather calm, determined.

Still, it was good to have most of her office separating them. "What lesson would that be?"

"That real men cherish and protect the people in their lives."

Gina stared at him without comment. This was one of the main deterrents to telling anyone what had happened. She was more than Alistair's victim.

"Regardless of whether she needs it," Hunter added, almost reading her mind.

Which was impossible, of course. *A warrior, who's made it through*, he'd said of the woman in Trisha's painting.

In the silence, his gaze shifted to the window behind her, and he winced. "Well, I'm not so sure about food trucks in the rain." Those deeply brown eyes returned to her. Either he had the best poker face she'd ever seen, or he really didn't judge her for everything he'd just somehow learned. "Are you sure you won't join me for some rainy day comfort food?" His shoulders notched up, and he tilted his head, lifting his eyebrows in an obviously practiced attempt to look charming. "I'll even let you pay, if that'll make you feel better."

A startled exhale escaped her, turning into a reluctant chuckle when she remembered her comments in the gallery. Maybe Sabella was right, and spending more time with him would be harmless. At the end of the day, he'd still be leaving Portland soon enough. And staying at the office with its anxious bustle, especially with the recent reminder of who was right upstairs, was entirely unappealing.

✧ ✧ ✧

"This is what you consider comfort food?" Hunter asked, looking around Vitto Ghiotto's clean lines and crisp linens with a bemused smile.

"There's some Italian in you somewhere, right? Or is the name a gimmick."

His gaze stopped on her with a slight nod. "My great-grandparents." His eyes narrowed. "Sabatino."

"You catch on quick." The sarcasm was probably a bit too biting, but Lina came up before Gina could backtrack.

"Benvenuto, Gina," she greeted with a warm smile. "Per due?"

"Si grazie, Lina." She followed the waitress past simple wooden furniture and impeccable place settings, and Hunter fell in behind her. "It's quiet today," Gina observed.

Lina glanced back over her shoulder. "You're here a little earlier than usual. But Marisa will be happy, she'll have time to come out and say hi."

Hunter waited until Gina slid into the booth before sitting himself. Lina twisted the menus toward each of them in a polished motion.

Gina shot her another smile. "Thanks, Lina."

"Enjoy," Lina added before melting away.

"It's your first time here, I take it?" Hunter commented drily.

"Portland's just a friendly place." Gina set aside her menu without opening it and reached for her glass of water. She knew exactly what she wanted today, at least when it came to lunch.

Hunter opened his menu but didn't look at it either. "Any suggestions?"

"What are you in the mood for?"

To his credit, he didn't go for the obvious suggestion, though his eyes did dip down her body. That little sign that he still saw her as attractive, and not as some distressed damsel, was surprisingly reassuring. "What are some of your favorites?" he asked politely.

"Their Pollo Ortolano is excellent, though you can't really go wrong if Marisa is cooking." She forced herself to maintain a politely blank expression. This was even more awkward than a bad first date, since they already had a history of sorts despite not really knowing anything about each other. Except now Hunter knew.

"Should I just close my eyes and point?" he asked.

"Sounds like a solid strategy. You do that with your business, too?" The tension of the day kept spilling out in her sarcasm, which wasn't entirely fair of her. Could she ask about his meeting? Did she even want to know?

Hunter's eyes narrowed, but he didn't otherwise react to the bite of her misplaced hostility. "Nope. My folks would kill me. I do tend to go with my gut, though."

"Is that what brought you up to Portland?" That was suitably casual. Probably.

"You know, I'm starting to think it might have been." His gaze softened on her for a moment, offering a sense of illogical comfort. He blinked, snapping that feeling, and exhaled. "I actually came up to look at some plots of land. Entirely different climate means entirely different wines."

She must have failed at hiding her confusion, because he answered the question she couldn't ask. "Since I was coming up to Portland anyway, I agreed to a meeting that had been requested, to discuss a potential collaboration. Which will not be happening," he added in her silence.

"Are you two ready to order?" Lina reappeared with impeccable timing, slipping a basket of freshly baked bread and some pesto butter on their table.

Thank goodness. "What do you think? Have you made a decision?"

"After you," he offered, looking down at his menu.

"I'll have the baked three-cheese artichoke ziti," Gina told the waitress.

"Oh, good call. I think I might have that later on my break. And your friend?"

"How about the honey-rosemary gnocchi," he said, with a pleasant smile to Lina.

She scribbled it down. "Anything to drink?"

Hunter looked to Gina.

"I'm all set with water, but please. You do have the day off." A soft red would have actually gone really well with the baked pasta, but drinking in the middle of her workday might be a bit too decadent.

"No, water's good, if you're sure?" He was being so courteous—living up to the family name.

Gina nodded, first at Hunter, then to Lina. The waitress gathered their menus and walked away, mouthing "cute," from behind Hunter.

Gina pressed her lips together to hide a smile. She certainly couldn't argue with that.

Hunter leaned back, relaxing in the faux-leather booth. "So."

"So?" Gina considered taking a slice of bread. It would be delicious, but Hunter might object to her eating unabashedly. Why had she brought him somewhere she actually liked?

"Did you grow up in Portland?"

"No, Boston, actually." The bread thing really shouldn't have posed such a dilemma, but apparently Alistair had already managed to get back under her skin. She stopped herself from drumming her fingers on the table. "What about you?" she asked, refocusing on the man across from her. "Did you always live in Sonoma?"

"No, I grew up a little further south, in Los Altos." He lifted the breadbasket, tilting it toward her.

"Thanks," she murmured, taking a slice. A pat of pesto butter soon melted into the fluffy warmth. "I thought we read your vineyard was a family legacy?"

Hunter deftly buttered his own piece of bread. "Yes, that's right. It was owned by my grandparents, and we did spend quite a bit of our time up there, but my parents weren't too interested in the day-to-day of working with wine."

"What do they do?" She bit into the bread, allowing the blend of tastes to play over her tongue. No telltale signs of disapproval flickered on Hunter's face, and Gina's muscles unclenched a fraction.

"My mother works for one of the big tech companies, and my father is a senior financial analyst. My brother followed in his footsteps, somewhat, going into financial management. I went the other way, learning from my grandpa." A sad smile accompanied his final words.

"You two were close."

Hunter nodded slowly. "He was the best. He taught me a lot, not just about wine, but about how to live life. That random coincidences probably happen for a reason."

Gina exhaled, holding back a smile. Despite herself, the distance she had tried to maintain was dissolving under his easy attitude. Something about him was comforting, almost soothing. But she had to remember not to let her guard down. She looked away from him, picking up her water glass.

"So what about you? You work in fashion?"

The ice water reinforced her professional demeanor, and she nodded. "I'm a fashion editor for a local women's magazine, though you may have noticed that."

Her phone ringing cut off whatever he was about to say. Heart pounding, Gina scrambled for her purse to silence it, shooting him an apologetic glance and seeking signs of anger.

"I'm so sorry." She'd been so flustered by the morning's events that she hadn't thought to turn off the ringer. *Stupid*. She knew better than to keep her phone on around someone like him. At least they were in public. "Really, I'm—"

Hunter gestured with one hand, palm up, cutting off her apology. "Please. I'm the one disrupting your day. You should take that if you need to." No tick jumped at his jaw, and no vise grip clenched her wrist, silently demanding she ignore the call.

Gina glanced at the caller ID. *Sabella*. "I really should," she murmured, slipping out of the booth. She walked toward the back and the restrooms as she answered the call, trying to breathe through the wash of anxiety. "Hi," she said to Sabella, leaning against the cushioned wall beside the ladies' room.

"Hey, are you all right?" Sabella asked. "Roger called, saying you left unexpectedly, with some guy?"

"I'm fine, just, uh. Just decided to go out for lunch." She debated for half a second before adding, "With Hunter."

"Wait. What?"

"I know, and it's a long story. I promise I'll fill you in, and I think I'm fine." *Liar*. "Or I'm making a ginormous mistake, but in theory, it's just lunch."

"With Hunter," Sabella repeated.

"Yeah. I might be crazy, but there are just these little things about him, that are so different from…"

Silence spanned between them over the phone. "Well, good, I think," Sabella said eventually, sounding a little at a loss for words which was virtually unthinkable. "Just, you know. Try to have a good time, and if you need anything, give me a call."

Sabella had gotten almost as overprotective as Gina's mother. She felt unreasonably guilty, for being out of town with Kane last summer and not intervening sooner, though of course she couldn't have known, and really, the intervention shouldn't have been necessary. Still, the protective presence was kind of nice. "Okay, thanks, Sab."

"And I expect you to fill in the blanks later!" Sabella added.

"You got it. I'll talk to you soon."

By the time Gina returned to their booth, their food had arrived. She was kind of regretting not ordering the wine, to calm her nerves a bit and because it would complement the pasta so well, but the dish would be superb all on its own.

"Is everything all right?" Hunter asked as she lowered back in front of him.

"Yes, thanks." He hadn't touched his food. "Please," she gestured to his plate.

"Ladies first."

The simple courtesy shouldn't have meant as much as it did. Gina picked up her fork, genuinely looking forward to the cheesy, perfectly seasoned, slightly crisped ziti. She slipped some onto her fork, blowing gently before sliding it into her mouth. At that first taste, a smile tugged at her lips and her eyes drifted shut, just for an instant. When they reopened, appreciative humor crinkled around Hunter's eyes.

He tried some of his gnocchi, and those eyes widened. He nodded as he chewed. "Wow," he said after swallowing. "Talk about comfort food."

By the time Lina slid the check onto their table, Gina decided this lunch had definitely been the right call. Marisa's food was reason enough to have slipped out, but Hunter had actually surprised her, too. He was warmly open, interesting, and interes*ted*. He seemed to have no expectations for who it was she had been or was supposed to be, and she found herself not worrying about who she now was. Their time together was limited either way, which helped this illusion of ease that his demeanor encouraged.

"So," he asked, not reaching for the little black folder, "am I allowed to pay?"

It seemed like such a trivial thing, but it was nice he hadn't forgotten. "I suppose," she tried to brush off. "I did drive." Taking her car had made more sense than getting a cab, especially since Vitto Ghiotto wasn't far from his hotel.

Cheeks rounding slightly from his smile, he seamlessly slipped his credit card into the folder without glancing at the check.

"Thanks," Gina said quietly.

"No, please. After that meal, I am definitely the one who should be thanking you."

On their way out, he held the door for her, then groaned when he joined her outside. "So much for exploring the city."

Gina bit back a laugh. "Welcome to Portland." Their rainy season was most of the year.

"Thanks," he said wryly. "So," he added, lips twisting to the side.

"Would you like a ride?" she offered, taking pity on his endearing disappointment, and his obviously expensive suit.

"Nah, it won't kill me." He paused, maintaining their light-hearted eye contact until it grew tinged with sensuality. "Unless you feel like playing hooky? I mean, we didn't have any dessert."

"We didn't..." she echoed, still processing his casual dismissal of the suit. And had he really proposed she skip work? Alistair would have had a stroke at the idea, and very nearly had when she'd made the mistake of suggesting it.

"I'm told that The Benson has this incredible molten chocolate cake that comes with homemade ice cream and home-made whipped cream." His eyebrows rose just barely, a shadow of his earlier attempt to appear endearing.

"That does sound appealing," she acknowledged, forcing him to spell out the implied invitation.

"Any chance you'd join me for some?"

They both knew he wasn't really talking about cake. But dessert, chocolate or otherwise, could be fun, significantly more so than returning to work. Besides, a couple more hours together couldn't be that big a risk. What could it hurt?

Twelve

Hunter slipped out his phone as Gina started her car. "Should I find a menu? Or does that molten cake sound good."

"Sounds like it can't be beat."

He could think of a better dessert, but suggesting it would be against the point of getting to know her better in a non-sexual way, and he was genuinely enjoying spending time with her regardless. Intelligent, witty, undeniably gorgeous, and charming, when she relaxed—she was obviously adored by the restaurant's staff, so much so the chef had made sure to come say hello, and he'd already seen her easy friendliness with those at the wedding.

Gina's head bobbed gently to the soft music running through the car's speakers, distracting Hunter enough that the hotel employee had to ask twice if he wanted anything other than the dessert.

"Would you like a drink?" Hunter asked, remembering his manners.

Her head jerked toward him for a second, sending her hair flying.

"Coffee? Wine? Anything?" he added.

Her lips parted at the mention of coffee, but she hesitated again before exhaling and confirming the suspicion. "A coffee would be lovely."

Hunter finished the order and hung up, watching her navigate the Portland streets.

Though she'd mostly relaxed as they'd eaten, a hint of tension returned to her posture once her keys went to the hotel's valet, gradually ramping up as they made their way to his room.

"Please, make yourself comfortable," Hunter said, opening the door. "I apologize for the lack of seating. I wasn't anticipating having company on this trip." The only options were an armchair, a desk chair, and of course the bed. He hadn't really thought it through when inviting her.

She smirked. "How incredibly disappointing." She hesitated briefly then strode to one of the large corner windows. Gray light filtered into the room through thin curtains, but with Gina's company, the weather didn't concern him in the least. Hazy light caressed her skin as she gazed out the window.

Hunter reached for his tie, loosening it slightly before catching himself. "Sorry," he said sheepishly, and she turned back toward him. "Would you mind if I got rid of the tie and jacket?"

Her hands did a little half circle around the room. "It's your home away from home."

"And you're the guest." He took a couple steps toward her. "In fact, should I be offering to take your jacket?" A bright, sort of blue-but-green top peeked from beneath the black fabric.

Wordlessly, she shrugged out of the jacket, revealing delicate chain straps that held the top in place, reaching over her neck and around her back. He swallowed roughly. She held the jacket loosely until he remembered to take it, draping it over the desk chair before peeling off his own. "So, what does one do on a rainy day in Portland?"

"Well, normally, one continues living life as usual on the many, many rainy days in Portland."

Hunter's eyes dipped briefly to the skin revealed by her backless halter before returning to her face. "And when one plays hooky?"

Gina shrugged carefully, shifting the draping over her chest. His eyes flicked down again, and she suppressed a smile. The top was perfectly demure under a jacket, but without one, it showed off almost more than it covered. She hadn't worn it like this in a long time. "That's the benefit of playing hooky, isn't it? Get to do pretty much whatever."

The room-service knock broke their eye contact, and Gina exhaled. He was being downright decorous, which made pushing his limits almost fun, but the lush surroundings still set her on edge. The Benson wasn't an inexpensive place, and this wasn't even their cheapest room. The reminder of Hunter's wealth, of that world, ate at the edges of the comfort of his company. Then again, she could walk out at any time, and he hadn't actually done anything to cause her anxiety. No, the sensations Hunter himself inspired in her were entirely different.

He wheeled the room service cart to the foot of the bed and lifted the metal cover, revealing a single dish that looked like it lived up to the hype. A little pot of additional chocolate sauce sat next to it, along with their coffees, a chilled bowl of ice cream, some utensils, and a pretty flower in a tiny vase.

"I hope you don't mind," Hunter said. "I was thinking we could share. Or order another, if you like it."

Faking confidence to match that of their first encounter, Gina settled on the edge of the bed, slipped a spoon into the whipped cream beside the cake, and stirred it into one of the coffee cups. Hunter smiled and lowered beside her. The unbuttoned vee of his shirt revealed tanned skin whose taste she could still recall. She sipped her coffee to replace the memory.

He picked up the second spoon but predictably didn't touch the dessert. Gina dipped her spoon in, scooping up a tiny piece so he'd feel comfortable trying it himself. She flipped the spoon, dropping the warm chocolate onto her tongue, then froze for a second with the metal still between her lips.

"That good?" Hunter teased, tucking his own spoon into the mound that had begun to ooze chocolate.

"It's pretty much worth getting a room here," Gina confirmed without thinking.

Hunter moaned his agreement, eyebrows drawing together in surprise. "We may just have to order another one. Or five."

Gina actually giggled.

"Should we add more chocolate?" Hunter asked conspiratorially, picking up the silver pot.

She nodded quickly, and he dripped some sauce over the cake and the ice cream then picked up his coffee. Gina slid her spoon into the soft mass of ice cream melting under the heat of the chocolate. The temperatures blended seamlessly, playing off each other in her mouth.

Hunter replaced his cup on the tray, and their spoons clicked, both reaching for more. His ingrained manners caused him to pull his back, and Gina gathered a bit more of the cake, with a dollop of whipped cream, then lifted her spoon out of the way for him. His wrist swiveled as he scooped bits of all three ingredients, and for a second, Gina just admired the dexterous motion.

Until a drop of chocolaty whipped cream from her spoon landed on his sleeve. Air froze in her lungs, and her free hand clenched. Carefully as she could, Gina lowered her spoon to the tray. "I—I'm sorry." The melted mess was already spreading, seeping between the fine fabric's threads. "I'm really sorry."

His brows angled together. Gina should have gotten up; she should have run, straight out the fancy hotel door. But she couldn't move. Hunter's bare torso flashed through her mind, the solid muscles flexing, their power controlled by nothing more than his will. The menacing image became the clang of dishes crashing, the slap of fabric thrown at her, the thuds of unforgiving flesh hitting hers. Gina's eyes closed against the memories as her shoulders braced.

Hands landed on her skin, and she flinched, until the soft warmth seeped through. Gently, Hunter's thumbs brushed over her shoulders, and the sound of him saying her name found its way into her mind. Her eyes opened to the color of the chocolate sauce, surrounded by thick lashes.

"First," he said, and her gaze dipped to his mouth. "That was not your fault. And second," he continued as her lips parted to protest, "it's just a shirt."

"Yeah, we, I—" She bit the insides of her lips, gaining focus from the localized bit of pain. Her eyes found the brownish blob. "I should try to wash that out for you, or I could go pick up a replacement, if you'd prefer, or—"

"Really," he cut her off quietly. "It doesn't matter."

Gina swallowed, trying to control her breathing as her lungs jerked. *This* was why she had avoided anything other than the most casual encounters. She couldn't do this; flawless social interactions were beyond her, and she absolutely never wanted anyone to see her like this.

Hunter's hand shifted up, fingers grazing her jaw with the faintest pressure. His thumb swept over her cheek. She exhaled, and his hand cupped the side of her face more solidly, though no less tenderly. Gradually, the flow of air through her body smoothed in the face of his steadiness.

He wasn't pulling away, and he didn't seem angry. His hand dropped to her shoulder, then both lightly slid down and up her arms. "You all right?"

Her eyes closed for an extended moment, heightening her awareness of his hands, their warmth, his controlled strength. When they reopened, she focused on the light lines between his brows, the tightness of his lips, before finally meeting his gaze. There was no criticism, no derision or disgust in his eyes. All she could see was patient concern that melted into something softer, contemplative, as she watched him.

Gina opened her mouth to say something, though she hadn't figured out what, and Hunter's gaze dropped to her lips.

She leaned slightly toward him, and then his lips met hers, slipping against them with a gentle friction. Opening her mouth further, she flicked her tongue out to taste his. Hunter's hands followed the invitation, rising to cup her head as he deepened the kiss. Their tongues met, sliding together lightly before twisting with each other in a slow discovery.

He pulled back with a hum, brushing her mouth once more. "You taste like chocolate," he murmured, so close his breath flowed over her.

Her cheeks twitched, briefly tugging her lips into a shadow of a smile. "I think that's the cake."

He smiled lightly, dropping his hands and looking down at the plate. Under the heat of the chocolate, the ice cream had quickly begun to melt, leaving two mounds floating in a shallow pool. A bit of whipped cream topped the blob that still rested on her spoon.

"Would you like some more?" he asked.

Gina glanced around the well-appointed room, folding her hands in her lap to prevent further mishaps. "No, that's okay." She clearly wasn't meant for this immaculate world.

"Would you like something else?" Hunter asked, faultlessly polite.

His eyes exposed no judgment or hidden anger, but Gina's gaze still fell to the smudged spot, and she shook her head.

"Gina." A hand dropped lightly on her knee, its warmth seeping through the thin fabric of her slacks. "I would pour the rest of that chocolate sauce all over this shirt to show you how little this matters to me."

She looked back to his face.

"But it kind of seems like a waste of the chocolate, don't you think?"

Gina's mouth opened and closed as she tried to figure him out. He hadn't said anything inappropriate, but the spark in his eyes didn't seem entirely innocent, either. That entirely familiar heat was the one thing she could make sense of. "I suppose there are better options."

He picked up his discarded spoon and slipped some of the melted mess on, casually bringing it to his lips. "Options, huh? Any suggestions?"

"You should probably soak that shirt."

He arched an eyebrow, lowered the spoon, then started undoing the buttons on his shirt. Cuff links clinked on the room service tray before he shrugged out of it and flung the fabric toward a corner of the room.

Alistair would have tossed it in her face and later had a fit at the crumpled, stained fabric.

But Hunter wasn't Alistair.

"Should I go find a clean shirt?" he asked, watching her carefully.

The implications were clear, but he was letting her decide. He'd already seen her weaknesses, multiple times, and right through her past back at the office, but he had yet to take advantage, leaving every step in her hands. And he would be returning to California anyway.

Gina picked up her spoon. "Probably shouldn't risk it."

His eyes crinkled, and he leaned closer, sharing the taste of the cooled spoonful in her mouth. Gina laughed against his lips as his fingers tangled in her hair.

Thirteen

Well, that got messy," Gina murmured beside him.

Hunter chuckled, lifting her hand to lick away a stray spot of chocolate on her wrist. She shivered delicately against him, turning the chuckle into a moan. Sleeping with her again hadn't been the point of inviting her out, but he sure as hell wasn't complaining. He dropped another kiss to her shoulder.

"Do you want to watch a movie or something?"

She arched against him. "I'm kind of sticky."

"Sorry," he smiled, brushing his knuckles over the slight curve of her waist.

"Are you?"

No hint of her earlier panic remained, replaced by a lightness and contentment that was infinitely better. "Not at all. But you're welcome to use the shower if you want."

"Probably a good call." She rolled away, the brush of her body tightening his as she rose from the bed and moved easily to the bathroom.

Hunter exhaled, dropping back onto the dessert-stained bedspread before pushing himself up off the bed. Their clothes lay scattered about the room. He went around, picking up the pieces, and brought them to the armchair, then wheeled the room service cart out of the way.

On the one hand, he should get dressed, so she wouldn't think his interest in her staying was purely physical. On the other, he could also really use a shower.

He came to the bathroom door and knocked softly. A few seconds later, she opened the door, still naked. Hunter's eyes slipped, and his body reacted without hesitation. "Hey there."

Her eyebrows lifted over humor-narrowed eyes. "Hi."

"I was just thinking." What had he been thinking? "If we showered together, we could conserve some water." The excuse was beyond weak.

"We are very eco-friendly here," she allowed generously.

Hunter's shoulders lifted. "When in Portland…"

The hissing of water streaming into the tub behind her filled their silence until she stepped back from the door, opening it more widely. Hunter followed her in, kicking it gently closed behind him.

Gina stepped into the shower, arching under the spray that flowed over her body, and looked at him with a hint of a smile, entirely aware of the effect she was having. The contrast with her earlier uncertainty was immeasurable. He stepped in after her, blocking some of the spray from her, and squeezed some body wash into his hand from the hotel's dispenser. The gel pooled in his palm with stray droplets of water, and he lathered it together, sending a light cucumber scent into the air around them.

Her hands came to his chest then slid up, already slick from the water. Hunter brought his hands to her waist, stroking the smooth warmth of her skin. Water beaded on her torso. She reached past his shoulder to the soap, eyes on his. His breathing grew heavier, his body tighter.

She lathered the gel against his skin, running her palms in uneven circles over his chest and stomach. Hunter moved his fingers to a lingering bit of chocolate sauce on the soft swell of her breast, covering it with his palm. Her fingers flexed into his shoulders as her lips parted. He trailed his hands over her torso, removing bits of stickiness but mostly teasing tiny shivers from her. She rose on her tiptoes, turning them so the spray beat at his back, and captured his lips.

Their torsos slid together as her hip pressed against him, and Hunter stifled a groan, tangling his tongue with hers. He flicked his thumbs over her breasts, and she tensed against him, gasping into his mouth. He broke their kiss to watch her eyes darken as his fingers circled her nipples, and she lowered back to the floor.

She reached for more body wash, slathering it over his back. The cucumber smell overtook his nostrils, and he slid a knee between hers, hooking one of her legs over his thigh. He braced on the side of the bathtub, stretching her, and her hands lowered to his hips, soap-slicked fingers drawing disappearing patterns on his skin. When he slid one hand down over her stomach, slipping it between her parted thighs, her fingers stilled, though her hips arched into his hand.

He stroked one finger over her with the faintest pressure, and Gina's eyelids drooped. Her chest rose as he stroked more firmly, palming her breast with his other hand. Her fingers dug into his hips as she ground against him. Hunter ducked his head, recapturing her lips and swallowing her moan as he slipped a finger inside, thumb flicking over her.

Her thigh tightened against his leg, and her head dropped back, breaking the kiss as her body sought air. Hunter dipped to her neck, licking up the beaded droplets as her breasts slid against his chest and she writhed into his hand.

Her hand slipped from his hip, and he smiled against her skin, until she gripped his length. He flexed his fingers inside her as his jaw clenched. She squeezed gently, and Hunter groaned, fighting to focus on the slickness of her on his fingers instead of the tormenting pressure of hers. Her breathless moan mingled with his voice as her hand slid over him, to his tip then down, gently hitting the base of his stomach.

Hunter matched the rhythms of his fingers on her breast and in her wetness, and she braced against his bicep, continuing her sure, slow stroke. He shut his eyes against the sensations, feeling her clench and shiver until her fingers squeezed and nails bit lightly into his arm. With one more stroke, he lost control, spilling over her skin as her climax danced through her.

He shifted his arm to her waist, holding her against him, and lowered his leg. Water still beat against his back. She blew her breath out in a puff, shivering against him once more.

"Well that was kind of counterproductive," she murmured breathlessly.

"Somewhat," he agreed, seeking any hint of discomfort in her expression. If anything, she looked languidly satisfied. He brushed her lips again and shifted away, raising the heat of the cooling water.

She hummed when the water hit her.

"Guess I should let you get cleaned up." He turned into the stream, letting it clean away the leftover body wash.

Her lips stretched in a teasing smile as she glanced down his body. He slid his thumb in an arc on her hip and pressed a kiss to her temple before stepping out of the shower, followed by a hint of cucumber.

Gina wrapped the fluffy white towel around herself and ran her fingers through her dampened hair, before swiping them under her eyes to catch any stray makeup. For all her other concerns, Hunter was really superb at this particular method of stress relief. Little surges of pleasure still tingled through her as she moved, drying her exposed skin with an extra towel.

Hunter's eyes opened when she left the bathroom, and he sat up on the bed, wearing only a pair of drawstring lounge pants. His half smile disarmed her further.

"So where'd we land on that movie?" he asked.

Gina chuckled, not moving further into the room. "I should probably get going."

"You could stay."

She'd already crossed so many lines today, but staying seemed like going too far. If she left now, they would have had barely more than some great sex. And a little bit of easy, comforting connection.

"Watch a movie, get some dinner, maybe show me around the city if it ever stops raining," he coaxed when she didn't comment.

"I'm not the one with a change of clothes," Gina pointed out, seizing the excuse. It was just too much.

"There are robes somewhere, if you'd like. Or I could loan you a tee shirt."

The intimacy he was suggesting tensed her shoulders despite its apparent innocence. They weren't close enough to lounge in robes, watching movies in an extremely pricey hotel room. And technically, she should still go back to work for a couple hours, though if she were honest, that probably wasn't going to happen.

"Okay, well, what about tomorrow?" he asked before she could formulate her refusal. "Dinner, in the evening? I could push back my flight."

"Why?" she asked before thinking better of it. With the question out there, she forced herself to maintain eye contact.

He pushed himself up off the bed, taking a couple steps toward her but maintaining a reasonable distance. "Because you're smart, interesting, unbelievably sexy. Something keeps throwing us together, and I'm definitely not complaining. I'd like to spend more time with you." His lips pulled lightly to one side. "And I'm hoping you wouldn't object to spending a little more time with me, either. You could show me your favorite food truck."

Gina exhaled, dropping her gaze to the floor. She'd assumed the idea of eating from a food truck would horrify him, which was precisely why she had suggested them, though they were actually quite popular. So much about him defied her expectations, even if the budding relationship he was suggesting felt like a trap. Dinner was just dinner. What was one more day? "Okay," she agreed finally. "Dinner, tomorrow, if you're sure about changing your flight."

His eyes crinkled slightly with his easy smile. "I'm sure."

Gina crossed the room to the armchair, sorting through the pile of clothes he'd picked up to fish out hers. When she spun back toward the bathroom, Hunter had turned to her, though he hadn't moved closer.

"So. Do I get your number?"

Her glance flew to her purse. What options did she have, here? This was what she avoided, any sense of ties, lasting connections.

"Or, I could give you mine," Hunter offered.

"Sounds good," she agreed, swallowing the lump that had grown in her throat. He was either ridiculously perceptive, or extremely thoughtful, but that effortless ability to adjust for her comfort, without making her feel like a pathetic victim, was at once reassuring and somewhat eerie. She didn't know what to make of him.

"Good," he echoed, stepping away from the bathroom door so she could pass him to go get dressed.

Gina fingered Hunter's card as she drove to Sabella's apartment. She'd called to make sure she wouldn't be disturbing the newlyweds, and Sabella had seemed eager to hear about Hunter's unexpected appearance. She loved a good story, and Gina could use some perspective. Idealistically romantic as Sabella could be, she also had a firmly pragmatic side.

Gina's phone chimed as she pulled into a guest parking spot, and she slid it out of her purse.

`Postponed meeting for tom at 9.`

She'd completely forgotten about the afternoon check-in. She might give him a hard time, but Roger did a great job filling in when she needed him, without waiting for minute instructions. She sent back:

`You're the best.`

Other than following up on some emails later, work could officially wait until tomorrow.

She knocked perfunctorily on Sabella's door and twisted the knob, heading inside. Kane sat at the island, staring at some papers with a scowl. The sound of the door closing brought his frustrated attention her way. Gina stiffened to avoid taking a step back.

Kane had always been respectful, and protective. When he'd stepped in on her behalf, he'd taken down Alistair with precise blows, easily fighting off the other man. That lethal strength was seared into her mind. Even though she logically knew he'd never hurt her, her instincts hadn't forgotten his utter physical dominance. Breathtaking was one way to describe it. Petrifying, another.

"Sorry, bad time?" she asked.

Kane's eyes focused on her, and he shook his head, letting the papers fall to the island. "You're always welcome here, Gina. Just tryin' to figure out some problems we're having, problems with the tour."

Gina exhaled, tossing her purse over the short bookshelf that divided Sabella's living room from the entryway and onto the couch. "I thought Mitch took care of all that stuff for you guys?"

"Yeah, he does. We're havin' some venue schedulin' issues, last minute. It happens, sometimes, somethin'll come up, and he's tryin' to make sure we can still hit all our spots, and make it to the weddin', get all the promo in so people show up, and all that." He shot her a tense smile. "Can I get you anythin'?"

"Hey." Sabella came out of the bedroom. She smiled at Gina but walked over to Kane, who put his arm around her on autopilot. "Is everything okay?"

"I'm good," he said, pressing a kiss to the side of her head. "It'll get figured out."

Sabella stepped away, coming to Gina. "You look nice," she said, leaning in for a hug.

Gina ran her hand through her hair, resettling it, but apparently she'd put herself back together passably enough before leaving Hunter's hotel room. "Do you want to go grab a coffee? Leave your husband in peace?" Great as Kane was, what she needed was girl talk.

"You're not in my way at all," Kane said.

"We could go talk in the bedroom?" Sabella suggested. She was still wearing yoga pants and a tank top, which was one of the undeniable benefits of being able to work from home. "Or I could change, and we could go out. Your call."

"Bedroom's fine, if you're sure."

Sabella nodded, and Gina slipped off her jacket, draping it over her purse.

"Do you want anything?" Sabella asked, turning into the kitchen. "I have a box of dark-chocolate truffles. Not as good as your mom's, but they're not bad."

The mention of chocolate sent a shiver of remembered sensations through her. "No, thanks." She walked further into the apartment so she could see both of the newlyweds. "Just some water would be great."

"No, to chocolate?" Kane teased beside her. "You feelin' all right?"

Gina rolled her eyes at the ribbing. "Sounds like you could use some, though."

Kane grimaced, glancing back down to the printed schedule, which was covered with scribbled corrections. "It's all yours. I'll take beer over chocolate any day."

Sabella pulled a bottle from the fridge when she replaced the pitcher of water. She set a glass of the cucumber water and the beer on the island for them, then turned to pour some coffee for herself.

"Thanks, Bella," Kane said, opening the bottle.

Gina tilted the glass, letting the chilled liquid refresh her mouth. Sabella inclined her head toward the bedroom door, and Gina walked into the familiar room. Outwardly, very little had changed in their apartment since the wedding, though the closet now housed plenty of Kane's clothing, and his guitar sat in one corner of the living room. And, their fridge now pretty much always had beer.

Sabella shut the door after following Gina in, and they settled on the bed.

"So tell me about lunch," she instructed curiously. "What's Hunter doing here? Did he fly out to find you?"

Kane had done that, after briefly meeting Sabella in Nashville. It had been incredibly romantic. "Not everyone is a stalker like your husband," Gina teased.

"Oh, shush you."

"He said he's here to check out some land, for expanding the vineyard I guess." It had only been a few hours, but lunch itself seemed ages away.

"So how did you run into him?"

Gina's fingers clenched against the solid cylinder of glass. "He had a meeting with Alistair."

Sabella blinked, eyebrows lowering into a concerned vee. "With Alistair?"

"Yeah, I know. I don't really understand either." She sighed, twisting to set the water on a nightstand. "He saw me downstairs, when I was in the lobby. Then Alistair came over, because they had a meeting scheduled. Hunter actually offered to blow it off, though, for lunch. Isn't that weird? I mean, if he flew all the way up here?"

"Kind of," Sabella confirmed. "But you said he was here to look at land, what could that have to do with Alistair?"

"Right, so, I guess he combined two trips into one. He was in that meeting for maybe a half hour before coming to ask again about going out." It made almost no sense, now, thinking over how he'd convinced her to join him.

"But you did go out with him."

"Yeah." Gina kicked off her heels and slid further onto the bed, careful not to bump Sabella's laptop. "He figured it out, about…"

Neither of them finished that thought. "What did he say?" Sabella asked quietly.

"He offered to punch him."

Sabella smiled, her approval clear. "Did you take him up on it?"

"No!" Gina's lips tugged up at the mental image, but she shook her head. "He would have gotten tossed out by security, or maybe even arrested."

"But that convinced you to give him a shot?"

"No." Sorting through what had happened was difficult in retrospect. "Or not just that. He offered to let me pay, and I know, it sounds ridiculous. But he'd remembered my being upset about the money slash bartender issue, and he seemed okay not throwing his weight around with it, you know? And I was really sick of being in the office, so, I said yes."

"And…?"

"And, we went to Vitto Ghiotto, and it was sweet. He really does seem like a nice guy, I think."

"So, do you think you may spend more time with him?"

"Well, technically, I already have."

Sabella's eyes widened.

Gina reached for her water, taking a sip before answering. "He's staying at The Benson."

"You went to his hotel? Is he really that good?"

Gina hummed. "He *is*. Though, technically, I went up to have dessert—this chocolate lava cake, which was delicious." She smiled at the memory. "Especially when I was licking it off him."

Sabella's jaw dropped, before she forcibly closed it, blushing.

"You guys should try it," Gina added.

Sabella groaned, rolling her eyes. "We are doing just fine, thank you."

"What?" Gina said with fake innocence. "You could surprise Kane."

Sabella sipped her coffee, trying to hide her wholesome shock. "Well, at least you seem like you're in a good mood."

"Sex with him is pretty great."

"And everything else?" she asked, dependably down-to-earth.

Gina's smile dropped, and she sighed. "I don't know, Sab. It's fine, I guess. I mean, he has this calming effect on me, you know? I relax around him, and not just after sex. But, he lives far away, and he's ridiculously wealthy, and what are we even doing? Even if he is actually a nice guy, and not just good at faking it at first, I'm so not the right person for him in any way other than the sex." She could still see the chocolate dripping onto his sleeve. He probably thought she was insane for freaking out like that. It wasn't even something she could tell her best friend.

Sabella's hand landed on her leg. "How about letting him decide that? I didn't think I was right for Kane, either," she reminded.

"You're not. You're way too good for him."

They shared a laugh. "He's plenty good for me, too. And if Hunter is someone you feel comfortable around, why not focus on that for now? Or the great sex, which was, if I recall, your selling point for my going out on tour with the guys last year. And back then, it wasn't even a guarantee."

"True, but I was right, wasn't I? But Hunter lives in Sonoma, and I actually have a day job that requires showing up, for now anyway."

Sabella's nails clicked on her coffee mug as she considered the situation. "How long is he here?"

"I don't know. 'Til Saturday, I guess. He pushed his flight back so we could have dinner tomorrow night."

"Wow. Well, why don't you talk to him about the distance thing. If he's doing business up here, he'll probably be back pretty soon, right? And what did you mean, 'for now'?"

Gina shot her a look, and Sabella sobered.

"You think he's going to fire you?"

"I don't know. What would be the point of making me lose my job? But he might, or he'll be unbearable, or I don't know what."

"Really?"

Gina shrugged.

"What I mean is, do you even know the current owners? Does the owner really have that much of a day-to-day impact?"

"Not right now. But why else would he have bought the magazine? We do okay, but we're not exactly the most profitable financial investment, and we can say a lot about him, but he's not an idiot, fiscally." She flopped back onto the bed, staring up at the ceiling. "I think Vivian might kill me for walking out today, anyway."

"I doubt it. The entire fashion department would go haywire in a second."

"Thanks, but, I'm not sure I'm doing that great a job right now as it is."

"Well, you know I disagree." Sabella paused for a drawn-out moment, probably licking her lips in her habitually nervous way before speaking again. "What if he does decide to make your life difficult at work. Would you quit?"

"I don't know. Would I really have a choice? Be controlled by him again, or lose my job." The former wasn't an option, even if she didn't love the idea of leaving *PDXX*.

"Or find a different job? Or, you could consider legal action. A restraining order?"

Gina lifted onto her elbows to regain eye contact. "We work in the same building. In a little while, he'll own my magazine. How exactly would that restraining order be phrased? If anyone even agreed to grant it, a *year* later."

Sabella's lips tightened. "Maybe the sale won't go through. And even if it does, we'll figure it out. He hasn't actually approached you, right?"

"No." She was going to plop back down on the bed when a thought struck her, and she sat up instead. "He did. When I was talking to Hunter downstairs, he came over, and the first thing he said was to me."

"What did he say?"

"It was stupid, it doesn't even matter." She knew better than to listen to him, now.

"Maybe," Sabella said a bit hesitantly, "Hunter could be a fun way to take your mind off all of this? We can't worry about what game Alistair is playing until he makes some kind of move."

"And then it'll be too late."

"No, it won't. We'll figure it out." Sabella sighed. "It might cost us our jobs, though."

"Us?"

"I wouldn't write for a magazine stupid enough to fire you."

The support wasn't unexpected, but it was still reassuring. "You'll be too busy writing your tell-all: 'How I Snagged Country's Hottest Rising Star.'"

Sabella kicked her gently with her toe, laughing.

A knock at the door quieted them. Sabella glanced at Gina, letting her decide. "Come in," Gina called.

The door swung open, but Kane didn't come inside. He did look like he was in a better mood, though. "D'you want to stay for dinner?"

"He's cooking for you?" Gina teased.

Sabella smiled, her shoulders tugging up. "Apparently."

"It's why she married me."

"She always was the smart one."

"Okay, enough," Sabella interjected.

Kane's cheeks rounded, and he leaned against the door-jamb. "So, dinner?"

"No, thanks, though. I should probably call Roger, take him out or something after today." There was undoubtedly drama and some pouting heading her way otherwise. "Did you figure things out?"

"Mitch's workin' on it. I'm thinkin' about checkin' out a local open mic night tomorrow, if you're in the mood to come hang out, tolerate a country song or two."

"She has a date," Sabella informed him.

"Maybe. Probably." She still hadn't made up her mind to call Hunter.

Kane lifted an eyebrow. Sabella slid off the bed and padded over to him. "Stop it." She put one hand on his arm and turned back to Gina. "I think you should go, have a good time with Hunter."

Kane kept his eyes on Gina. "You could bring 'im by."

She didn't miss the implication. "You know I have a big brother, right?" Though really, she appreciated the protectiveness.

"Yeah, well. He's on the other side of the country, and me, I'm right here."

Sabella smiled at her husband, and he looped an arm around her waist. Roger was right, seeing them together was enough to make anyone want what they had, even someone who knew it wasn't possible—not for everyone, and certainly not for her. But it was wonderful to see her best friend so happy, finally. And Gina didn't actually mind having another protective brotherly type, especially one who wasn't a quick-tempered Italian.

Fourteen

Hunter brushed the dirt from his fingers and stood, pulling his vibrating phone from his pocket. The number wasn't recognized. He gestured to the broker who stood a little ways away with the owner, then turned his back to them. "Hello." Solid clouds gathered over his head. The sky up here lacked the expansive infinity of California's, but the differences in the climate were precisely what made developing a satellite vineyard here such a promising option.

"Hi. It's, uh, it's Gina."

A smile spread across his face. "Hey there."

"Is this an okay time?"

"Of course. I'm glad you called." The properties he'd seen so far weren't terrible. This one had been the best yet, but he hadn't quite been able to focus, wondering if he would see her again. He'd told himself that he wouldn't pursue her if she hadn't called, but that decision had soured his mood. "Can I take this to mean I'll get to see you tonight?"

"If I don't get a better offer."

He smiled wider at the easy confidence, even if it was augmented by the distance of the phone. "I will definitely try to make it worth your while. Should I come pick you up?"

"I can meet you somewhere."

"All right, well, what are your thoughts on Carafe? Or, perhaps Higgins?" He'd researched some of the local restaurants last night, hoping she'd call. There were plenty of popular places within walking distance of his hotel.

"Whichever you'd prefer."

After yesterday, he should have expected that answer. Picturing the possibilities of what Talbot had put her through still made him itch to retaliate on her behalf. "I imagine you know the area a bit better," he pointed out. "And after yesterday, I definitely trust your choices."

"I have never actually been to Higgins." She sounded almost apologetic, as if she'd somehow failed by not knowing every restaurant in Portland.

"Would you like to change that? If you don't like it, we could always go somewhere else."

"I'm sure it'll be fine, be good."

Was that a yes? "So, Higgins, then. What time would work for you?"

"Would seven be all right?" she asked.

"Seven sounds great. I'm looking forward to seeing you again."

"I'll try not to disappoint, then."

"I doubt you could."

Gina paused for a second before he heard her exhale. "See you tonight."

"You bet," he answered as the connection broke. Truth be had, he didn't know where he was going with this. Nothing about trying to be with Gina would be easy—not the geography, or the scars she was still getting over, if she ever would. Or her ex, though he was the least of Hunter's concerns. But something kept throwing them together, and he couldn't turn away from the feeling that somehow…

It had taken his grandpa three days to propose to his grandma and less than two weeks for them to marry, and their love was unlike any other Hunter had seen, because his grandpa had known when he'd found the woman for him.

Hunter tried to consider practicality and reason, but frequently, following in his grandpa's footsteps, trusting his instincts, that's what worked out best. Maybe he was wrong about Gina, but he was willing to deal with the logistics of finding out. Because, well, maybe he wasn't.

Roger's syncopated knock sounded as he stepped into Gina's office.

"What's up?" she asked, without looking away from the email she was writing.

"It's five thirty."

Gina glanced at the time at the top of her screen then pinched the bridge of her nose before passing her hand up over her forehead. She reread the last sentence she'd written, hit send, and pushed back from the desk with a grateful smile. "Thanks."

Roger shrugged.

"Are you okay?" Gina asked. He looked particularly lackluster, with his shoulders hunched around some files and the corners of his mouth slightly downturned. "What's going on, Rodge?" He'd already had plans with Michel when she'd invited him to dinner the night before, and they hadn't really had an opportunity to talk about anything but work lately.

"You said you had to go," he reminded.

"I have time for you." Plus, if she was late, it would be a sure test of Hunter's patience. "Come sit. Talk to me."

He lowered to the chair across from her, dropping the files on his lap. "Things are tough with Michel. I know, you don't really want to hear about it—"

"What are you talking about?" Gina interrupted. True, she hadn't wanted the two to get involved, in case Roger grew bored, but she'd seen his overly dramatized melancholy act right before he'd ended things with previous boyfriends. This was something different. "Of course I want to hear about it. What do you mean, 'tough'?"

"He's been through some things, some serious things, you don't even know. And I don't know if I'm enough for him. I mean, I didn't have the easiest time of it in high school or anything, but…" He sighed, more solemnly than she had ever seen, belying the cheerfulness of today's yellow tie. "Nothing like what he's been through. And someday, probably soon, he'll realize there's really nothing more to me than this." He gestured around her office for emphasis.

"Does whatever he's been through scare you? I mean, does it make you think otherwise of him?"

"I dunno. Maybe."

Gina's fist clenched on her lap, thankfully blocked from Roger's sight by her desk.

"What if I can't be there for him the way he needs me to be?" Roger asked.

Gina exhaled, forcing her fingers to loosen. "What if what he needs is someone who wants to try?"

Roger didn't say anything, staring over her shoulder at the city outside her window.

"I didn't realize you two had gotten serious enough for this to be a concern," Gina said when his silence continued. They'd met less than a month ago.

Roger's gray eyes swiveled back to Gina. "He has this scar, on his neck. It's hard to miss, when…well, you know."

Gina's eyebrows rose. Roger wasn't exactly circumspect when it came to discussing sex.

He ignored the motion. "It's why he wears a scarf all the time." His head shook with a tiny jerking movement.

"Do you think he's worth it? Learning to get over it, to deal with what happened to him?"

Roger looked at her as if she'd just suggested spotlighting burkas in their summer edition. "It's not about getting over it. I mean, not on my end. I just don't know if I can do this, can support him through it. Be who he needs. What if I say the wrong thing? Or hurt him, somehow, without meaning to."

"He'd probably appreciate the fact that it matters to you, keeping him from that hurt." Gina paused. "If you really care about him, that's probably all he needs from you. And the only thing you can do is make sure his experiences with you are good."

"I want to be with him, but…" Roger blinked, and his gaze dropped with another sigh, his jaw shifting before he looked back to her. "What if I'm not enough to make him happy, so he knows nothing like that will happen to him again? I can't guarantee that, but maybe someone else could. Maybe someone else can wipe that miserable memory away, make his smile real."

Gina swallowed past the growing dryness and reached for the lukewarm coffee on her desk. "I doubt that's what he wants, a guarantee. Being loved, if you end up falling in love, of course, without his past deterring you, that will probably go a long way to helping him with whatever it is he's been through. He's more than that experience, and as long as you know that, you'll be okay."

"You think so?"

Gina shrugged, glancing down at her desk briefly to avoid the intensity in his eyes. "You're right, I don't know him all that well." She straightened the stack of sticky notes beside her mug. "But it sounds right to me. You might need to be a bit more thoughtful, but otherwise, you still have to take this relationship as it comes."

"What if he thinks I'm too superficial?" he said flatly, so it wasn't really a question.

"Well, he's still human. But there's more to you than telling Portland women what to wear."

His lips pinched.

"I've never seen it," Gina teased, smiling to lighten the mood.

Roger rolled his eyes, opening his mouth to protest with a tilt of the head.

"But I'm sure it's there," Gina finished before he had a chance.

Roger's lips curved, with a lingering tinge of sadness. "Thanks." He exhaled dramatically and stood. "Anyway. You're going to be late for your mysterious evening plans!" he announced with a hint of his usual enthusiasm.

Gina glanced at the time bouncing around as her screensaver and winced. She wasn't going to have time to get home and change. Talking things out with Roger was obviously worth it, but now she would have to improvise. "It's just dinner," she told him. "What about you? Fun plans tonight?"

"Seeing Michel again."

"Wow, two nights in a row?" It shouldn't have been surprising, given everything they'd just discussed, but it was practically a record.

Roger's head tilted unevenly from side to side, and an idea popped into her mind.

"Kane has a thing tonight. I don't remember the details, but we could ask Sabella, maybe all meet up? It'd be good for us to hang out, get to know the new man in your life."

A grateful smile grew shyly over his face. "Thanks. I'll ask him."

"Good." She and Sabella were immeasurably closer, but they never intended for Roger to feel left out. Maybe Michel and him joining them tonight would help remind him of that.

"Although," Roger added, "country music?"

"Oh, I know. The things we do for her."

He chuckled, and Gina smiled in return.

"So, is that what you're wearing?" Roger asked, fully slipping back into his normal self.

Gina glanced down at her outfit. It was acceptable enough for a day at work, but she'd passed on the accessories, so she looked kind of drab for a Friday night out. "I guess so."

"We should check out what we've got in the closet. We both know you can wear anything the models do."

Gina narrowed her eyes. The "closet" was really a storage room full of racks and boxes of accessories, where they collected pieces for upcoming shoots, or kept pieces that didn't have to be, or just hadn't yet been, returned. "Is this something you suggest often?"

"Not allowed. My boss has this strict rule, but as long as you don't tell her, you could get away with borrowing something." He smiled mischievously.

Gina had put in place their current policy for dealing with leftover clothes: donation, usually to women's shelters. But if she brought something back on Monday, it couldn't hurt, right? It wasn't as if the magazine itself had rules against it—the clothes used to be up for grabs once shoots were over.

"You know you want to, and there's nobody here," Roger coaxed.

"Ah, okay," she relented. She glanced back at the dimmed computer screen, then stood. "Just this once, we can go play dress up."

Less than an hour later, Gina stood outside Higgins in a sleeveless champagne top that bloused from an intricately gathered neckline. Roger had found a lovely pair of tarnished-gold-and-purple hoop earrings, and an interesting wrist cuff with a Celtic weave. She'd kept her simple black slacks, and she'd even had a chance to touch up her makeup. Everything had come together, but Hunter was nowhere to be seen.

Granted, since she hadn't gone home, she was a few minutes early. Meanwhile, she'd underestimated the evening chill and left her cute asymmetrical jacket lying on the passenger seat of her car. She'd definitely regret that later tonight. She could head back to the car to get it, but then she would end up late.

"You look—"

She spun around to find Hunter's smiling eyes.

"Gorgeous," he finished, holding out a single lavender-tinged rose, offset by a fern leaf and a sprinkling of baby's breath. "Not that I'm surprised."

She brought the outstretched rose to her face, inhaling briefly to steady her thoughts. Just seeing him again sent a wave of warmth coursing through her, and the understated flower was quite a sweet gesture. He'd even had it placed in a plastic tube of water so it wouldn't wither. The thoughtfulness had her returning his smile. "Thank you."

His arm swept toward the entrance. "Shall we?"

Fifteen

He looked good. There had been no lulls in their conversation since entering the restaurant, but now, as Hunter signed for their check, Gina had a few seconds to really look at him. He wore his John Varvatos effortlessly, unquestionably at ease, unlike some men who looked itchy and uncomfortable in suits. For that matter, Hunter had been just as comfortable with no clothes on at all.

He slid the check to the corner of the table and picked up his port. "I have to admit, I hadn't planned anything beyond dinner. Didn't want to jinx it."

Gina didn't comment, watching his lips part around the edge of the glass, welcoming the garnet liquid.

"I've heard there are some good comedy clubs around, if you'd like," he added, setting down his glass.

"Karaoke is also quite popular around here," Gina said, picking up the remnants of her sweet white wine. Alistair had once visibly balked at a similar suggestion.

"Do you sing?" Hunter asked curiously.

"I don't think people would run the other way screaming, or anything, but no, not at all. Do you?"

"No." He chuckled, shaking his head. "Believe me, no one should be subjected to that."

A scene from *My Best Friend's Wedding* flashed through her mind, and Gina shrugged. "Karaoke is about guts as much as talent."

"Fair enough. Is that where you would like to go?"

Was it? She'd made the comment offhand, not as a suggestion. On the other hand… "Would you sing?"

"If you asked me to," Hunter answered without hesitation, making her smile.

Gina shook her head at the mental image. Karaoke could be fun enough in a private room with a bunch of friends, but on a date of sorts and surrounded by strangers? Not so much. "Maybe another time."

Hunter's eyebrows rose at the implication. "All right. What shall we do tonight then?"

The assumption was there, that their night wasn't over, but it didn't feel presumptuous, or demanding. "How about listening to some music instead? Kane's playing at an open mic thing tonight, not too far from here." And she'd already agreed to go.

"Sounds like a plan." He stood and came around to her side of the table, then placed one hand on the back of her chair.

Gina stood too, lifting her purse and the rose that had survived their dinner admirably. Her bare shoulder grazed the soft fabric covering his chest as she headed toward the exit. Hunter followed without comment, reaching around her to open the door. She shivered at the blast of chilled night air and turned in the direction of Dante's. The walk would take them past his hotel, but unfortunately not past her car.

Hunter silently slipped off his jacket, holding it just beside her. Gina twisted to face him. His warm eyes didn't slip from hers as he settled the fabric, still heated from his body, around her shoulders.

"Thank you," she murmured.

He paused for a moment, holding onto the edges of the jacket. A stray lock of hair had fallen over his forehead. Little laugh lines by his eyes deepened as he watched her. Gina broke their eye contact first, her gaze falling for an instant to the cushion of his lips before following the movement of a passerby.

Hunter let go, taking a miniscule step backward. Gina resettled his jacket, wrapping her arms around her torso to help keep it in place. He turned slightly, facing the direction she had been headed.

"So you're a fan of country music?" he asked as they started down the street.

She slanted a look his way, though she shouldn't have been surprised. Hunter took such a hands-on approach to the goings-on at the winery that of course he'd remember what type of music Kane—an artist he'd scheduled for two appearances—played. "It's one of those things that grows on you. You know, when your best friend marries a country singer."

Hunter laughed, openly and unabashedly. Gina smiled slightly at the sound and curled into his jacket, inhaling the trace of his scent that lingered in the fabric.

Hunter followed Gina as she wove through the chatting groups in the downtown club. She stopped by a familiar blonde, who slid off her barstool with a smile, leaning in for a quick hug.

"Mr. Cavaliere," she greeted warmly when her eyes found him.

Hunter smiled. "Mrs. Hartridge." For the life of him, he couldn't remember her first name, though he knew it was something uncommon. "Lovely to see you again. Can I get you ladies some drinks?"

Gina's friend stepped back, gesturing to a wine glass behind her. "I'm all set, but thank you for offering."

"Gina?" Before he could finish asking, a pair of men joined them. A flurry of kisses and half hugs were exchanged. Hunter hung back, watching the almost choreographed activity.

Gina pulled away from the other three first, placing a hand on Hunter's elbow. "Hunter, this is Roger, and Michel. Guys, this is Hunter."

He held his hand out, shaking briefly with each other man. She hadn't included last names or even affiliations. Were these casual acquaintances, here by coincidence, or also friends? He couldn't help wondering if she had spoken to any of them about him, juvenile as that was.

"Should we grab a table?" Roger asked, filling the somewhat awkward silence that had fallen after the introductions.

"Great idea," Mrs. Hartridge said, searching for an empty table.

"Would anyone like a drink?" Hunter offered again. "Or we could share a bottle?"

"Hunter works with wine," Gina explained.

Mrs. Hartridge threw her a look that lasted less than a second. What did she think of Gina's vague statement, omitting Hunter's role at the vineyard? No one else seemed to notice.

Roger's eyes narrowed on Hunter. "That's right. Didn't I see you, at the wedding? A few weeks ago, in Sonoma."

"That was me," Hunter confirmed. "I'm in town for some business."

Michel stood a little behind Roger, silently. He wasn't exactly avoiding looking at Hunter, but he did seem to be keeping his distance, until Roger turned to him. "What would you like?"

"Anything is fine," Michel answered with a light French accent and a tight smile. His gaze flicked toward Hunter then down to the floor.

Hunter looked to Gina, unsure what he was missing.

"We could start with a bottle and see where the evening takes us?" she suggested. "It *is* open mic night."

Everyone chuckled, diffusing the earlier tension.

A bartender sidled up behind them. "What can I get you folks?"

The amusement died down. "White or red?" Hunter asked.

"Red," Gina and Michel said in unison, then smiled at each other.

"Oh! I think I see a table," Mrs. Hartridge said. "Let's go grab it?" she added to the other men.

They nodded, moving obediently across the room. Hunter picked up the laminated drink menu, scanning the wine list. The bartender waited with a courteous impatience.

"Maybe this one should be on me," Gina offered once the others were out of earshot.

It should have been a nice change, her not assuming that he would always pay, but simultaneously it bothered him that she associated his money with a desire to control—that she still, in any way, compared him to her ex. "If you'd prefer. I definitely don't mind, though," he felt compelled to add.

She shrugged, driving his attention to the line of her bare collar. "You can get the next one. But you should probably still choose."

Hunter inclined his head and glanced back down at the list, before addressing the bartender. "How about a bottle of the two thousand nine Willamette Valley Pinot Souris."

The man nodded, tapping the bar twice before moving away. A similar tapping thumped through the sound system, and Hunter and Gina both turned to face the stage.

✧ ✧ ✧

"You slept with him at the wedding, didn't you?" Roger accused almost as soon as Hunter had excused himself.

"Roger!" Sabella exclaimed in her best schoolmarm voice.

Michel placed a hand on Roger's elbow, not commenting on the dramatics. He'd actually been uncharacteristically quiet most of the night.

"I'm right, aren't I?" Roger added. "Why didn't you tell me?"

Gina raised an eyebrow. She hadn't *not* told him, it just hadn't seemed worth mentioning. Behind Roger, a new act settled in front of the microphone.

"Did he follow you up here? Something's wrong with the two of you, luring men across state lines." Roger looked reproachfully at her and Sabella.

"Actually,"—Gina took a sip of the wine Hunter had picked—"it's kind of a weird coincidence."

They quieted as the girl on stage started singing. Their conversation had followed that weird rhythm all night, chatting as the singers changed places, listening politely as they performed. It wasn't particularly conducive to socializing, but it probably took a little bit of pressure off of Michel and Hunter.

The latter settled quietly back at their table, flashing her a smile when she looked at him. He brought one arm to the back of her chair. One finger brushed softly at the base of her neck, and her lids drooped heavily. When they lifted, Hunter was watching her with a disquieting affection. Gina's breath caught, and she turned back to the stage, forcing her lungs to work. Hunter's finger stilled with a bit more pressure on her skin before dropping away.

Faint applause greeted the end of the song, quickly followed by the reawakening of various conversations.

"So how do all of you know each other?" Hunter asked.

"Well, Gi and I met in college," Sabella explained.

"And I work at the magazine," Roger added.

Michel stayed silent, so Gina jumped in. "And Michel is the best hairdresser in Portland, or possibly the U.S."

His head tilted back as he flashed her a small, grateful smile.

"That's quite the endorsement," Hunter said. "You must have a great eye."

"Thank you," Michel murmured after a brief pause. "That is nice of you."

"I can't imagine being able to look at someone and see what style may suit them best, and how to bring that to life."

"He's an artist," Gina agreed.

Michel seemed like he would protest, but the club's representative announced Kane as the next performer, so they all returned their attention to the stage.

He settled on the single stool, fiddling briefly with the mic. Then his eyes found Sabella, and he smiled. "This is, uh, this is a song I wrote after, well, after I got married. I hope y'all like it."

Gina glanced at Sabella, who was smiling contently as Kane began strumming the guitar. As he sang, table after table seemed to quiet, drawn in by the ballad. Gina still wasn't the biggest fan of country music, or even Kane's music, but watching him singing his love, the effect was undeniable. The quiet earnestness was beautiful. She even glimpsed Roger's hand slip toward Michel, their fingers tangling together.

The hush of the crowd lingered for a heartbeat after Kane finished, until he straightened from his guitar. Applause spread through the room, and he flashed everyone another smile, ducking his chin. Everyone at their table looked at Sabella.

"That's one talented cowboy," Roger commented as Kane started another song.

"At least you're half right," Sabella rejoined, but the sarcasm was tempered by her pleased smile.

Kane played two more songs before ceding the mic to the club's announcer. She went down a litany of reminders, and Kane wove his way to their table, still holding his guitar. Sabella stood, tilting her chin up toward him. He hugged her with his free arm, dropping a chaste kiss to her lips, then nodded to the rest of them and lowered onto the chair Sabella had freed. She perched on his knee.

"That wasn't horrible," Gina told him before the awkward round of introductions could start. Kane undoubtedly knew who the other men were, through his wife.

"High praise," he drawled.

"It was a lovely song," Michel defended.

"Thank you," Kane acknowledged with his easy smile.

"Kane, this is Michel." Sabella gestured across the table. "And you remember Hunter."

"Glad you both made it out," Kane said, nodding to each of them in turn. "Let me go tuck my guitar away, and I can come join you properly."

"We can't really chat here," Sabella pointed out. "Should we head somewhere else?"

"A quiet bar? Any suggestions?" Roger asked Gina.

"Quiet isn't really in my repertoire," she reminded. "The only place that comes to mind is Bartini, but that's kind of far if we want to walk."

"There's Palm Court," Michel suggested softly. "They have a late happy hour, and it's not far."

"Sounds perfect." Sabella glanced around at everyone. "Any objections?"

A mix of shrugs and nods decided it.

"I'll meet you outside in a few minutes, then?" Kane and Sabella stood, right as the next performer started tapping a rhythm on his guitar. Sabella smiled apologetically, and her husband melted away into the relative darkness as the rest of them pretended to listen, waiting for a pause in which to leave.

"Looks like we should maybe let them close up," Sabella said, glancing around the emptied lounge. The Palm Court had turned out to be on the ground floor of Hunter's hotel, but Michel's description had been spot on, and it had been a great place for them all to talk.

Still, Michel and Roger had left a little while back, and even the jazz pianist who had been playing earlier had packed up. Only the clean lines of the polished wood paneling and emptied armchairs surrounded them.

The couples walked out of the bar then paused in the hotel's lobby. Bright chandeliers overhead held off the darkness of the night, reflecting off the marble floor.

"This was lovely," Sabella commented, putting on her jacket.

"It was a pleasure," Hunter agreed, holding his hand out to Kane. "I look forward to having you back at the winery."

Kane shook the offered hand. "Appreciate it."

Gina reached out to hug Sabella. "I'll see you tomorrow," she murmured. They were spending the afternoon, and maybe evening, helping to put together gift bags for Melody's shower.

"Do you want us to walk you to your car?" Sabella asked.

"I'd be happy to walk her," Hunter said.

"Gina?" Kane looked to her. He seemed to like Hunter, but it was clear where his allegiance was.

"Seems like I'm all set," Gina assured.

Kane held her gaze for a moment, before offering a shallow nod and picking up his guitar case. "Come on, Bella," he said, wrapping an arm around his wife.

"We should do this again," Sabella said with a genuine smile.

Hunter inclined his head.

"Good night you two," Gina called softly as they headed to the door.

Sabella twisted back to wave at them.

"Good people," Hunter commented. He'd taken everything in stride tonight, though she was starting not to be surprised by his laidback manner.

"Some of the best."

"Would you like me to walk you to your car? Or are you up for a nightcap?"

She spun in a half circle, taking in the molded ceiling and their lush surroundings. "They do say this is quite an impressive hotel."

Hunter stepped up beside her, hands in his pockets. "Just wait 'til you see the rooms," he teased back. His good-natured eyes waited patiently for her decision.

He was leaving tomorrow, and thankfully he hadn't brought up the question of any type of future, but more importantly, his company tonight had remained easy, comfortable. Almost effortless. There was no reason to end the night quite yet. Gina glanced down at the rose he'd gotten her, then headed toward the elevators. She would have bet that a slanted smile curved Hunter's cheeks as he followed.

Sixteen

Gina drifted up languorously from the depths of sleep. A nearly perfect silence surrounded her in the darkness she could feel behind her eyelids. She couldn't remember the last time she had slept restfully while in Portland. Cool sheets shifted over her body, their silken caress interrupted only by a hand on her naked hip.

Her eyes flew open. A hint of the city's lights streamed through the thin curtain of the hotel room's windows. She hadn't meant to fall asleep. Staying with Hunter overnight wasn't an option. She held her breath, carefully rolling so his hand fell to the mattress, allowing her to slip out of the bed.

She brushed her hair back from her face, squinting as she searched the room for the discarded pieces of her clothing. At least the jewelry she had borrowed was still on her, so she didn't have to fumble for it in the dark. Better yet, the pale color of the top helped it stand out against the wooden dresser that had caught it when Hunter had thrown it off her. Her bottoms had to be crumpled in a pile over her heels, somewhere by the bed.

She scanned the floor for any irregularity in the shadows, then scooped up the clothes and padded to the bathroom to get dressed. She left the door slightly ajar so there was no *click*. It wasn't that she wanted to sneak out, exactly, but there was no reason to wake him. And technically, her number should be in his phone's history, so he could reach her if he wanted to. And if she at some point no longer wanted him to have it, she could always change the number. Simple.

She flicked the light off in the bathroom before opening the door.

"You okay?" Hunter's groggy voice asked from the darkness.

Her head jerked toward him, and she forced herself to exhale. "I'm fine," she whispered. "Go back to sleep."

He sat up, the faint light from the window setting off the silhouette of his torso. "You should stay."

Gina closed her eyes. *It isn't a command*, she reminded herself. "That's all right, I should really go."

Hunter scooted to the edge of the bed, running his palm over his face and letting the blankets fall away from him. "Okay, give me two minutes. I'll walk you to your car."

"You really don't have to. Please, go back to sleep."

"Gina, it's"—his head turned toward the glow of the hotel's alarm clock—"three in the morning. Even if we were in Newton, Massachusetts, I'd still want to walk you to your car."

Gina smiled despite herself. He seemed to have that effect on her rather frequently. "Really? In just about the safest city in America?"

"Really." He got out of the bed and found the nearest light switch. A golden glow spread over the tanned muscles she had gripped, brushed against, tasted. Their first time together had been good, but as they learned each other's bodies, the sex only got better.

He grabbed his pants, pulling them directly onto his naked body, then strode over to the closet. A sweatshirt he grabbed from his compact suitcase soon hid his sculpted arms from view. He turned toward her, hesitated, then crossed the room to pick up his jacket from earlier, holding it out for her. His hair was still sleep-rumpled, but apparently his thoughtfulness was so ingrained that even the grogginess didn't prevent it.

The silence of the late hour covered them as they moved, first through the hotel and then down the darkened street. Hunter kept his hand at the small of her back, but he didn't say anything until they reached her car. Its windows were coated with a light frost, but Gina started slipping off his jacket anyway.

His hands landed on her upper arms, stopping the motion. "Will I see you tomorrow?"

"I have a gift-bag-making party in the afternoon for a friend's bridal shower," she answered, equally quietly.

A dog's bark echoed in the distance. Hunter's hands moved up and down her arms, warming her.

"How about brunch? Or I could come help, if I wouldn't be intruding."

Gina laughed at the mental image: Hunter surrounded by pastel tissue paper, a miscellany of tiny gifts, and Melody's bridal party. Still, even the somewhat comedic offer held layers of that consideration. "Brunch sounds lovely."

He smiled, hands stilling. "I'll call you in the morning, then?"

Gina nodded, and he bent slightly to brush her lips. He stepped away, and Gina slid the jacket off, then climbed quickly into her freezing car. Despite the cold, Hunter waited on the sidewalk until she'd driven away.

Wind ruffled Gina's hair as Hunter tugged her toward him and laced their fingers together. Even dressed simply in jeans and a pink tee shirt, she was stunning, especially when she smiled. Saying goodbye again wasn't easy, but at least they were leaving things on good terms, ones with a potential future. He would have to remember to call Paige and cancel their date.

"You sure you and your friends don't want the questionable assistance of my clumsy hands? I could single-handedly double the time it'll take." Her grin would be more than sufficient compensation for the afternoon if she accepted, though he doubted she would.

"Oh, I don't know." She stepped a touch closer. "Those fingers are pretty dexterous from what I've seen."

"Yeah?" He wrapped their arms behind his waist.

Her head tilted, shoulders lifting coyly. "Maybe I'm misremembering."

"Think so?" Hunter leaned in to kiss her once more. The chaste brush was entirely suitable for the street, until her mouth opened and her tongue flicked out against his lower lip. Hunter squeezed her hands gently, deepening the kiss. The tip of his tongue slid against hers, teasing softly at first before delving deeper, tasting the honeyed remnants of the waffles she'd had at brunch. Her tongue twisted with his as her fingers squeezed back. She hummed into his mouth, the sound just barely vibrating through and into him, before she pulled away.

The kiss had darkened her lips, sobered her expression. Hunter slid his hands up her arms, over the fabric of her jacket. Her arms remained looped at his waist.

"So what're you going to do before your flight?" she asked.

Hunter sighed. "I don't know. Probably get some work done." If he could stop thinking about her, which was highly unlikely.

She nodded slowly, lips pressing together. Her eyes stilled on his, framed by a thin purple he hadn't noticed before. A moment later, she looked away, her hands unclasping.

"I'm not certain when I'll be able to come back up," Hunter said. He would have to visit the plots he liked again, with a viticulturist this time around, but that would take time to arrange, and in the meantime, he still had the main vineyard to take care of.

Her eyebrows angled together. "Of course."

"Meanwhile, can I call you?"

Her eyes found his again, and he felt her shoulders drop as she exhaled. "You may."

"What're the chances you'll answer?"

Humor touched her eyes. "Guess you'll have to try it and see."

"You sure you have to go?"

Her phone chimed before he'd even finished asking. On the plus side, she didn't flinch this time. "When it comes to assembling gift goodies, I can't be beat," she joked.

"Guess I should stop trying to tempt you away."

"Probably so. But thank you for brunch."

He considered dropping his hands but moved them up to cup her jaw instead. "Thank you, for gracing me with your charming company this weekend."

"You're welcome," she murmured against his lips.

This kiss was more leisurely, both of them content to take their time with the warm slip of their mouths sliding together. He caught one lip between his teeth, and her hands trailed up his torso, stopping on his chest. Her phone chimed yet again, and Hunter stifled his groan, pulling back.

Her lips twitched with humor as she fished her phone from her pocket. Hunter brushed his mouth against her forehead, lowering his hands.

"I should really get going." The disappointed apology in her expression was reassuring.

Hunter nodded, stepping back. She licked her lips, and his gaze fell back to her mouth. Caitria was right—she really had gotten under his skin.

"Have a safe flight," she added.

"Thanks." He tucked his hands in his pockets so he didn't reach for her again. "We'll talk soon."

"Okay." Her phone chimed again, and she shook her head. "Bye," she exhaled.

For the second time in twenty-four hours, Hunter watched her drive away.

"Is that everything?" Sabella asked, running her fingers over the various bags in Gina's trunk. There were two hours before the official start of Melody's bridal shower, and so far everything seemed to be going according to plan. Though Sabella wasn't officially a bridesmaid, she had, predictably, volunteered to help them pull everything together.

"I think so." Fifty tiny gift bags they had made the day before sat in a box, beside which rested a collection of plastic champagne glasses, pastel napkins and matching balloons, and a few serving trays. Melody's future sister-in-law and her best friend were bringing in the rest of the supplies.

"Great!" Sabella shut the trunk. "So we can get going."

"Eager to share your wifely wisdom?" Gina asked as they got in the car.

Sabella snorted delicately. "I've been married for all of four weeks."

"True. Is it getting old yet?"

"You're hilarious," Sabella said, deadpan. "So we didn't have a chance to talk yesterday. How'd you leave it with Hunter?"

"Vaguely." Even focusing on the road, she could see the wry look Sabella shot her. "He said he'd call, presumably in the near future."

"So you're going to see him again?"

"I honestly have no idea. Not everyone's long-distance fun turns into something long-term, you know."

Sabella faked nonchalance by playing with the radio. "Would it be so bad if it did?"

"Are you really trying to play matchmaker?"

"He seems like a great guy!" Sabella defended. "And he makes you smile."

True. And frequently.

"And you said from the start that he's satisfactory in other ways."

"Oh, more than." Gina glanced at her best friend. "I'll spare you the details, though. Unless you're looking for inspiration? Isn't Kane's birthday coming up?"

"In a couple weeks, but don't change the subject. If Hunter's that great, and sweet, and obviously intelligent, where's the harm?"

"There is none, while he's out in California. But there's nothing else, either."

"You don't think he'll call?"

Gina sighed. Sabella meant well, but Gina was doing her damnedest not to consider all of these questions. "Honestly? I don't want to think about it." She pulled into an empty spot directly across from Melody's parents' house and turned to face Sabella. "I'm just going to let whatever happens, happen. Sort of, anyway. If he calls, and if we see each other again, there will hopefully be some yummy sex, and maybe some fun other stuff, if we can tolerate each other. I'm not looking for something more complicated or commitment-centric here."

Sabella's eyes narrowed. "You smile when you talk about him, you know."

"He did this thing, with his tongue last night. You'd smile, too."

For once, Sabella didn't react to the blatantly sexual comment. "I'm sure that's it," she said wryly, then paused. "You're allowed to be happy, you know."

"There's a blushing bride waiting to hear raunchy stories and celebrate the end of her single life, right inside that house, and she also happens to be a friend of ours. I am happy," she assured.

Sabella obviously didn't believe her, but she nodded, letting it drop. Gina exhaled, shutting off the car. She was honestly pleased for Melody's sake, and that was all that mattered today. The murky future could wait.

Seventeen

Gina silenced the ring of her phone as Roger came into her office.

"Well someone's happy," he commented smugly. He nodded to the phone, placing a memo in front of her. "Hunter?"

Gina covered the screen, trying to appear focused though the stretch in her cheeks was undeniable. "Thanks!" she called as Roger strolled back out of the office, shutting the door. Her finger tapped the green button almost of its own accord. "Hello?"

"Hey there."

Her smile grew a notch wider. She turned away from the reflective computer screen and picked up the memo. "Hi."

"How's your week starting out?" His voice was enough to distract her from scanning the words.

"Not too terribly." Melody's shower had gone off superbly, earning even the bride's approval, which was quite the feat. Gina had returned to work yesterday in a great mood, and people's updates on their next features had kept that mood light, despite the rain now beating against her window. "How about yours? Missing that beautiful Portland weather yet?"

His chuckle rumbled through the phone. "Of all the things I might miss about Portland, the weather's pretty low on the list."

"I don't know," she teased. "I don't think your California sunshine can compare to our downpours."

"Maybe it grows on you."

Hunter kept talking, but Gina's eyes stalled on the memo before her. Her smile disappeared, and she blinked, rereading the words. Her fingers clenched the seemingly innocuous sheet, crumpling it.

"Gina?"

"What?" she answered automatically before remembering the phone in her hand. "Oh, Hunter, I'm sorry. Something just came up at work. I completely missed that."

He redirected instantly. "Is everything okay?"

Good question. "I… I'm not sure, I'm sorry. What were you saying?" *One-on-one meetings with each of the senior editors.* She hadn't been in a room alone with him for nearly a year, and she certainly had no desire to change that, but he'd decided not to give her a choice. She should have expected that from him.

"Nothing too important." The warmth in Hunter's voice from moments ago had seeped away. "Do you need to take care of whatever it is?"

Meaning try not to have a panic attack? Or, better yet, find a way to tell him to go to hell? Yes, yes I do. But she couldn't.

"Is it Talbot?" Hunter asked in her silence.

She shouldn't have been surprised by the guess. But she also couldn't stand him dominating this relationship, or whatever it was, too. "It's complicated." She sighed. "I'm sorry. Can we talk some other time?"

"Of course. Can I call you later?"

Her shoulders drooped slightly at the question, and she tossed the crumpled sheet on her desk. "Thanks. I'm so—"

"Don't apologize," he cut off. "You don't need to. I'm the one who keeps pulling you away from your work." He paused. "Let me know if I can help at all, okay?"

"It'll be fine," she assured on autopilot, then exhaled. "Thanks."

"You bet."

After awkwardly exchanged goodbyes, they hung up. Gina dropped her phone lightly onto her desk then pushed her chair as far back as possible, as if the distance could protect her from the memo.

She rolled her shoulders, trying to work out the tension. Outside the glass door of her office, the usual buzz of activity continued, and of course there was no reason it shouldn't. He wanted to meet only with the senior editors, safely ensconced in their offices, not to mention the fact that to everyone else, the notification probably seemed commonplace. Was that how she should take it? A perfectly reasonable request from the magazine's future owner? It didn't even necessarily have to mean that he would be heavily involved in the future, since it could be a one-time, pro forma thing.

Or she was deluding herself.

Her chair spun as she stood and stepped back to her desk. She smoothed part of the page, looking for relevant details. *Tomorrow.*

"You okay?" She nearly jumped at the familiar voice that came from the office's doorway. Roger's eyes narrowed, and he shut the door, coming toward her. "What in the world was in that memo?"

"You didn't read it?" Gina twisted it to face him.

Roger scanned the page. "It's a meeting," he half-asked, shrugging.

"With the new owner."

Roger sobered but didn't comment.

Gina turned away to look at the miserable city outside her window. "I haven't been alone with him since… Since I broke things off."

Roger's silence was interrupted by a sharp knock on the door. Gina twisted to see Nikki, their lifestyle editor. "Are you two fighting again?" she joked with her usual grin.

"Us? Never," Gina said as nonchalantly as she could manage. "What's up, Nikki?"

"Oh, just had that meeting with the new owner. Thought I'd pop my head in." She rested one hip against the doorjamb. "When's yours?"

"Tomorrow."

"How was it?" Roger asked. It was entirely plausible that Roger, known for his gossip, was simply curious, but maybe he was asking for Gina's sake, just a little bit.

"Oh, you know," Nikki said, shrugging. "Vision for the future, maintaining the quality readers have come to expect, while increasing our visibility and the reach of our work, et cetera."

That did sound pretty standard, possibly even good to refocus the magazine.

Nikki scrunched her nose, shifting her green-rimmed glasses. "He's kind of cute, don't you think?"

"Who?"

Her eyes widened. "The new owner," she said pointedly.

Suddenly, Gina would have been warmer out in the rain. "You know, I think he's married." The lie came smoothly, out of nowhere.

Roger crooked an eyebrow.

"Oh. Darn." Nicki shrugged good-naturedly. "Dating the owner could have been fun. All the scandal, the secrecy. Could have made for a good story, too."

Gina's nails dug into her arms.

"Oh, well. I'll let you get back to work. We should grab lunch sometime!"

"Sure thing." Gina forced a smile as Nikki left.

Roger shut the door behind her. "Married?"

"He's bad news, Rodge. Let's leave it at that." Gina sank back into her chair.

"He wasn't right for you, doesn't mean he won't be good for someone else, right? Jackass or not." He leaned against the door, blocking most of the office from view. "No one's irredeemable."

"Some are worse than others," Gina muttered, rubbing her temples. "Just trust me, okay?" she said more clearly. "No one should be put through that."

"I bet there are people out there who would say that about the two of us." His proud smirk didn't help her growing unease.

"I'm sure you've never…" Gina pressed her lips together, stopping herself from speaking.

Roger's smirk dropped.

Gina sighed, feeling so much older than her friend, though Roger actually had a few years on her. "People may be redeemable, Rodge, but they'd have to want to be redeemed, know that it's necessary. It'll be better for everyone if no one we know messes around with him, okay?"

Roger watched her for a drawn-out moment before finally nodding. "All right, Gi. Whatever you say."

Gina exhaled at the mild sense of relief. If Roger spread around that their new owner wasn't one to be approached, the rumors would grow on their own. She couldn't prevent anyone ever from making her mistake, but she may be able to make his next target a little less accessible. Then again, other women were probably less susceptible to his façade to start with. Her eyes fell back to the crumpled memo. "So what do I do about this meeting?" she murmured, not really expecting a response.

Roger plopped into one of the other chairs and crossed his legs out in front of him. "If you don't want to be alone with him, why don't you just ask an HR rep to sit in on it?"

How incredibly simple. "That may be the most brilliant thing you've ever said."

"Wow, I hope not," he fired back.

Gina's chuckle surprised her.

"You want to hang out with Michel and I this weekend?" Roger asked once the tension broke.

"Michel and me."

He rolled his eyes. "You sound like Sabella. And that's not an answer."

"There are worse things. And thanks for the invite, but, can I get back to you?" She couldn't think past tomorrow morning's meeting. "How're things holding up with Michel?"

Roger's head tilted from side to side. "All right."

Another knock sounded at her door. Roger's gaze fell to the ground.

"Let's go out for lunch later, okay? We can chat." Gina waited for Roger's nod before gesturing to Tristan and refocusing on work.

When his cell phone buzzed in his pocket, Hunter told himself he wasn't hoping it was Gina calling him back. He also wasn't dwelling on that call from this morning. He glanced at the display before answering. It wasn't Gina. "Hey, Tucker."

"Hunter!" his brother's unusually chipper voice responded. "Am I pulling you away from anything?"

"Guess I could find some time for you." Hunter walked out to the terrace, to look over the land that had become his life. "What's going on?"

"I'm hoping to plan a little family celebration, out at the vineyard."

"Celebration?" Hunter grinned. "Don't tell me you tricked Nora into saying yes." They'd been together for years now, so it was about time to make things official. Nora had instantly hit it off with their entire family.

Tuck laughed drily. "Not yet. We're going to be out there next week, so hopefully she'll accept, if I get up the nerve to ask her."

"You want to ask her out here?" Their parents would be thrilled.

"Probably back home. But I was thinking we could do a sort of engagement party thing, surprise her. Or I could get hammered when she turns me down."

"If she has any sense, she will." Hunter turned away from the view and headed around back to his office. "When were you thinking?"

"A week from Friday, or Saturday. So we can fly back out on Sunday."

Hunter flipped through the calendar on his desk. He had a computer system accessible to the main staff that tracked everything that went on in the winery, but he still preferred keeping a paper calendar with his own scribbles, like his grandmother had when she'd run the winery's events. "When are you coming out?"

"Tuesday. Figure I'll need the time to work up to it, let Mom and Dad soften her up."

Hunter's finger landed on the weekend Tuck was talking about. "I have a concert that Thursday." It was actually Kane Hartridge's return to the winery. His first performance, a couple days before the wedding, had even gotten some decent buzz going. The discount the band's manager had negotiated for the nuptial festivities was definitely worth the additional influx of bodies. "Some tours scheduled to drop by Saturday afternoon, too, but otherwise it's your call. You want to check with Mom?"

"You're the best, Hunter."

"Well, one of us has to be."

Tuck laughed again. "I'll let you know as soon as I get things figured out."

Hunter grabbed a pen to note the dates, then groaned. "I should expect a call from Mom, shouldn't I?" Their mother would probably have very specific ideas about how to mark the occasion.

"I wasn't planning on telling her why, just when."

Hunter snorted.

"You don't think I can pull it off? As long as you don't tell her when she calls."

"You got it." She'd probably figure it out before calling him anyway.

"You know she's going to ask about your lack of a suitable relationship, right?"

Hunter grimaced. "Relationship" may be questionable, but "suitable" definitely wasn't the way to describe whatever he had going on with Gina. "I think I can take it." He lowered onto his desk chair.

"Caitria hasn't set you up with the perfect woman yet? Will you invite her, by the way?"

"Your party, and you have me doing all the work? Why am I not surprised."

"Hey, at least the engagement will take some of the heat off you. Mom'll be too busy having opinions on flowers and asking us about babies and whatnot."

"You love the attention." And their mother had enough persistence and focus to keep her mind on both her sons' lives at once.

"Yeah!" Tucker called to someone on the other end. Hunter smiled at the coincidence. "I have to let you go," Tuck said back into the receiver a moment later. "Thanks again, Hunter."

"No problem," he said to the sound of the line clicking off. At least someone would enjoy all the romance of the vineyard. It hadn't bothered him much before, seeing the parade of couples. He was glad to be a part of their happiness, to help them create romantic memories for a lifetime.

After meeting Gina, he kind of wanted that too. Not with her, necessarily. Or at least not right away, that would be too fast.

Or at least not before she was less scared of the idea of commitment.

"Ladies." The chill his voice sent through her was only worsened by his dispassionate examination. "As I mentioned, Ms. Sabatino, I would like to meet with each editor one-on-one." He turned to Janelle. "So, if you'll excuse us."

"Actually, Mr. Talbot," Janelle said, "considering your and Ms. Sabatino's personal history, I'm sure we can all agree that it would be most prudent for someone from Human Resources to sit in." She gestured with the notepad she held, rotating it partially away from her body. "That would be me."

A tic jumped in his jaw, but he inclined his head. "Of course. Please," he motioned into the simple office.

Gina swallowed and walked in silently. If anything could be said about Alistair, it was that he was the consummate profes-sional. He wouldn't do anything questionable with an HR representative around. Hopefully, this meeting would be brief.

The women chose chairs beside each other's, and he predictably sat opposite them, flipping open a waiting leather portfolio. "So, Gina," he started, looking between the two women. "As you can imagine, when ownership transitions, we will be working toward an expansion of the magazine's reach. Ideally, this will mean more women will be impacted by the example we set, particularly, of course, by the fashion and lifestyle sections." He fixed her with a cold stare. "While one can't argue with the results you have achieved, I'm sure you will agree there is nevertheless more work to be done in solidifying the content."

Gina curled her toes to avoid clenching a fist. "Did you have particular concerns?"

"It's important to encourage women to embrace a more elegant, refined look. Of course, I would expect you and your department to lead by example, both in the office and through your selections for the magazine." He didn't move as he spoke. *Movement equals uncertainty*, he'd told her once.

"I'm not sure I follow. Do you have particular objections to the styles we have historically selected? I can assure you, we represent the best of modern fashion, carefully ensuring we remain current and relevant, encouraging women to express themselves through their wardrobes, and not to fear branching out or experimenting with exciting, distinctive looks." Which was precisely what he found so objectionable.

Janelle scribbled silently on her notepad.

Alistair picked up his pen. "You are in a position to help shape the lives of thousands of women, who turn to these pages to help guide them through the myriad of choices awaiting them in terms of fashion. As navigating the ambitious, if sometimes unsuitable, selection offered by the world may be overwhelming without your guidance, you have a responsibility to ensure the options you recommend remain tasteful."

Gina knew exactly what he was trying to say, but she was past having it. "I assure you, we are quite careful in our selections. I personally oversee each piece included in the shoots, and then each shot chosen for a given spread, for maximum impact."

"I don't doubt that." His pen arced through the air, catching the sunlight that seemed out of place streaming through the window. "Going forward, however, I will expect a higher standard in your selections, and, certainly, the manner in which you represent those standards."

"While I appreciate your input, Al." His jaw visibly clenched. It was a petty triumph, but he hated nicknames, believing they lacked dignity. "I hope you will understand that, as my department has, in fact, been quite successful, we will continue to answer only to Vivian, who, as far as I am aware, trusts my judgment unreservedly."

"While I can understand your resistance," he said, leaning back in his chair, "I must insist you consider my vision for polishing up the magazine. Sanding the rough edges, as it were, to enhance its brilliance in the future."

Gina swallowed roughly at the phrasing, steeling herself against the memories. Her chin notched up slightly. "While I do not doubt your experience with women's clothing, my position exists precisely to ensure the quality of our fashion spreads. This department and our readers have relied on my expertise in guiding our choices for over three years now. I appreciate your interest, but those daily details cannot, as I see it, concern you overly as long as the magazine continues to perform. Our department does not underperform."

That got Janelle's attention. She stopped scribbling to glance nervously between them, as if waiting for someone to slip up and say something reportable.

"As with my other acquisitions, I have a vision for the potential of this magazine." He wove his fingers together. "A hesitance with regards to changes is understandable, initially, though I do expect you to lead your department in coming around. If necessary, of course, additional measures could be implemented to ensure your process results in pages that adhere to the new standards." He stood, shutting the portfolio that had clearly been intended as nothing more than a prop. "That will be all."

Gina rose from her chair, her jaw clenching. Janelle chewed her lip anxiously, also standing.

"Always a pleasure." Gina turned away and strode smoothly out of the room.

Roger looked up from his desk, and Gina lifted her eyebrows slightly. They'd been working together long enough that he instantly stood to follow her into her office. "What did he say?" he hissed, shutting the door.

"That we should encourage women to wear burkas." Gina pulled past issues off one of her shelves.

"You're joking." He took the magazines from her without being asked. "Did he actually say that?"

"Of course not. But he would be happier that way. Apparently the pieces we've been spotlighting have not been 'sufficiently tasteful.'" Gina closed her eyes, forcing herself to slow her breathing. He was attempting to assert control, and she wasn't about to submit to his preferences. *Not again.* She couldn't allow him to worm his way under her skin. It was one meeting, and it was over.

Eighteen

It was only eight, so it was way too early to go to bed, but Gina couldn't find anything to occupy her time. She'd flipped through every channel, and the automated guide. Twice. She'd run her fingers along the spines of her books, which was of course incredibly useful for choosing one. If she was honest, she didn't really feel like reading.

Now her laptop sat beside her on the couch, displaying her fairly organized inbox, and solitaire. She'd already played four games. Groaning, she pushed off the couch and strode to the fridge to refill her wine glass. Her phone rested on the dining table. She could call someone—anyone, really, but she didn't feel like talking about anything. She picked the phone up anyway, bringing it with her back to the couch.

Technically, she owed Hunter a call back, possibly with an explanation, not that there was a sane way to explain. For that matter, he might not want to hear from her after she'd blown him off.

Then again, there was a chance he was trying to give her the space she did in fact want. Probably wanted. What was the big deal about calling, anyway? It was a phone call, not a strategic decision in a battle plan. He might not even pick up if she did call.

Gina passed a hand over her eyes and through her hair, shaking her head at nothing in particular, and turned on the TV again.

"Yeah," Hunter answered the ring, staring at the indecipherable puzzle of his staff's summer schedule.

"Hi."

The soft voice caught him off-guard. Hunter almost checked the phone's display to confirm, but he didn't want to be wrong. "Gina," he said quietly, pushing back from his desk.

"Am I pulling you away from something?"

"Nothing more important than you." He winced at the cheesy line.

Then he heard her chuckle. "That's laying it on a bit thick, don't you think?"

"That wasn't my smoothest moment ever," he agreed, wracking his brains for a normal thing to say. "How was your day?"

"Fine." She paused. "Sorry about yesterday."

"Don't be. Did everything work out?" He was pretty sure that whatever had drawn her away had included her ex, though he couldn't figure out quite how. Then again, the man did work in the building.

"Just a complication at work." She sighed. "I don't want to think about it." She paused again. "How are things down south?"

"Going fairly well. Wrestling with staff schedules at the moment." Phone conversations were apparently not their forte. Talking in person hadn't been this bad, had it?

"Not the fun kind of wrestling."

The comment froze him for a heartbeat. "You're right about that."

Silence stretched out over the line.

"Should I let you focus?" she asked eventually.

"No, please, you're saving me." He got up from the desk and strode out to the silent lobby, then out to the benches in their entryway. "Tell me about your day."

"Just the usual mess of meetings and decisions. Nothing quite as fun as dealing with schedules."

The comment was probably intended as humorous, but she sounded more despondent. "I thought you liked your job?"

"I do, most of the time. The magazine's getting a new owner, it's making things…" She trailed off.

"Complicated," Hunter finished for her. It was the word she kept using. "The bumps will get smoothed out."

"You think so?"

"You're still in charge of your people, right? It's still your vision. The new owner might need some time to see how great you are at your job, but I doubt that'll take long." He stretched out on the bench as he spoke, staring up at the stars.

"What makes you think I'm any good at my job?"

"I've met you," Hunter answered simply. Silence answered the statement. "I have no doubts you're irreplaceable. And if the new owners think otherwise, they're idiots." It wasn't empty flattery. She was intelligent, and she obviously cared about her work. Roger and Sabella had both subtly mentioned how unique yet determined her vision was. Hunter couldn't judge the fashion side of things too well, but she looked stunning and classy every time he saw her.

"That's sweet of you," she murmured. "How about at the vineyard? Are things going smoothly?"

"Pretty well, yeah. We're getting more firmly into the wedding and bachelorette party season. Plus, the weather's been beautiful, so we've had a good stream of people out for tastings."

"Can't blame them. The views from your terraces are pretty phenomenal."

Hunter smiled, remembering her flitting about the wedding. "You're welcome to come visit any time," he found himself saying. *Damn it.* He should have thought about that one. He didn't want to sound like he was pressuring her. At the same time, he didn't want to have to watch every word he said.

"Tempting. Have you decided against a satellite vineyard then? Did the rain scare you off."

"Nah, I don't scare that easily. The soil drains the water surprisingly well, but it's a long process, checking out the land, doing what we can to ensure the yield would be good."

Actually, he needed to check in with Vince, his viticulturist. "Anyway, I don't want to bore you."

"You're not. Not that I know much about wine."

"As I recall, you know what you like."

She chuckled, low and deep. "Someone told me once it's all about the experience."

"What a coincidence. My grandpa used to say that. About wine, I mean."

"You don't say."

Hunter smiled again, inhaling the life-filled air. "I'm glad you called, Gina."

"You must really hate dealing with those schedules."

"Or really like talking to you." He could almost see the small smile that followed his compliments before she found a way to brush them off.

"Which one sounds more plausible to you?"

Hunter laughed, picturing the raised curve of an eyebrow, the sparkle of humor in her eyes. "So what do you have going on this week?"

"It'll be kind of quiet, actually. Hanging out with Sabella before they leave, you know."

"Oh, Kane's tour is starting, right?" His mother had yet to call him, which meant Tuck had yet to call her.

"Yep."

"You know you miss country music enough to come out for his concert here in a little bit." Although maybe it was way too soon to risk having his family possibly around her. They'd definitely scare her off.

She laughed outright. "You know it. His music isn't what would bring me down there."

"No?" He sobered.

She hesitated for a prolonged moment.

Hunter's breath stilled.

"No," she finally murmured.

Nineteen

Ooh, I remember this one," Gina said, pulling a little sapphire number out of Sabella's closet. They'd purchased it right before Sabella had left to join Kane on tour for the first time. She tossed it onto the growing pile on Sabella's bed.

"I do not think I'll need that this weekend." Sabella plucked it from the pile, moving it aside. She reached for a green sweater, folding it before dropping it into the open suitcase beside her.

"Why not?" Gina added a pretty purple top. "If I recall, it was quite a hit the first time."

Sabella blushed. She'd surprised Kane with this negligee on his birthday last year. "He doesn't seem to mind me without it," she said primly.

Gina crooked an eyebrow.

Sabella grinned through her wince. "You know what I mean!"

"I certainly do. Have you even worn it since? And anyway."

Gina moved the item in question back to the pile waiting to be packed away. "It's not like it takes a lot of room."

"That's true." The agreement was lackluster.

Gina lowered onto the corner of the bed. "Is everything okay with you guys?"

"Oh, of course." She shook her head then worked the band out of her hair to redo the slipping messy bun. "He's been stressed, about the start of the tour. And I don't want to throw anything off for him, but I'm not sure how I could help."

"Half of his songs are about you." Gina picked up another sweater from the pile. "I think you're plenty helpful."

"It's his first time going on tour, since the wedding. Well, obviously." Her fingers fidgeted in the skirt she was folding. "I simply don't want his fans to be disappointed, or put off, or anything." The concern literally lined her forehead.

"Is Kane worried about it?" It didn't seem likely. He adored his wife, though Gina knew without a doubt that appearances could be deceiving.

"He hasn't said anything," Sabella admitted. She pushed off the bed to gather makeup from her armoire into a travel case.

Gina tried not to smile. "So this is you being ridiculous? He loves you. And wasn't there all this concern last year about his fans not being okay with him dating you, which turned out to be completely untrue? Being capable of being in a committed relationship is an attractive feature in a man, in theory."

Sabella's eyebrows lifted. "Convincing."

"Well, you shouldn't really care about people's possible reactions. Kane loves you, and that's not about to change. And it could have a mixed effect anyway, right? Women who hate the fact that he's married but love that he's the type to marry. Men who are impressed that he got a hottie like you."

Sabella rolled her eyes, but a smile tugged at her lips.

"Just don't worry about it unless it actually becomes a problem. Which I doubt it will," Gina added for good measure. "Besides, Seattle was fun."

"They're playing in Spokane first." She shook her head. "But you're right, I'm probably stressing for no reason." She plopped back on the bed, dropping the makeup bag beside the suitcase. "Anyway, fill me in on the goings-on at work."

Gina scrunched her nose. "Nothing good." It had taken less than two days for rumors of an impending dress code to start flying about. "He's obviously trying to assert his dominance. And he'll probably succeed."

"You don't think Vivian will stand up to him?" Sabella opened a drawer to pull out lingerie and socks.

"I don't know. She seems to be on board with his plans, or at least willing to play along. Or maybe she doesn't care." Gina looked at the top she was folding, then shook it out to try again. "Some people actually seem smitten, though I guess I shouldn't be surprised." She'd found something about him appealing, once.

Sabella worked the top out of her fingers, covering Gina's

hands with one of hers. "He'll slip up, and people will see him for the monster he is."

"Right. And meanwhile, one of the single girls will fall in love, and our magazine is going to start telling women that colors are evil."

"You won't let that happen. He isn't omnipotent, and you know that." Sabella's lips pursed, twisting to one side.

Gina recognized the sign. "What? What are you thinking?"

Hazel eyes considered her for a prolonged moment. "Well, I could pitch an article, to Heather."

Heather was the magazine's features editor, but other than that, Gina wasn't following.

"About the warning signs of women in, well, unhealthy relationships. Or advice for intervening. It's an important women's issue, so it wouldn't be surprising for her to choose to print it."

Gina ignored Sabella's obvious hesitation in suggesting it. She hated the fact that Sabella treated her with kid gloves now, though it was nice that she considered the impact of that kind of article. It would almost certainly touch on the personal. "He could just tell her not to," Gina pointed out.

"If he's that involved, which he might not be with other departments. I think he's pretty fixated on you." Sabella's inhale hitched. "Sorry, I mean…"

"You mean he only bought the magazine because I work there, and he's only picking on the fashion department because it's mine. And I can't stop him," Gina finished flatly.

Sabella exhaled, her torso drooping. "I think he might actually have those ludicrous, puritanical opinions on what women should and shouldn't wear, but I also think his predominant interest is in making you squirm."

"In controlling me, you mean." Gina shifted her shoulders to work out the knot that never seemed to leave anymore. Well, almost never. Sex with Hunter left her entirely knot free.

"And you said the HR rep was useless?" Sabella asked, dropping the subject of the article.

"I don't know about useless, really. He probably would have been worse without her there. But I can't exactly sew her to my side." She thought a second. "Though that could be an interesting new fashion trend."

Sabella's response was more exhale than chuckle. "What about leaving? I know you like your job, but it's not like you couldn't handle a position somewhere more prominent. You had intended this to be a stepping stone, once upon a time."

"I wouldn't have expected you to suggest running away." Not that the thought hadn't crossed her mind. Standing her ground seemed like a losing battle.

"It's not running. And there's no point in staying for the sake of proving something, if it's to your own detriment. You could put out some feelers, see what's out there, maybe switch over to a magazine that focuses exclusively on fashion," Sabella tempted.

"Maybe." Gina stood, walking back over to the closet. She

was there to help Sabella pack, after all, not steal the focus. "I doubt he'd let me leave."

"He can't stop you."

They'd had a similar conversation when Sabella had helped her break things off. Gina slipped another top off a hanger and folded it. "I like working at the magazine, with Roger, even if it wasn't supposed to be forever." There was nothing wrong with climbing the food chain in a small pond.

"It can't hurt to see what else could be out there, though, right?" Sabella added the folded top to the suitcase. "I'm certain between the two of us, we know people in some other local magazines. Oh! And I think my mom knows someone at a magazine in the Bay Area. She could probably set up a meeting."

"In the Bay Area?" Gina repeated skeptically. The weather here might not be the greatest, but she liked the life she'd built in Portland, for the most part.

"Portland isn't exactly a fashion capital," Sabella reminded. "Plus, living in the Bay Area isn't so bad, and more importantly, it's only a meeting."

"Roger would kill me," Gina deflected.

"Roger would want you to be happy."

Gina snorted. It wasn't so much untrue as only half the picture. He'd definitely be less than pleased if Gina chose to leave the magazine, much less Portland.

"Okay, well, we'll cross that bridge when we get to it. You could probably switch him over with you, or recommend him to Vivian as your replacement, or something." Sabella paused. "You seem scared, to leave."

Gina plopped back down on the bed, beside the diminishing pile of clothes. "I have a good job, and I'm good at it. Why rock the boat?"

"You *had* a good job, until ownership changed." Sabella sat on the other side of the pile. "And you always wanted more anyway, because you can continue climbing upward in the industry. Why are you settling?"

"What if I can't hack it," Gina pointed out.

Sabella literally shrugged off the possibility. "Of course you can. You basically built the fashion department here, and you'd be an incredible asset at a larger magazine."

"Maybe." Gina fell back on the bed, staring up at the ceiling to avoid Sabella's concerned gaze. She did that a lot lately.

"In either case, you don't have to make a decision right this second. But honestly, I think you should see what's out there." She nearly jumped with her next idea, shaking the mattress. "Maybe my mom could arrange a meeting the same time Kane's playing in that area, and you could come hang out for a while."

"That could be fun," Gina agreed. *And it would be just a meeting.* "Hunter actually suggested I come down for the concert at the winery."

"Yeah? You guys have been talking?" Sabella tried to hide the hopefulness in her voice, but Gina knew her too well.

"We talked." Gina twisted onto her side, propping her head on her hand. "I don't really know what's happening there."

"Taking things as they come seems like a good plan. And I imagine you and Hunter would enjoy hanging out again."

"Interesting euphemism, Sab."

Sabella smiled wryly, shaking her head. "That, too."

It wasn't the worst idea in the world, and if she had a business meeting, it wouldn't be as though she was going down just to see Hunter. "Are you sure your mom wouldn't mind? I wouldn't want to put her out."

Sabella grinned before Gina even finished. "I'm absolutely certain." Her shoulders lifted, and Gina couldn't help smiling back. "This'll be fun!"

Hunter checked his watch as he lowered into the rental car. Vince, his viticulturist, was staying another day to get a better sense for the land Hunter was considering, but his own flight back was in a few hours. Things looked good, on the surface. Hunter had focused on oenology in his time at Davis, but he'd known Vince for decades, and there was no question he could rely on the man's take on the land. That was why they'd flown up to Portland this morning.

Unfortunately, going round trip in a single day didn't give Hunter much leeway. Still, he could probably manage to swing by Gina's office. The question was whether he should. He had a bad track record of pulling her away from her work. On the other hand, the possibility of seeing her, even for a few minutes, was too tantalizing to pass up.

He punched in her work's address on the car's GPS then did a quick search for a local coffee shop.

Luck seemed to be on his side, as about a half hour later he found a parking spot beside her building, with the coffees and absolutely no problem. He bypassed the security desk and strode straight to the elevator. One thing his upbringing had taught him was no one questions a confident man walking purposefully, especially not one in a good suit.

Anticipation had him tapping his finger against the cardboard carrier as the elevator ascended. A bustle of bright colors surrounded him as soon as he passed through the magazine's doors. He scanned the room quickly, trying to remember which one was Gina's office.

"Hunter," a familiar voice called.

Hunter smiled, turning to the flash of green. "Roger," he acknowledged. "It's good to see you again."

Roger's eyes fell to the coffees, and the single iris Hunter had also stopped to get. "Those for me?" he teased with a cheeky smile. If Hunter hadn't seen him so comfortable with Michel, he might've interpreted it as flirting.

"Is Gina available? I only have a few minutes," he explained, hoping Roger wouldn't take the direct question as rude.

Roger turned away, glancing toward what had to be her office. "Her door's open."

"Thanks." Hunter inclined his head, since his hands weren't free to shake.

"No problem." Roger gave him a once-over before walking away.

Hunter dodged a quickly moving employee with a handful of files and strode to Gina's office. She wore a striking, brightly patterned top in an array of pinks and was intensely focused on a spread of sheets before her. He paused to admire her before brushing his knuckles against the doorjamb.

"Yeah," she acknowledged without looking up.

"Hi there."

Her blank gaze found him, followed by a wash of recognition. "Hi." She glanced back at her desk for a second then shook her head. "What are you doing here?"

"I had another meeting up here, things are moving with the land. I don't really have a lot of time," he explained, approaching her desk. "My flight back's in a couple hours, but I wanted to come say hi, maybe tempt you with a brief coffee break."

Her lips curved softly, and she stood then stepped around the desk. Hunter held out the iris first, taking the opportunity to look at her more closely. Rainbow earrings decorated her ears, and a simple black skirt swirled around her hips. She brought the flower to her face, inhaling as she reached out to shut the door.

Hunter smiled, offering her the coffees. "You look beautiful, by the way."

"Why, thank you." She tilted a paper cup to her lips, gesturing to the chairs beside them.

Hunter lowered into one and worked the second coffee from the carrier, carefully placing the cardboard on the edge of the desk.

Gina settled into the other armchair beside him. The flower remained in her hand. It wasn't a bad sign. "How was your meeting?" she asked.

"We're making some headway. I have a pretty good feeling about this land, and there's a decent cottage on-site that could be converted into headquarters while the cellars and tasting room are built."

Her eyes widened. "That sounds like quite the undertaking."

"It's a long-term project." *To put it mildly.* "If everything works out, we'd plant next spring. Even then, we wouldn't produce anything drinkable for at least a few years."

"But you obviously think it's worth it." Her eyes reflected interest and not the polite detachment most people outside the business tried to maintain when he went into details.

"It would be an investment," Hunter agreed. "Branching out, both geographically and with the varietal, but ultimately, it will help my grandfather's name, his legacy, gain even more traction in the wine world. Or at least, that's the plan." One of several, any of which would require a fair amount of work. But anything worth having was worth working for.

"I can certainly understand why you would be so careful with choosing where to focus your efforts."

Hunter nodded, distracted by the apparently rare glint of sunlight that streamed through the window, blending into her hair. He sipped his coffee to regain focus. It had already been a long day. "What's going on in your world?"

She glanced behind them, out at the activity in the main room. "Just the glamorous world of fashion. Did you fly up only for the day?"

"Yeah. It's a long day, but it's fairly doable with such a short flight. Hopefully next time I'll be able to stay longer, if you'd grace me with your company, of course."

"Of course," she repeated sarcastically, though humor danced in her eyes.

Hunter ran mentally through the winery's schedule. "Maybe I could come back up this weekend?" It would take some doing, but it could happen.

"That wedding I mentioned is this weekend. And Melody isn't one of those brides who would welcome a last-minute addition to the guest list."

"Shame." At least the idea of inviting him had crossed her mind. It may have been wishful thinking, but there seemed to be honest regret in her voice.

"I was considering possibly flying down for Kane's concert, though," Gina added softly, eyes trained on him.

"Yeah? Any chance you'd be interested in spending the weekend?" he asked before remembering Tucker's plans.

"I have a meeting, that Friday in the city, but otherwise I might be able to be convinced."

Hunter felt his mouth stretch into a grin before his brain caught up. "I have to warn you, though, my brother's planning on proposing and, in theory, having a small engagement party at the winery that Saturday night."

"Oh, well, I wouldn't want to intrude," she backtracked immediately, and predictably. "And congratulations to your brother."

"You wouldn't be. Intruding, I mean. If you were still interested in spending the weekend, I wouldn't want you to be blindsided by my family." Considering that, thus far, they'd spent maybe a total of five days actually around each other, it may seem premature, or pressuring.

Gina sipped her coffee, her gaze flicking to different spots around the office as she considered. "We could play it by ear," she said finally. "I could always sneak away to Davis for Kane's concert that night."

As far as compromises went, it definitely wasn't bad. At least he'd have a chance to see her again, and maybe convince her to stay. "I do know how much you love his music," he said.

Gina burst out laughing, and Hunter smiled again, warmed by the sound. This was definitely worth the detour.

Twenty

A comfortingly familiar rhythm surrounded Gina the second she stepped into the magazine's offices. With Melody's wedding and Kane's birthday, it had been a party-filled whirlwind of a weekend. Life wasn't half bad. It was almost enough to make her forget the jackass had purchased the magazine.

Almost.

Still, she hadn't seen him since their unfortunate meeting, and though the rumors of a dress code continued to circle, nothing official had been announced. Her coworkers had easily transitioned to a vibrant, summery wardrobe, which was perfectly suitable for June.

Roger met her at her office door, handing her a mocha.

"Gather everyone for an update in twenty, okay?"

He trailed her into the office. "You're not even a little bit hung over, are you?" he accused.

"Well, some of us can hold our liquor." Roger and Michel had joined in on celebrating at Kane's combination gig and birthday party. Roger had tried to keep up with the general consumption of beers and whiskey. "Besides," Gina added, "didn't Michel take care of you when you guys left?"

"He was very sweet."

Gina paused her perusal of this morning's proofs to really look at him. "I'm glad things are going well for you two."

Roger smiled shyly, and his shoulders danced. "Doesn't seem like I've messed it up yet."

"Give it time," Gina retorted on autopilot.

But this time, Roger just rolled his eyes. He was really growing up with Michel in his life.

"Gina," Vivian's voice spun them back to her doorway.

"Good morning, Vivian," Gina said brightly.

Roger shrank somewhat into the background, like he always did with their editor in chief around.

"I'd like to speak with you," Vivian said almost emotionlessly, then turned away, barely waiting for Gina's nod.

She turned to Roger, who shot her a curiously worried glance. "Get started without me," she instructed. "Get an update on the stories, the bookings for the shoot, everything. Make sure we're on track."

His head tilted to the side. "Whatever you say."

Gina shook her head slightly and made her way over to Vivian's office, then rapped her knuckles on the open door.

"Please shut the door," Vivian said without looking up.

Gina pushed it closed before settling in one of the leather chairs. The office was bigger than Gina's own but decorated more sparsely, with clean lines and without the tack boards, clothing racks, or shelves of past issues. It was an office made for meetings.

"All our years working together," Vivian started, lowering her pen and leaning back in her own chair. As always, her graying peach hair was impeccably styled, her makeup and outfit kept tidy, cutting-edge, and tasteful. "You have been a wonderful asset for our magazine."

"Thank you."

"However, it seems you have created friction with our new owner."

Gina froze in the face of the steely gaze. She didn't have a clue how much Vivian knew, or what specifically had prompted this meeting, so she didn't respond.

"I would have expected better from you, stirring this ridiculous rebellion to perfectly reasonable requests for a standard of professionalism, refusing outright to consider the new owner's vision, and then drawing me into it."

He did have a way to spin things, and convincingly. "You have trusted my judgment, my taste, for a long time, Vivian," Gina reminded, trying to keep her voice calm. Remaining professional was her only hope. "We've garnered a growing amount of respect, expanded our readership. There is no reason to curtail our stylistic choices to the baseless demands of someone who understands nothing about fashion."

"He owns the magazine," Vivian stated bluntly. "I have seen you be charming, be vague, be so subtly manipulative that men fall over themselves to give you what you want. And instead, you threw a gauntlet in Mr. Talbot's face. What were you thinking? And taking a Human Resources representative with you into a simple meeting?"

Gina curled her fingers into her thighs, out of Vivian's sight. "You aren't seriously considering altering our content to kowtow to his puritanical notions of women's roles and appropriate attire."

Vivian arched a single, perfectly plucked eyebrow. "My decisions with regards to the future of this magazine are only your concern in adhering to them. There is nothing wrong with encouraging women to reclaim tasteful, elegant options, nor with accepting a re-envisioned future for the magazine. I expect you to show more deference to Mr. Talbot's vision, as well as to set a more appropriate example to your staff." Her glossed lips thinned, pressing against each other. "This magazine wasn't built for you to destroy in an attempt to do whatever it is you're trying to do. I don't know what game you think you're playing, but I'm incredibly disappointed, and furthermore, questioning your future here."

"Vivian, you have always been a visionary, encouraging women to experiment with their sense of identity, both through fashion and with regards to other aspects of modern life." Gina swallowed to tamp down her mounting disbelief. "While I regret if my intention to stay true to the tone of our magazine despite the change in ownership came across as disrespectful to your vision, that is all I have intended. If people are reacting to rumors about the impending increase of so-called professionalism, that is their choice, and it certainly wasn't instigated by me." Unless you count leading by example, but she wasn't known for demure, bland outfits, or hadn't been before she'd met him. More importantly, some part of her had expected Vivian to stand behind the assertions she'd made during that meeting. And including an HR rep in a business meeting when the parties involved had any kind of personal history *was* professional.

"Change in ownership frequently results in changes in staffing, Gina. Some less disastrous changes in the direction of our content and image are inevitable. Keeping Mr. Talbot happy for the few weeks or maybe months he will be interested in anything other than the numbers of our sales means saving jobs, including yours." Vivian sighed, outer corners of her lips drooping and heightening the lines in her gracefully aging face. "And including mine."

Gina blinked at the admission. She'd considered the possibility of Alistair firing *her*, but it made no sense in his apparent quest to control some part of her life. He wouldn't think twice about removing and replacing anyone who stood in his way as he tried to exert his dominance.

"I can see it's finally sinking in. I expect you to make amends."

Normally, Gina would have panicked, but right then, everything inside her stilled. "Elle Savvy had an interesting idea for an article, about the reach of domestic violence and abuse," she told Vivian, using Sabella's pen name. "She was going to pitch it to Heather, of course, but in case you still value my opinion, I think it would be a great issue for us to address."

"It's a touch of conservatism, Gina, not abuse," Vivian said, picking up her pen in a dismissive gesture.

"It's an important women's issue."

Vivian sighed, dropping the pen back onto the stack of papers before her and making eye contact. "Talk to Heather, get your department back in line. We'll discuss it at our next meeting."

Gina nodded, fighting the clench of her jaw. Vivian glanced toward the door, then resumed marking up the mock-ups from various departments. Gina left the office in silence.

She had actually considered quitting right there, but the impetuous decision was bound to have consequences for her staff, and for Roger, and it deserved a bit more thought. It wasn't likely Vivian would fire her in the immediate future, which gave her time. Now she was even more grateful Sabella's mother had set up that meeting at *Bay Fashion*, and even more motivated to reach out to her own connections.

A change did in fact seem inevitable, simply not the one Alistair had in mind.

"Damn it!" Hunter barreled his fist into the surface of the cherry-wood desk after hanging up. That was the second time in three days that a regular distributor of Cavaliere wines had decided they no longer wanted to stock his label. The first time had blindsided him, until he'd learned the restaurant had a new sommelier. As with everything, politics played a role here, and he'd already planned to take the man out to a nice dinner to renegotiate the role of Cavaliere wines on his menu.

This time, however, it was a small, local wine shop that had been stocking their wines for almost as long as the winery had existed. He couldn't begin to imagine what had caused them to suddenly up and decide they no longer wanted their quarterly orders to continue. It definitely wasn't for lack of sales, and he was absolutely certain it didn't have to do with any kind of quality lapse.

This backing out wouldn't be great for the winery's quarterly numbers, but it wouldn't devastate them either. It was the step backward that really bothered him. He'd been steadily making headway, gaining name recognition and slowly respect. He had award-winning vintages, sure, but even his less-renowned wines were recommended among the locals, which was an endorsement he'd worked hard to maintain after his grandfather's passing.

He had to figure out what was driving people away, whether it was a faux pas on the part of one of his staff, or perhaps an enticing deal by one of his competitors, though neither was usually sufficient to cause his regulars to stop buying. If he didn't know what the problem was, he couldn't fix it.

His hand still smarted when Caitria strode into his office without preamble and perched on the corner of his desk.

"I'm sorry, Caitria, but it's not a good time."

"We need to talk." Her tone allowed for no argument.

Hunter redirected his focus to her, trying to shake off his anger and the slight sense of betrayal. He'd worked hard to become an active member of this eclectic community, but apparently that word meant nothing anymore. Still, the winery's problems weren't Caitria's fault. "What can I do for you?"

"I received an interesting offer today." She reached out to swirl one of his pens around their wooden cup.

"What kind of offer?"

"An investment, of sorts, in the gallery." Her eyes found his, and the movement stopped.

Hunter's gut clenched. "Why do I take it this isn't good news."

"All the costs of refreshments for my openings, or other events, would be covered, or donated, or something along those lines, as long as I agree to use this person's providers, for things like cheese and crackers." She paused dramatically. "And for the wine."

Hunter's teeth grated against each other, and he tried to get his jaw to relax. He didn't doubt Caitria's loyalty, but it wasn't a small offer. They had a pretty good deal in place already, but he couldn't afford to give her all those cases for free, either.

She slipped off the desk and turned to face him. "I told him I wasn't looking for any kind of exclusive agreement with a provider, of course."

"Of course," Hunter echoed. He hadn't missed the word *exclusive*.

"And that if he wanted to do a trial run, he was welcome to send along a few cases for my next opening. You wouldn't believe what he said next."

Hunter leaned back in his chair. "Try me."

"He told me that he wasn't interested in having the products he would provide served alongside Cavaliere wine." Her eyes narrowed. "Now why is that?"

Hunter shook his head, exhaling. "I wish I knew."

"Whose toes have you stepped on so badly they would target an art gallery's purchases?" Caitria held regular events, but it was true the sales weren't truly worth going after, except of course for the name recognition garnered.

"Trouble is," Hunter confided, "you're not the only one. We've had a couple major cancellations lately. And it no longer seems like a coincidence." Maybe he was being paranoid. "He didn't give you a name or anything, did he?"

"Gunnar Hackett."

Hunter shrugged. "Doesn't ring a bell."

"I'd ask about upset fathers and brothers, but that's not your style."

Hunter's mind flashed to Paige, but that wasn't likely. She was a sweet girl, who'd sounded very understanding about him cancelling. Besides, it wasn't like she would have a difficult time finding a date. If he had pissed someone off enough that they were going after him, that was a problem for his subcon-scious to figure out. He'd also need to look into Gunnar Hackett, see if there was some connection he was missing. "Speaking of brothers," he redirected, "has Tucker called you about Saturday yet?"

"He left me a message, but I haven't had a chance to call him back. What are you going to do about this?"

"I don't know. But I'm working on it." He needed a change of scenery, so he stood to walk her out of the office. "Anyway, if Tuck gets his act together, we'll be celebrating Nora's wise decision to tell him to go to hell."

Caitria's lips curved into a pleased smile. "He's finally going to propose?"

"That's the plan." Hunter led her to the tasting room then stepped around the bar, scanning the bottles to find Caitria's favorite. At her nod, he grabbed a clean glass and poured. "You know we would all love to see you there."

She tilted the glass toward him before taking a long sip. "Whatever it is that has someone targeting you, it's not your wine." She reconsidered a second, lips pressing into a protective frown. "Or maybe it is. Especially if it's a competitor, you need to nip this in the bud."

"I will," Hunter assured. He had no idea how, but that would come. He wouldn't let his grandfather's name be tarnished. But he also didn't want Caitria to spend time worrying. "So, Saturday. Can we count on you being there?"

"I might be able to be convinced. I did always like your brother," she teased.

Hunter grinned. "I knew it." At one point, both boys had had crushes on her, and you could still see why. Her black hair reached elegantly down to her waist, shifting around her with every movement, and she had gorgeous, pale-green eyes that had once sparkled with life, and now held wells of wisdom. She'd easily maintained her fit, modelesque shape, which showed through even in the loose blouse she'd paired with figure-hugging jeans. Her warm, loving nature hadn't hurt either. It was a shame she hadn't found someone for the long term, but she'd always have a family with the Cavalieres.

"So," Hunter asked, pouring himself a glass, "what's coming up at the gallery?"

Twenty-One

ou're here!" Sabella shot up from the bench beside the smaller of the winery's parking lots almost as soon as Gina had opened the door of her rental.

Gina smiled at the enthusiasm, especially since they'd seen each other four days ago, though it had been quite the long week since Kane's birthday. The California sunshine warmed her already, seeping through her top and into tense muscles as she opened the trunk to pull out her small suitcase. Sabella had crossed to her side by the time she locked the car. "Admit it, you're just bored on tour," Gina teased as they hugged.

Sabella smiled. "I have no doubts this will be even more fun with you here." She nodded to the suitcase. "Do you want to drop that in the bus for now? We can figure out sleeping arrangements later."

"Sounds like a plan." Between the bed on the bus and the rooms reserved for the band, they had only vaguely discussed where Gina would be staying tonight. They also hadn't really covered where she would stay tomorrow after her interview, since the musicians would be moving on to Sacramento. Sabella had mentioned off-hand that Gina could stay with her parents in the South Bay, and in theory Gina could rejoin her and the band, but then there was the question of Hunter's involvement, though she wasn't sure spending the night, or several, with him would be the best idea. The only fixed points of the next few days were her meeting tomorrow in the city, and her and Sabella's flight back to Portland on Sunday, but it felt kind of nice to play it by ear like she used to.

"Where are the guys?" Gina asked as Sabella unlocked the tour bus that had been tucked as far out of the way as possible in this lot.

"Finishing up the sound check, before people start arriving." There were a few hours left before their show. "Or were you asking about Hunter?" Sabella asked, though the up-turn of her lips showed she knew better.

"Of course not." The idea of seeing him had kept a steady stream of anticipation coursing through Gina ever since she'd woken up that morning. It was amazing she'd managed to get any work done before heading to the airport.

Sabella gestured to the short flight of stairs revealed within the bus. "After you."

Gina stepped inside, expecting a mildly dilapidated and entirely cramped space, but the interior of the bus was neither. Everything had been set efficiently, allowing the illusion of comfort. The relatively small vehicle encompassed a compact kitchen and a cozy-looking seating area. The back half of the bus, presumably with a bed and a bathroom, was closed off from view by a door painted or covered to resemble wood. Everything appeared clean, and the only signs of occupancy were a deck of cards on the table and a couple mugs beside the sink.

"What do you think?" Sabella asked behind her.

"It's not terrible." Gina'd thought Sabella, being Sabella, had been making the best of the situation for the sake of being with Kane, but it really didn't seem that bad. "Okay, I know it's none of my business," Gina asked as Sabella tucked the suitcase out of the way and they headed back outside, "but do they actually make anything from these tours? Seems like they have pretty high expenses."

Sabella shrugged. "They definitely break even, but most of their income comes from downloads and such, so the tour lets them get their music out there, to boost sales. I know at least in some places, they make a decent amount over the expenses, but you know musicians—it's a labor of love. Steve and Bobby play with other groups when Kane's not touring or in the studio. And Mitch has other clients, too."

"And Kane?" Gina prompted casually as they crossed to the main winery building. Though she hadn't been back since the wedding, the space felt strangely familiar.

"Kane makes a little more than the rest of them," Sabella admitted, "since he writes the songs and all that. They're in the middle of negotiating a contract for his next CD, and that should mean financial backing for recording and some promotion, concerts, plus maybe an advance. It does help that Nashville isn't as expensive as out here."

Though the tasting room was filled with chatting visitors, memories of the empty space, of seeing Hunter for the first time, and of everything they'd done since hit Gina, tightening her body in places and ways memories shouldn't be able to. She had to mentally shake her head to refocus on what Sabella was saying.

"It's not like I make oodles of money either."

"I'd pay you more if I could," Gina told her honestly, though she knew that wasn't the point.

"Speaking of," Sabella said, finding an empty spot by the bar. The bartender was busy pouring for a trio actively debating which wines they wanted to try, but the two of them weren't in any kind of hurry today. "Are you excited about your meeting tomorrow?"

"Somewhat. I'm still not sure what may come of it, especially since this one's down here. But." She took a deep breath. "I think you might be right."

Sabella's eyes widened.

"It may be time for me to leave, to move on."

Sabella didn't have a chance to comment as the bartender appeared beside them, flipping two glasses before setting them down beside the girls' spot at the lacquered counter. "What are you ladies interested in today?"

"Should we get a bottle?" Sabella suggested. "Sit outside?"

"Sure. What're you in the mood for?"

The bartender tried to hide his grin at the easy sale behind a polite look.

"Riesling? Or, remember the Muscat?"

"Are we celebrating something?" Gina asked.

"Your arrival," a familiar, deep voice interjected.

Gina spun around to see Hunter, framed by the beams of the doorway, wearing a simple gray tee shirt and jeans. A hint of stubble covered his jaw, and she couldn't help remembering the gentle scrape of it on her skin as his mouth and tongue played over her.

He stepped closer but spoke first to the bartender. "Darian, anything these ladies want, it's on the house."

"Oh, you don't have to do that," Sabella protested instantly.

"It's my pleasure, really. Wonderful to see you both again." He finished the phrase with his gaze stilled on Gina, and she had to suppress a shiver. She was almost disappointed that he hadn't moved to touch—or kiss—her in hello.

"That's rather generous of you," she said.

"Well, I have to make your trip out worth it somehow," he said quietly, so the other patrons wouldn't overhear. They maintained eye contact for an extended moment, and Gina looked away from those knowledgeable eyes first, swallowing. A hint of humor touched the corners of his lips.

"Perhaps I should go find my husband," Sabella offered.

"Alas, I only popped out for a moment. Though I'm glad to have run into you both, I do have to get back to work." His tone had shifted seamlessly from intimate to professionally friendly. "Maybe I could join you later?"

"That would be lovely," Gina said, matching his cool tone.

Sabella tried to hide her amusement, fighting a losing war with her expression.

"A bottle of Muscat, then?" Darian repeated, reminding them of his waiting presence.

She and Sabella exchanged a wordless agreement, and Sabella looked to the bartender with a smile. "Please." When Hunter excused himself, she added, "I haven't forgotten what you said, you know. Though I think you might have."

Gina didn't bother denying the obvious suggestion. "He is pretty cute, isn't he."

"Definitely not bad," Sabella agreed, watching her expectantly. "Did something else happen?" she asked when Gina didn't resume their previous topic.

They hadn't actually talked since her meeting with Vivian. "He might not be interested in firing me, but he could run the magazine into the ground. Vivian pointed out that everyone's jobs, meaning everyone else's apparently, are on the line." The bartender set an opened, chilled bottle on the bar. They both shot him smiles before grabbing it and the glasses and heading outside. "Maybe with me gone, he'll leave it alone, and this won't destroy everyone else's lives," Gina continued. "I mean, the magazine wouldn't interest him anymore, right?"

"And you?" Sabella asked, ignoring the last point.

"I will try to find a different pond. Maybe somewhere that might actually send me to fashion week in L.A. or New York." She sighed as they settled on cushioned metal chairs beside a little round table. Like in the bar, a poster promoting Kane's concert sat in a little plastic cover. Gina picked it up to get a closer look. "Good picture." It showed Kane standing slightly offset from his band in front of a mountain, with wind puffing his hair.

Sabella hummed noncommittally, filling their glasses. "So are you okay, with possibly leaving? I know you love the magazine."

Gina traded the photo for her glass. "It's better than trying to stand up for something that wouldn't need defending if I wasn't there, and better than costing people their jobs." She tilted the glass to her lips, letting the refreshing, delicate sweetness wash over her tongue with a light play of bubbles. "Besides, I can't even imagine how nice it would be to go to work without worrying about seeing him, or having a useless meeting with him, or wondering what manipulative thing he'll do next."

Sabella also sipped her wine, quietly, which meant she either didn't know what to say, which was unlikely, or was trying to find a way to word something.

"I pitched your article idea to Vivian, by the way. Hope you don't mind."

"What did she say?"

"To bring it up with Heather and then also at the next meeting. *If* I can get my department in line."

"You're kidding," Sabella blurted. Vivian was known for bolstering women's rights, supporting important causes enthusiastically if not unreservedly.

Gina shrugged. "She's falling in line. She doesn't want to get fired, not that I blame her for that."

"She should have given you the benefit of the doubt," Sabella contradicted.

A chilled bubble seemed to surround them despite the sunshine and lively greenery that felt just beyond their reach. Gina took another sip of wine. "Something's bugging you."

Sabella licked her lips, then sighed. "Benny's boss said he's been getting pressure, to let him go."

Gina nearly spit the wine out, forcing it down with a rough swallow. "What?"

"Apparently his boss pointed out his impeccable record, and that there was no actual cause, even the complaint itself was rather vague. He stood up for him, and gave Benny a heads up, but it seems odd, don't you think?" Worry flattened the line of Sabella's brows.

"How do you know all of this?"

"Melody was anxious, and you know how chatty she gets sometimes. I didn't really think Alistair would be involved, until you brought up Vivian."

"You think he's targeting people who have a connection to me," Gina said flatly. As a control tactic, it made sense. She was so tired of considering battle tactics, wondering what his next steps may be. Meanwhile, he was slicing away at her life.

"I think," Sabella said slowly, "that you transitioning to a less volatile work environment with more potential for growth may be a really good idea." She picked up the bottle to top off the glasses they had both abandoned on the table. "I also think that we're at a beautiful winery, with some gorgeous men waiting for us, and that we should take full advantage." She lifted both glasses, and Gina obligingly reached for hers. Sabella smiled. "Everything else can wait."

Gina exhaled and clinked their glasses together, hoping the earlier warmth would soon seep back in.

Hunter wasn't really listening to the music. The seating set before the slightly raised stage was completely filled, though the open air prevented it from feeling stifling. The setting sun washed this entire part of the vineyard in a glow of colors that would gradually be replaced by strategically placed lights. This was only the second of their biweekly summer concert series, but attendance was a marked improvement from last year's, so the event seemed to be gaining traction.

He scanned the audience, looking for any disturbances, but really trying to find Gina. He'd meant to get away to join her and the others for a quick dinner, but with the influx of people, he hadn't been able to. Although for the winery's sake, it was a good problem to have.

A swell of applause spread through the audience as he caught sight of Gina and Sabella, sitting at the outside edge of one of the picnic tables set around the perimeter of the area. Not wanting to draw attention, Hunter waited for the musicians to launch into an upbeat song before moving toward the women. He hadn't intended to distract her, but Gina's head turned, finding him only a few steps away, and Hunter smiled at the instant upturn of the corners of her mouth. He slid onto the edge of the bench beside her. "Mind if I join you?" Unfortunately, she was wearing a jacket, and the night wasn't particularly chilly anyway, so he had no pretense for slipping his arm around her.

"I suppose it's too late to protest," she said quietly, though she didn't turn back to the stage.

Hunter rested an elbow on the table behind them, wanting to bring his fingers to the nape of her neck. The trio sitting on the other side of the table prevented the motion. He leaned a little closer instead, lowering his voice further. "I know how much you love Kane's music, and I hate to disrupt your enjoyment, but perhaps I could steal you away?" He wanted to say a proper hello, not to mention find out what her plans were for the weekend. He definitely knew what his were, but she'd objected so strongly to spending an entire night with him in Portland that suggesting it here didn't seem like the smartest idea.

Gina turned briefly to Sabella then stood smoothly, heading toward the outdoor bar. Hunter followed, as he frequently seemed to do with her, not that he minded. The view wasn't half bad, either. Despite it, Hunter sped up slightly so he could slip a hand onto the small of her back and lead her to a more secluded area, behind the reach of the lights. Her long legs matched his stride effortlessly.

When they were safely out of view of Kane's audience, Hunter swung around to face her, lacing their fingers together. "Hi there."

She chuckled, just barely, pressing her lips together to control the impulse. Even in the dimmed light, looking at her stilled something inside him. All the issues with his distributors melted into the background. She was here with him, and his brother was getting engaged, and despite the recent headaches, life was good.

On heels, Gina was nearly as tall as him, tantalizingly close. Her fingers tightened in his, and Hunter closed the insignificant distance between them, brushing her lips. Her strawberry-tinged lip gloss heightened the slip of their kiss. Only an ingrained sense of decorum prevented him from deepening it to inappropriate levels, since they were still very much in plain sight of anyone who might wander toward the bar or lose their way to the restrooms.

"It's good to see you," he said after pulling back.

She glanced up and around them at the growing darkness, cocking her weight into one hip.

Hunter smiled. "You know what I mean." He wanted to ask if she had come down for the entire weekend, and where she was planning on staying, but was there a good way to bring it up?

"You don't mind missing the concert?" Gina asked.

Much as he loved country music… "If it wasn't rude to your friends, I'd do my best to steal you away right now."

She stepped a hairsbreadth closer, and the temperature between them shifted just barely from the heat of her body. "Why's that?"

"Let's say I could use some stress relief."

Her eyes widened at the allusion, before a line appeared between her eyebrows. "Is everything all right?"

"Better with you here."

She stepped away, frowning lightly and loosening her fingers from his.

Hunter repositioned their hands, brushing his thumbs over her palms. "It's just some hitches with the winery, distributors pulling out suddenly." He could feel his own frown growing, but she'd stopped pulling away, which meant his hunch had been right. It wasn't a bad sign, her wanting more between them than physicality. "But I'd really rather not worry about it tonight." He hadn't done much thinking about anything else in the last few days. "It'll get sorted out."

"Denial, huh? Sound business strategy."

"Faith," Hunter corrected gently. "And it is tonight."

Her lips curved slightly, but her gaze fell.

"Where are you leaning toward spending the weekend?" he asked, and her eyes jumped back up to his face.

She hesitated a second. "I'm open to hearing options."

"Option one." Hunter stepped closer. "Stay with me. I live in a little apartment on the other side from the guest suites." She didn't respond, but he could see her swallow. "Option two, stay in one of the guest rooms, at no charge of course." A vague memory tickled at the edges of his mind. "Did you say you have a meeting tomorrow? Do you need a car?"

Though only their hands touched, he could feel tension seep out of her. "I have a rental."

"Okay. Why don't we get you a room key, so you can decide later." He'd rather they spent the night together because she wanted to, not because she felt there wasn't an option.

"Are you sure? I could always stay with Sabella, or on the guys' bus."

"I'm sure. I'd rather spend as much time with you as possible, but if you'd prefer the separate room, that's definitely not a problem." The room was available, and if she'd feel better with her own space, even if she didn't end up using it, that was easy enough to arrange. He let go of her hands so he could cup her jaw. "It's your call, and you don't even have to make it right now."

Her eyes danced between keeping his gaze and dropping to his mouth, before she leaned into him, lifting her hands to his hips and bringing their lips together.

Twenty-Two

"This is nice," Gina murmured almost automatically as Hunter flipped on the lights in his apartment. The clean, wooden lines of the rest of the building were enhanced in here with an eclectic collection of décor—cozy quilts and hand-painted tchotchkes, placed on what seemed to be hand-knit doilies. She stepped further into the space, taking in every mismatched piece of stuffed furniture. Everything had clearly been chosen for comfort rather than style, which was at once relaxing and endearing. Two solid wooden doors, one partially ajar, were set in the far wall. It wasn't at all what she would have expected for someone of his means. Nothing about this room said luxury, so much as homey welcome.

"Sorry about the mess," Hunter said, shooting her an apologetic grin as he picked up a single dish and mug that had been left on the round, wooden table set within the corner that was the kitchen. The layout was actually kind of like her apartment's, with the kitchen and living room areas separated only by the placement of furniture. "I meant to clean up, but things got really hectic today."

"Please, don't worry about it." The reasonable set of priorities was actually reassuring. Alistair would have flipped if a dish was left on the table, not to mention at the mix of colors and textures easily spread about the room.

Hunter joined her beside the tan couch, looking her over with a subtly smoldering gaze. "Can I take your coat?"

Gina shrugged silently out of the cream moto jacket. They'd already brought her suitcase and purse to a guest room, after saying goodbye to Sabella and the others. Keys to the room and to her rented car jangled as Hunter stepped away to hang the jacket behind the door. Though awareness still flared between them, it was the bits of new information, the little touches of consideration, that really amplified her comfort around him, transforming the spark from their first time into a more constant, solid warmth. She still didn't want any kind of ties or commitments, but he hadn't made any actual demands, though the possibility of meeting his family had some implications she didn't want to consider right now. *Denial* seemed to be the word of the night.

Hanging out with Sabella and the band had been purely fun, the concert had gone well enough, with the audience enthusiastically demanding two encores, and the prospect of some fantastic sex with Hunter had coursed anticipation through Gina until all she really wanted was to feel the press of his solid, naked warmth against her. He and Sabella were right—all the problems of the outside world could wait for the night.

Hunter padded back toward her, keeping a chaste distance. "Can I get you anything?" His voice was low, not disturbing the still quiet that permeated the winery's main building.

"I'm all set." She could spend ages looking at the clean lines of his face, the warmth of his eyes, the soft curves of his lips. The yellow glow of the overhead lamp washed over him, almost deepening the even tan of his skin. He didn't move closer, but tension pulsed between them.

Gina took a step toward him and brought her hands to his chest, sliding them over his cashmere sweater. Hunter watched her alertly, living up in that moment to his name. Though maybe, she wouldn't mind being caught by him awhile.

His hands settled at her waist, but he kept waiting patiently. The scent of vanilla, or maybe honey, or some interesting mix of both floated to her as she leaned in, lightly tilting her chin up to graze her lips against his.

Hunter's fingers tensed slightly, but he didn't deepen the kiss, letting their lips brush with the faintest pressure. Gina slid her hands up over his shoulders to the back of his neck. His hair tickled her fingers as the gentle kiss and the hint of warmth emanating from him deepened her breathing.

With the barest movement, Hunter broke the kiss, bringing an almost nonexistent barrier between them. "Gina."

She felt him speak as her lungs kept dragging in air filled with the scents she still couldn't quite discern but had come to recognize as his. Her fingers trailed down his neck as her hands came back to the strength of his shoulders. The softness of his sweater caressed her skin, reminding her of the layers still separating them. She slipped her hands down to its hem.

He brushed her lips again, more firmly, then stepped back, stripping the sweater and his tee shirt off in one smooth motion and tossing them to an armchair. That golden light played over the revealed planes of his torso, flowing over the swell of his biceps and deepening the shadows in the shallow valleys distinguishing his muscles.

He stepped toward her as her tongue flicked out, moistening her lips. A hand came up to her neck, skimming over her jaw and into her hair. Her head dipped slightly back, following the movement, and his lips recaptured her parted ones, his tongue thrusting inside in foreshadowing of things to come. She gripped his belt for a point of balance, and he stepped even closer, one leg coming between hers. Her hips bucked into the solid pressure, and she arched against him.

His hand slipped from her hair, grazing against her breast and meeting his other hand at her waist. She skimmed her palms up his torso, and he lifted her so she could wrap her legs low around his hips. He broke their kiss, dipping his mouth to her neck. His tongue flicked out, and a moan escaped her. Her top rubbed between them and against her, the friction further heightening the desire that had been thrumming through her all day.

His mouth continued teasing at her collarbone as he walked through the apartment. The light jostling bumped him against her, and she dug her fingers into the suppleness of his shoulders. He lowered her onto a bed in the darkened room, bracing over her, then leaned back, kneeling on the edge of the mattress and pressing his hips into her.

Gina lifted slightly, stripping off her top, and he groaned at the motion, or the revealed flesh, or possibly both. His hands skated over her torso, up to her breasts, teasing lightly, then down lower, to undo the clasp on her slacks. Gina unwrapped her legs, leaving them draped over his thighs, and sat up.

Even in the moonlight, she could see his jaw clench, his throat work as he swallowed, gaze unmoving from her torso. She smiled, sliding her hands over his heated skin and leaning against him. His eyes skipped to her mouth, and she licked her lips purposefully. His hands clenched at her hips, and she felt his lungs expand.

He pushed back, rising from the bed to kick off his shoes and strip away the remainder of his clothes. Gina's gaze stilled on his length, and her breath puffed out. She leaned down, nudging the straps of her shoes over her heels so she could slip out of them, then stood, relishing the directed attention of his gaze as it flowed over her body. Gently, she moved her fingers down her waist, to her hips, sliding them below the loosened waist of her pants to let them fall, leaving only her string bikini in their place.

Hunter closed the distance between them, seeming taller now without her heels, his length pressing against her belly. His hands skimmed down her back until they reached the scrap of fabric, warmth seeping through as they cupped her ass. Gina rose on her tiptoes, deliberately letting the movement stroke him, and a low growl echoed in his throat.

He leaned his hips away enough to slide one hand between her thighs, brushing a finger over the thin barrier of her panties before slipping it inside. She gasped against his mouth as it closed over hers, and her muscles clenched around the subtle pressure.

He knew her body better now, expertly teasing her with lips and teeth and tongue and fingers as his thickness throbbed against her. She arched into both movements at once, and then his other hand found her breast, lightly squeezing the sensitized nipple before circling it, and she broke the kiss, lungs seeking a wash of air as his fingers flicked her over the edge.

Humming softly, Gina leaned against him, the pressure almost torturous. He stroked her back as her breathing slowed. Her arms loosened from around his waist, skimming over his hips, the delicate brush challenging his control. Her mouth moved against his chest, teasing lightly, and Hunter's hands stilled. Her tongue joined her lips, tracing a burning pattern over his skin.

His breath hissed out as her fingers gripped him, and he dropped his hands, closing his eyes under her ministrations.

Her head lifted from his chest, replaced by one hand as the other stroked slowly. Knowledge sparked in her eyes as she pressed him down, letting go and allowing a hint of clarity to work its way into his mind. She lowered as well, kneeling between his legs, and what little sense he had left at the visual alone let him cup her jaw gently, drawing her gaze up to him. "You don't have to—" he said hoarsely, but her hand closed around him again, and her tongue flicked out, tasting him and stealing any remaining thought. Her hair floated against his inner thighs, adding to the sensations piercing through him.

Her fingers stroked with a gentle pressure as her lips closed over his tip, and Hunter froze. Her tongue swirled around him, and his lungs had to fight to breathe. Merciless, she angled her head, sliding her hand to his base as she took him in her mouth. She pulled back a bit, squeezing with a light pressure and sucking gently, and Hunter's fists clenched in the bedspread. She took him deeply again before drawing almost wholly back, letting the cool air tingle against him as her tongue swirled over him once more.

Her teeth grazed faintly, and Hunter groaned, fighting an obviously losing battle for control. "Gina," he forced out.

Her hand replaced her mouth, and she gazed up at him, though he still felt her exhale on him. Hunter watched her, fumbling through the jumble of words tumbling at the outer edges of his consciousness. She pursed her lips as she waited, blowing a breath over him as her hand continued its slow, sure stroke. He closed his eyes on the visual of her striking eyes watching him as her mouth hovered near him, scattering the fragments of his last thought. Her tongue flicked out in his silence, drawing a prolonged groan.

He could feel her smile against him, and his eyes snapped open in time to see her lips slip over him. His focus narrowed on the sensations of her fingers. Her mouth. The skim of her teeth. The slow, moist stroke of her tongue. She moaned around him, the sound vibrating through her throat and over him. With the barest leftovers of consciousness, he lifted one hand to her head, fingers brushing lightly through her hair.

His hips flexed of their own accord, and she chuckled lightly, and then there were only her lips, the swirl of her tongue, the shallow stroke of her fingers at his base, and a gentle sucking that stole the shreds of his control.

Hunter was spent, wrung dry by the passion between them. Gina was curled against him on the cool sheets, fingers playing idly on his stomach. A beam of moonlight cut across the foot of the bed, slanting over them.

She pressed a light kiss on his skin before lifting onto her elbow. Hunter brought his hand up, brushing back some silken hair that had fallen over her eyebrow.

"I should probably go," she murmured softly.

"You should stay."

She shook her head. "All my things are in that other room."

Hunter groaned. "I could go get them." Other than the getting up and moving part, it was definitely doable.

"That's all right, really."

Hunter exhaled, reaching to switch on a light before sitting up. "Okay, well, let me walk you at least."

"Through the dangerous halls of your winery?"

He chuckled. "The lights are all out for the night. I'm pretty sure I know the building a tiny bit better."

"You're just worried I'm going to re-appropriate some of your wine, aren't you?" She smiled as she slid off the bed, wrapping the sheet around her.

"Honey, you can have any bottle you want."

Her head snapped toward him, the humor disappearing from her expression as if he'd imagined it.

"Sorry, are you opposed to terms of endearment?" It was a quirk he could live with, as long as she didn't mind one slipping out occasionally. She didn't actually look offended, though.

Her shoulders inched up, and she turned away. "I didn't used to be."

He crossed to her side in seconds but had to hold himself back from touching her. "Would it help if I said you can call me whatever you want?"

Her eyes flicked up to him for a heartbeat, cheeks twitching in an attempt at a smile.

He crooked a finger under her chin. "You could even call me Bob, as long as I knew you meant me."

She froze, then exhaled through a small smile.

Something in him uncoiled, and Hunter dropped his hand to her shoulder.

"What about baby cakes?" she asked, trying to joke, though a tightness around her eyes betrayed her apprehension.

Hunter snorted. "Whatever you want."

Her head tilted slightly. "Snuggle bunny?" Her timid smile dropped as she faked seriousness. "Love muffin."

"Sure." He grinned. "But turnabout is fair play."

She chuckled with uncertain relief, and Hunter swept his thumb over her collar, exhaling. He wanted to ask her to stay again, but this conversation only reinforced the need to take things at her pace, and he could wait. He pressed a kiss to her forehead and stepped away, going to the dresser to pull out a pair of sweatpants.

She moved too, going around the room to find her clothes. "Uhm."

Hunter's head twisted toward her.

She hadn't begun dressing, clutching the discarded clothing to her chest along with the bed sheet.

"What is it?"

"I can't find my, uh…"

Hunter didn't bother hiding his smile. "Sorry about that." After recovering from that first time, he'd tossed her panties somewhere. His gaze swept the room, but nothing stood out. It took some doing before they finally found the pink bit of fabric tucked in amid the heap that the bedspread had become.

Hunter's grin widened as Gina rolled her eyes at him, snatching the panties with a suppressed smile.

Twenty-Three

The drive back to Sonoma wasn't horribly long, but it still gave Gina way too much time to think, and not about her meeting. Oh, that had gone well enough, and she should have been thinking about practical things, like whether she would be leaving *PDXX*, if she would consider moving if, for instance, *Bay Fashion* offered her a job, or if she should put some more feelers out back in Portland, or even in Boston or maybe New York, though she didn't relish the idea of returning to Northeast winters. Then again, no matter how discretely she reached out to her contacts, word would spread, and she would have to consider how to handle informing Vivian, and Roger, if leaving actually was the right way to go.

And despite all of that, her thoughts kept jumping back to Hunter. She honestly enjoyed spending time with him and talking to him, and everything else with him. He still had an uncanny soothing effect on her, but they hadn't transitioned into an easy comfort, not really. They'd never touched without it leading to sex, or following up after sex, which was just fine, because she did not want this to turn into any kind of true relationship.

Sometimes, though, it seemed Hunter did. Especially when he did things like invite her to meet his family.

She couldn't even imagine what they would be like. Probably upper crust, wealthy, refined—nothing at all like the loud, boisterous family she had, who'd feel comfortable eating snacks with their fingers in front of a TV or a board game. Hunter's parents would probably balk at the idea of eating a meal from large, shared dishes. Although, there was at least some Italian in his blood, so perhaps not.

But that whole line of thought was moot since she was not going to interfere in their family celebration. Whatever this was, it wasn't a "meet the parents" kind of thing, and she didn't even want to speculate as to how he would introduce her—his "friend"? His "lover"? Obviously not his "girlfriend."

There was a strange persistence about Hunter, though, a patient caring she didn't want to consider too deeply. Some little part of her still wanted the tenuous possibility of a dedicated, reciprocal relationship. Good thing most of her knew better, no matter how insistent that small part was.

Gina sighed, cutting the ignition. It was early in the evening, and she'd actually managed to beat most of the traffic back. She'd declined having breakfast with Hunter, not wanting to run late or look disheveled from whatever non-breakfast activity would likely happen, so they'd made plans for dinner instead. It was still early enough that he'd be working.

She made her way over to her guest room, trying to find something to do. She could check out some of the other local wineries after changing, but going tasting alone would make driving a questionable decision. She could enjoy the sunshine flooding this winery's terraces, maybe take her laptop out and get some work done, if she wanted to be productive.

Her phone chimed. Gina unzipped her dress and glanced at the display. "Hi, Ma," she said, slipping out of the black fabric. She'd chosen this dress for its interesting yet subtle geometric shapes, woven throughout in the cut, stitching, and even a little bit of beading. "Yeah," she added, sitting down on the plush bed to take off her turquoise pumps. "The meeting went well, I think. We talked for almost two hours, and it felt pretty comfortable, but of course it was just an informal meeting. Not an interview or anything like that."

Her mom started asking questions about the future that Gina couldn't answer, but the phone buzzed in her hand.

```
Looking forward to tonight. Hope your
meeting went well. Let me  know  when
you're back. -H
```

Her lips twitched, and she shook her head, trying to refocus on the phone call.

"Even listening to me," her mom finished saying.

"Sorry, *mami*. I was distracted for a sec. Tell me what's going on back home." She rifled through the options in her suitcase, even though she knew them by heart. "How's Donny?"

A casual knock sounded at her door minutes after she'd responded to Hunter's message, so it was a good thing Gina had taken time to finish talking to her mom and get dressed beforehand. When she swung the door open, Hunter smiled, cheeks rounding to create crinkles around his eyes, and the whirlwind of Gina's thoughts stilled.

She froze, one hand still on the door, until he blinked, reminding her to step back and gesture for him to come in.

"How was your meeting?" His voice flowed over her, which was the kind of naively idyllic way Sabella would say it, and yet the description felt right.

"Good, I think. How was your day?" Her eyes dipped to the tanned skin exposed by his unbuttoned collar before she turned away to grab her purse.

"Torture." He waited until she looked back at him before continuing. "All I could think about was you."

Gina ignored the light flutter inside her chest. "That is a horrible line."

His head tilted. "I'll try harder."

"Good." She brushed away the hair that had fallen over her forehead in all the turning.

Hunter stepped closer, humor gradually seeping from his expression, though to his credit he never looked below her face. "Hi," he said quietly.

A smile twisted and tugged at her mouth, before he ducked his head to kiss her. The gentle slip of their lips infused the ease between them with just enough anticipation to snake a flash of heat through her.

That comfort and heat blended into a penetrating warmth that suffused their dinner. The anxious whirl had floated away. They chatted effortlessly over a delicious enough meal she didn't quite remember in the face of his smile, his voice, the brush of his fingers on her hand.

It wasn't all that late, but the winery was hushed when they returned, with only the soft yellow of a single light glowing in the spacious entryway. Hunter walked her through the guest room hallway, resting his palm on the small of her back.

"So, do you feel like a nightcap?" he asked outside her door.

"It is pretty early."

They stood, facing each other in the darkness. "We could grab a bottle, maybe play a board game? Up in my place, or we could find somewhere down here."

"Board game?" Gina didn't move to unlock her door. Respectful as he was being, she didn't want to say good night just yet.

"We keep some around, for the guests. I think I might have checkers upstairs."

"Entertain frequently, do you?"

A wry smile slanted his lips.

"We could go outside," she suggested. "Enjoy the view." It was so impossibly romantic, but it seemed a shame to pass up the opportunity to take in the uninterrupted sight of stars twinkling over the slopes of the vineyard. His vineyard, though there wasn't an oppressive sense of her being on his territory.

His gaze stilled on her, but to his credit he didn't go for the cheesy line this time. "I'll go grab us a blanket."

Hunter woke a few minutes before six as always. Sunlight streamed through the thin curtains, and he stretched, working out the bits of tightness within his muscles—reminders of the night before. From dinner, to sitting silently, gazing at the stars in the gradually chilling air, to a late dessert of sorts, he loved simply being with her.

The sheets tightened around his legs, and Hunter's head twisted instantly. The sight of Gina beside him drove late-night memories up through his consciousness.

She'd shivered deliciously against him as he'd trailed his fingers up and down her spine while sweat cooled on their skin. Her languid hum had vibrated through him.

"I should go," she'd murmured eventually.

"You could stay," Hunter had answered, though he'd known the words wouldn't sway her.

"All my things," she'd pointed out predictably. They'd had almost the same conversation the night before.

"I could go get them," he'd offered again.

"You sure?" she'd sighed against him, stilling his hand on her back.

He'd almost questioned what he'd heard but quickly thought better of it. Getting up right then hadn't been his favorite idea, but sleeping next to her, waking up with her in his bed, was entirely worth it. He spent so much time smiling with her, it was getting to be a little ridiculous.

Hunter slipped out of bed rather than reach for her, letting her sleep. He tugged on a pair of sweats and went out to the kitchen. He should make coffee, and breakfast. Maybe breakfast in bed. It was cheesy, but he was having a hard time being anything else around her.

Having her here, in the apartment his grandparents had shared for so many years, put the point on how right this seemed. Not that there weren't practicalities to consider, but those could be worked out. At this point, he'd probably be spending a fair share of his time up in Portland regardless, and maybe she could come down for the weekends. Or, she could move down here and stay in touch with her Portland friends by going up with him on some of his trips. He did own an apartment in the city they could use, if she decided to work for one of the local magazines, though that would mean a somewhat annoying commute for him. They could also find a place out near Novato or San Rafael. Either way his schedule would be complicated if the land purchase went through, and if it did, he could move up to Portland, if that was where she wanted to stay.

Hunter shook his head and scooped some beans into the coffee maker. He was getting ahead of himself, all things considered, especially given how understandably skittish Gina was after her previous perversion of a relationship. Still, if they moved toward a pattern of seeing each other regularly, he could wait until she felt comfortable with a more defined commitment. Meanwhile, he'd take things as they came. Saying the time they spent together was enjoyable wasn't doing them justice, and he loved knowing that even at that moment she was in his bed. There were definitely worse ways to start the day.

Twenty-Four

Gina stretched before opening her eyes, letting the soft sheets glide over her skin. For a second, she didn't recognize the sparse room. Sunlight picked out colorful flecks in the worn, wooden walls. She swept a hand up the empty side of the bed. Where had Hunter disappeared to? It couldn't be that late.

She lifted onto her elbows, searching for a clock, and a soft thump sounded outside the bedroom, quickly followed by a muffled, "Dammit!" She glanced at the door then caught sight of her suitcase. He'd even grabbed her toiletry and makeup bags, both of which rested on top. Too bad his bathroom wasn't accessible directly from this room. That really was one of the best things about her own apartment.

Still, she should probably make herself moderately presentable before leaving the bedroom. She finger-combed her hair—one of the convenient advantages of it being short—and got out of bed to grab the oversized tee shirt she had brought in lieu of pajamas for the weekend. Quick swipes under her eyes ensured stray makeup didn't make her look like a raccoon.

She opened the door quietly, in case the sounds she had heard were indications of a foul mood.

The scent of coffee drifted toward her, but it wasn't even half as appealing as the sight of Hunter, standing in his kitchen with his hair still slightly mussed from sleep and sunlight playing over his bare torso as he made a face at whatever was in his fridge. "G'morning," she ventured, attracting his attention.

The pensive twist of his lips melted into a smile. "Hey there." He let the fridge door drift shut. "Did I wake you?"

Gina shook her head and sank into the doorjamb, letting it support her sleepy weight, though seeing Hunter, shirtless and smiling, was stirring in every way imaginable. "Whatcha doing?"

Hunter shot the fridge an exasperated glance. "I was going to make some breakfast, but I don't have much. Not that I actually know how to cook."

Even his sheepish grimace was tinged with that endearing smile. Gina focused on the problem at hand. "You live on your own and don't know how to cook?"

"I can manage the very, very basics. And some pretty amazing tomato sauce."

A chuckle escaped her throat, and Gina took a few steps toward the kitchen. "So, there's nothing in the fridge?"

"I've got some eggs, so we could do omelets or something, but there isn't anything to go in them. Hard-boiled eggs and some toast?" Tension narrowed his eyes, and Gina bit back a smile. "I'm sorry, I wasn't really—" He faltered as she walked toward him. "Thinking ahead." His gaze stilled on her face before dropping down to the hem of her tee shirt. The question that was undoubtedly flashing through his mind showed in the hyper focused lines of his face.

Gina stopped in front of him, close enough to feel the heat of his torso. She curled her fingers rather than graze them through the morning stubble that colored his jaw. Her chin tilted up as she breathed in the hint of his scent that just barely overpowered the coffee now that they were close.

"Hi," he said, angling his head down.

"Hi," she repeated into the kiss that met her parted lips.

Only the gurgling of the brewing coffee sounded around them. Hunter's hands settled over her ribcage, drawing her tee shirt up just enough to make it indecent, especially with nothing on underneath. She shifted into the caress of the cool air, gripping Hunter's muscled shoulders.

The coffeemaker buzzed, and Gina drew back with a hum, lowering from her tiptoes. She took a steadying breath, but neither of them moved away. "So," Gina said, redirecting them back to the topic at hand. "You have eggs, and bread."

"And butter, for the toast," Hunter added adorably. His thumbs brushed up to the base of her breasts, distracting her momentarily.

"Do you have any sugar?"

"For the coffee, yeah." He was still intensely focused on her mouth.

"All right, well." Gina finally backed away, putting at least a false sense of distance between them. "If I could get some coffee, I could make breakfast, if you'd like."

"You don't have to do that," Hunter said without hesitation.

Gina crooked an eyebrow.

"I promise to give you coffee regardless."

"Don't trust me?"

"I'm not exactly giving you much to work with, and you're a guest." He stepped toward her, leaving them even closer than before. The soft fabric of his sweats grazed the tops of her thighs. "We could go out. Or order something in?"

"Or…" Gina rose on her tiptoes again, deliberately pressing against him. "I could make breakfast. And then we wouldn't have to get dressed."

Hunter's groan followed her as she turned away.

"You're a genius," Hunter said, popping another piece of French toast into his mouth.

He hadn't had any jam or anything, so it hadn't occurred to him as an option for breakfast. But French toast dipped in sugar was surprisingly and simply delicious.

Gina chuckled, leaning back in her chair. If she hadn't been there, he'd have probably skipped breakfast altogether. Then again, he'd considered doing that precisely because she was there, until she'd put some shorts on.

"I'm serious. Thank you."

She sobered, eyes narrowing before she forced a smile. "It's just French toast."

"It's life-changing," Hunter said, swiping another piece through the pile of sugar on his plate. "You've basically doubled my breakfast options."

"You could just go shopping, you know. Buy some groceries."

"Can't argue with that. It never seems like much of a priority. I do have a frozen pizza in the fridge, for emergencies," he admitted, making her laugh. His mind stalled for a moment at the sight. The sound of the main doors being opened echoed up to his apartment, reminding him of the real world, and his very real obligations. He downed what was left of his coffee to gather his thoughts.

Gina still cradled her mug, watching him.

"So, listen," Hunter said. "I'm not sure if you had plans for today, but I do have to spend at least a couple hours down at the bar. We have some groups scheduled to come in, and…"

"Oh, of course." She set her coffee on the table. "I'll get out of your way."

He stilled her upward motion with a hand on her knee. "The last thing you are is in my way. I'd rather spend the day with you, but we get a lot of people in on the weekends."

"I don't need to be entertained," she said quietly.

"Well, you're entirely welcome to stay, enjoy the sunlight, save me from the giggling bachelorettes."

"I'm sure you can handle them."

Hunter kept his hand on her thigh, bracing himself internally before reminding, "And my family will be showing up at some undetermined time in the afternoon."

Her muscles bunched under his hand. "Right. Well, I was thinking of going to Kane's show, out in Davis, so you can celebrate with your family."

"I'd say you're welcome to join us, but that's not quite it." How should he word this? "I'd strongly prefer you stayed." *Shit,* that could sound pressuring. He leaned back to give her space. "I mean, it's obviously up to you, but it's not that I wouldn't mind you being there, or that I'm being polite. I think it'd be great if you met everyone. And I'm absolutely certain it'll be more fun with you here, and I'd rather spend more time with you than less."

"I don't know," she murmured. "I wouldn't want to intrude on what is obviously a private celebration, and I'm sure I'm not exactly up to your parents' standards."

"What are you talking about?" If anything, his parents would be overly enthused to see her with him. How long had his mom lamented his bachelor status?

She shook her head lightly, lips parted, then sighed. "I come from a very different world than you, which will be very obvious to your family. I mean, for crying out loud." She unfolded her legs from the chair and sat up straighter. "Just look at how I was sitting."

Hunter would have objected, but it was true his mom would have noticed her posture, even if that wasn't what mattered. As much as it irked him that they'd come back to the money issue, she wasn't entirely wrong.

Her hand came up to brush through her hair, disheveling it more than anything else. "My family is the loud, family-style dinner type of Italian, all right? We're not—"

"Stop," he interrupted quietly, needing to cut off the rising panic. "I will admit my parents are a little more formal than, say, my grandparents were, but that doesn't mean they're as bad as you seem to be picturing." She did look really worried. Hunter reached for a hand that was busy tangling her fingers in a complicated pattern. It stilled in his. At least she wasn't protesting on relationship-defining grounds. "Listen to me: they are nice, and you're amazing. This'll just be a quiet dinner, nothing to worry about."

"Oh really? Who's making dinner?" she asked with a bit more of her usual sass.

"It's…" Hunter paused as her point sunk in. "Being catered," he finished lamely. "But that's only so we could stay here instead of going out somewhere."

Her skepticism was obvious even with only a hum as her response.

"Okay, fair enough. But I promise, they'll surprise you. Plus, there'll be plenty of wine. And,"—he wove their fingers together, stroking her palm with his thumb—"the second you want to, we can say you have an early flight or something, and sneak away."

"Oh, so they're wonderful, but you're already planning ways to get away?"

Hunter smiled wryly. "Let's just say, much as I love my family, I have my priorities in order. And I'm actually pretty confident I'll have to drag you away rather than anything else."

She still seemed skeptical, but at least the jittery tension had disappeared almost as quickly as it had come on.

"Obviously, it is up to you," Hunter said. "I do know how much you love Kane's music, so if you'd like to see him perform twice in three days rather than spend another night with me, far be it from me to stand in your way."

She nearly choked on a quiet burst of laughter. "Shut up. You probably should have started there."

Hunter stood, leaning on the table to bend toward her. "Yeah, probably," he agreed, meeting her upturned lips for a kiss.

He really was adorable. There was an undeniable charisma to Hunter's manner of dealing with his customers, a flirty friendliness that effortlessly maintained an invisible barrier of professionalism. Everyone seemed sociable and happy, and though the wine probably played a part, there was also something about the atmosphere he cultivated here.

Gina still wasn't entirely sure about staying to meet his parents, but she'd agreed to think about it. The glances he snuck her way and stolen moments interspersed among serving customers were helping his cause. The memory of the soft hint of bristles that covered his jaw scraping over her when they'd showered wasn't hurting either. Even sitting on a stool out of the way at the bar, the lingering sensation sent shivers through her.

Technically, Hunter was working, but for Gina, it was turning into a remarkably relaxing day. She was even reading a book—a rare luxury nowadays. The difference between their first meeting in this bar and now was staggering.

"Can I top that off for you?" he asked with a softer smile than the ones he'd exchanged with the various visitors who had been wandering in and out of the tasting room, which had now emptied.

"I'm all set, thank you. Two glasses before lunch might be my limit."

"You're at a winery." He slid a platter of cheese cubes and crackers closer to her. "We have different rules here."

Gina smiled, leaning slightly over the bar while they were alone. "And what are these rules? Is there a list somewhere?"

"Come closer, and I'll tell you." He bent down to her, shifting her still partially filled glass out of the way before kissing her through their smiles.

"How utterly unprofessional," a man's voice said from the doorway.

Gina pulled back instantly, but Hunter brought a hand up, resting it on one of hers. "Feel free to complain to the management," he said, unconcerned.

"I would," the man retorted, moving closer to the bar. He wore obviously expensive gray slacks and a navy button-down shirt with the collar thrown open in deference to the sunny day outside. "But he's incredibly thick-skulled."

The man's lips curved, drawing a mirroring smile from Hunter's. Gina relaxed slightly in the face of their bewildering calm.

Hunter squeezed her hand gently. "Gina, this is my brother, Tucker, who has some nerve calling me thick when it took him five years to propose to the best thing that's ever happened to him. Tuck, this is Gina."

Tucker dipped his chin in a considering nod. His eyes found her and Hunter's joined hands, but he didn't comment.

"Congratulations," Gina ventured.

That seemed to snap him out of his contemplation, and he grinned, lips pulling into a lopsided curve. "Thank you, thank you." He drummed his hands on the bar. "So, are you at least going to pour us some champagne?"

"Not until I get some proof," Hunter said, obviously teasing.

"Proof of what?" a sleek blonde woman asked, coming to stand beside Tucker. Her wrinkle-free sundress screamed wealth even without the noticeable ring shining on her finger. The almost unbelievably pure, light blue of her eyes matched her dress flawlessly. Then again, the dress may have very well been designed with that effect in mind.

Hunter moved away when the blonde approached. "Proof that you lost your mind and agreed to marry him."

The blonde smiled sweetly, patting Tucker's arm. "I still have high hopes for this one."

"He's lucky to have you."

The woman tilted her head and slightly lifted her shoulders in that falsely self-conscious way that every high-society woman must learn as a young child.

Tucker threw his arm around those shoulders. "Oh sure, *her* you're happy for."

"Well, I actually like her," Hunter threw back without hesitation, though the bite of the words was entirely belied by the brothers' matching grins. Hunter's gaze caught Gina's, and he took a couple steps in her direction, drawing the attention of the couple to her as well. "I'm sorry, my manners escaped me. Gina, this is Leonora. Leonora—Gina."

The fiancés exchanged a curious glance. "Please, call me Nora," the blonde said politely.

"Pleasure to meet you," Gina murmured.

"So. Champagne," Tucker reminded in the resulting stretch of silence.

"What happened to Mom and Dad?" Hunter asked, leaning down to grab a bottle from the fridge below the bar.

Tucker answered, but Gina didn't hear, because Leonora asked, "So how do you know Hunter?"

"My best friend had her wedding here."

"Oh, that must have been beautiful!" Leonora settled fluidly on a stool beside Gina. "I would love to have our wedding here."

"Something tells me the owner would be happy to arrange that."

"Well, I would certainly hope so." She smiled then shook her head. "But, no, Tucker and I live in New York, and my family is there, as well as the majority of our friends. So it makes more sense to find somewhere out there and have the handful of people we know in California fly out, than the other way around." She seemed genuinely disappointed. And she had yet to react outwardly to Gina's casual violet halter and jean shorts, which was either a good sign or evidence of Leonora's impeccable mastery over her expressions.

"There are some gorgeous venues in and near New York, though," Gina pointed out.

"True." Leonora's lips formed that perfect smile. "It's not exactly a sacrifice."

"Marrying Tucker?" Hunter asked, bringing over champagne-filled glasses for them. "Of course it is."

"How's that exactly?" Tucker asked.

"There *is* a ritual involved," Gina added without thinking. She would have apologized immediately, but Leonora burst out laughing, and even Tucker faked a wince, groaning with his smile.

"I like her!" Leonora said sweetly.

"Yeah, me too." Hunter caught Gina's gaze for a moment, before lifting his glass. "To the happy couple."

The three of them copied his motion.

"It's about damn time," he added before they clinked their agreement.

"Don't say 'damn,' dear," a woman who could only be Hunter's mother chided as everyone sipped the bubbly liquid.

Gina set her glass down as the new couple approached. Mrs. Cavaliere had a pale-brown, perfectly coiffed asymmetrical bob and wore a pastel-green dress that was precisely on-trend with its peplum hem. She'd accented it with white pumps and a pearl choker for an ensemble that could have passed at a society garden party. On the plus side, the barely graying Mr. Cavaliere wore jeans, though with a crisp button-down shirt. Then again, the jeans alone probably cost more than Gina's entire outfit.

On their own, the brothers could have passed for vaguely similar friends, with Tucker's lighter hair and lankier build, but with their parents in the mix, the blend of features suddenly made perfect, unmistakable sense. They were a gorgeous, impeccable, upper-crust family. How the hell had she ever confused Hunter for a bar boy?

Breathe, Gina. They're just people. Polished people. Hunter might find her rough edges tolerable, or charming, but his mother's keen eyes wouldn't miss a single faux pas. She could practically see Alistair standing there with them, with his patronizing, derisive, pinched expression, gloating over her inappropriate overreaching. He'd been right; she lacked the finesse for this level of company. She was the mistress rich boys kept secret while they searched for their high-society wife.

"And this,"—Hunter's hand landing on hers snapped Gina back into the scene around her—"is Gina Sabatino. Gina, these are my parents, Bernardo and Florence."

Both of his parents considered her with politely detached expressions. Years of professionalism responded on her behalf. "It's wonderful to meet you both."

Hunter could see Gina panicking behind her poker face, but all he could do was lightly squeeze her hand again. He understood her nervousness, but her cool façade didn't lend itself to particular warmth from his family, who were clearly unsure how to respond.

His father drew focus before too much awkwardness could be felt. "Well, since you've obviously forgotten how to do your job, I guess it's up to me to pour your mother and me some champagne," he said, comfortably rounding the bar. He'd never wanted to make the winery his life, but he'd still spent his fair share of time working there.

"By all means, I defer to your expertise. Besides, I could use a break. It's been nonstop today." Hunter took the opportunity to come stand beside Gina, laying his hand on her back. He kept his fingers moving gently through the silky fabric of her top, out of sight of his family, to help dissipate her nerves.

"You should grab us a couple of bottles for lunch, if you have anything drinkable around," Tuck piled on meanwhile.

"For lunch?"

"We were going to have a picnic," Nora explained. "Enjoy the beautiful day."

"You're more than welcome to join us," his mom told Gina.

"Oh, I wouldn't want to intrude," she answered instantly.

"No, please do. We brought plenty with us, since Hunter never has any food," Nora said with a smile. "And if you helped your friend plan her wedding, maybe you'll have some tips for me? The proposal caught me entirely by surprise."

"And she abhors being unprepared," Tuck teased.

"I somehow already feel like I'm behind on planning." She smiled at her own silliness.

"We haven't even discussed a date yet," Tuck said.

"Exactly!" Nora explained, endearing worry crinkling the space between her brows.

Tuck brought his arm around her shoulders, and Nora looked up at him ruefully, drawing fond smiles from their parents. Hunter would have smiled too if it wasn't for the tension still vibrating through Gina. She'd seemed anxious about meeting them earlier, but nothing like this. In fact, she hadn't been this panicked around him since that moment with the chocolate sauce.

Damn it.

His family was nothing like her presumptive, elitist ex, but if the jackass was still popping up in her mind, it wouldn't be logical, and she wouldn't be able to relax enough to see that.

"So, what," Hunter said, drawing everyone's attention to

himself, "you'll all abandon me to have lunch, as I starve, neglected?"

"In here? With your overwhelming crowd of patrons?" his dad commented.

Hunter glanced at the clock. "I have another group scheduled to come in in about twenty minutes."

"We can easily make you up a plate if you haven't eaten," his mother said. "What am I saying, of course you haven't."

"You will join us, won't you?" Nora asked Gina. Finally noticing the hesitation, she added, "I promise to tell you some wonderful Hunter stories."

"Not unless I can steal her away to counteract the propaganda first," Hunter warned. "You want to help me grab a couple bottles?"

She slid off the stool before he'd even finished the question. "Of course."

"All right. We'll be right back," he said, leading her toward the back room. "Try not to break anything."

His father's keen eyes followed them.

Gina strode into the cellar without a word. Hunter nudged the door shut before following her down the steps. The mimicry of the day they'd met was hard to ignore, but it was almost as difficult to reconcile that confident, assertive woman with the anxious one now here with him. Some part of him hoped it was a sign of her coming to trust him more, that the façade had dropped, but it could as easily be the difference between how she felt with a working-class bartender and with the owner. Could this all really keep coming back to money, despite everything they'd shared? He couldn't, and wouldn't want to, change who he was.

"Talk to me," he said quietly, staying a few feet away to give her space.

She spun around, sending her hair flying. He could see the muscles clenching in her jaw. "This was a bad idea."

"Why?"

"I just—I don't want to embarrass you, with your parents. I'm sure they would expect you to be with someone more like—" She pressed her lips together, cutting off the phrase. "More refined."

Hunter moved toward her, intending to take her into his arms, but she nearly jumped back, wincing, before her chin notched up defiantly. In that moment, Hunter was entirely ready to use Alistair Talbot as a punching bag. Instead, he stepped back and lowered himself to the ground, back against the wall, in the least threatening pose he could think of. "First off, you could absolutely never embarrass me, and I'm certain my parents would like you exactly as you are. But Gina, if this is making you this uncomfortable, we don't have to stay. We could go have lunch in town, or steal some of their food and watch a movie upstairs…"

"You just said you're expecting a group for a tasting."

"Yeah, well. Three out of the four people out there know their way around the winery well enough to take care of it."

He'd just have to tell them what to pour, but really, it didn't matter as much as she did.

She wrapped her arms at her waist, but then swept a hand through her hair to break the defensive gesture.

"You want to come sit with me?" he asked.

Gina shrugged slightly, then turned to look around her at the shelves.

"I think about you pretty much every time I come in here, you know," he confessed, trying to remind her of more pleasant memories.

Her attention snapped back to him, and the corners of her lips twitched upward. "Not our best."

"But pretty great nonetheless." He paused. "And we could always try again."

She actually seemed to relax then, really seeing him. She considered a moment then stepped toward him. When she sank down next to him, Hunter reached for one hand, gently bringing her palm to his lips before letting their hands drop.

"It's something he said, isn't it," Hunter said quietly, fairly certain of the answer.

Gina's head bent, breaking eye contact. "It's a lot of things he said," she breathed.

"He was wrong," Hunter told her as calmly as he could.

She shook her head, but at least she didn't take her hand from his.

"He's a pretentious, self-aggrandizing moron," he added.

She finally looked back to him, her lips downturned and her eyes resigned. "I'm ruining your weekend."

"You're the best part of my weekend," Hunter said honestly.

Disbelieving humor gradually grew in her expression. "Where do you get these lines?"

Hunter smiled, relieved to see the panic gone, even if solemnity replaced it. "Sincerity can sometimes come across as cheese, but that doesn't make it any less true."

She exhaled visibly, shoulders dropping as she watched him. Hunter shifted, bringing their faces closer. Gina's lips parted, mingling their breath. Her fingers squeezed a moment before she tilted her chin so their lips met.

The kiss was almost entirely chaste, filled with a softer warmth than the intensity that usually consumed them.

"So what do you think?" Hunter asked when they pulled away. "Do you want to give them another shot, or should we sneak out the window?"

Twenty-Five

As Hunter went to grab the wine they had supposedly been selecting, though they'd been gone long enough it wasn't likely his family believed that, Gina swiped her fingers under her eyes to catch any mascara that may have smudged, then patted her cheeks and fluffed her hair. It was the best she could do without a mirror.

She shouldn't have let the jackass twist her up like that, yet again, but there was something about the impeccably dressed women and effortlessly wealthy men in such intimate circumstances where she was indisputably an outsider. Hunter had seemed to understand—more easily than she would have preferred, actually, which was par for the course with him.

Still, she was better than that. Stronger than that. Definitely able to handle a lunch that should quite naturally focus on the bride-to-be.

Only Hunter's father and Leonora were still in the tasting room when they finally emerged.

"Your group of ladies loved the suggestions of a few photos out on the main terrace, with the view," Mr. Cavaliere said, reorganizing the bottles on the bar. "Tucker's playing photographer."

"Not a bad idea, thanks," Hunter said, setting down the bottles he'd chosen.

Gina rounded the bar, which still held everyone's partially drained champagne glasses. Leonora had been looking around the souvenir area, but she turned toward them. If either she or Mr. Cavaliere had any opinions on Hunter and Gina's absence, it didn't show.

"The painting back here is beautiful," Leonora said. "Is it one of Caitria's artists?"

"Up on the wall, in the corner?" Hunter asked. "Yeah, it is. Actually, Gina knows the artist."

Gina followed his gaze to the painting they'd discussed at Trisha's opening. She'd forgotten that he'd purchased it. *A warrior who's made it through, and found her haven.*

Leonora threw it another glance over her shoulder then stepped toward the bar. "It's lovely. Is it for sale?"

"Not even for you, sorry," Hunter said. "That one's a personal favorite."

"Shame. Is the artist local?"

They both looked to Gina, but at least this was a topic she could easily handle. "She currently lives in New York. Beatrice is incredibly talented, in my entirely biased opinion."

"You should talk to Caitria," Hunter said. "She may have held some pieces back. Or I have another one by the same artist, hanging in the entryway."

"I'll have to remember to do that," Leonora said politely.

"When is she coming?" Mr. Cavaliere asked.

"Wasn't expecting you so early, so I told her around five."

"Oh good. I think Greg and the Wilsons will be here around then as well, so that's perfect," Leonora said. Her delicate hand landed on Hunter's. "Thank you again for letting us all invade."

"My pleasure," Hunter said, shaking his head a little. "It's great to see you."

His mother strode in then, carrying a small glass container and something wrapped in a napkin. "Tucker's leading the girls back, so you should place these out of sight," she said, setting it all on the bar.

Hunter smiled, taking the food and obediently lowering it to the counter behind the bar. "Thanks, Mom."

Giggling and Tucker's confident voice announced the arrival of the scheduled group. Hunter brought down and emptied the champagne glasses as his dad efficiently set out fresh ones. One of the girls asked Tucker to stick around, palming his upper arm and arching to give him a better look at her chest.

To his credit, Tucker simply stepped out of reach, flashing them all a neutral smile as he said, "Sorry, ladies, but my lovely fiancée awaits. I assure you, I leave you in expert hands."

A few pouts appeared, but the distribution of the tasting menu distracted them all, and soon the group was busy pointing and giggling. Hunter and his dad traded places.

Tucker took the bottles Hunter had brought out, and their father stacked some fresh glasses for their lunch.

"So," Leonora said, turning to Gina. "Are you from New York as well?"

All of the Cavalieres except Hunter seemed to be waiting for her response, rather than heading out for their picnic. It had been easier two minutes ago, when they'd all seemed to forget she existed.

"No, actually," she managed to say eventually. "I live in Portland, but I grew up in Boston."

Leonora smiled. "Don't tell anyone in New York, but I love Boston."

"It's a lovely city," Mrs. Cavaliere said. "Are your parents still there?"

As if on cue, the Cavalieres and Leonora moved toward the door. Gina shot Hunter a glance, catching a parting smile, then fell into step with his family as was clearly expected. A picnic lunch with the Cavalieres. This was so not what she'd had in mind this weekend.

"And here I thought I'd have time to join you," Hunter said as Gina walked back into the bar with Nora. The others had split off to change or otherwise prepare for that evening's dinner. All in all, lunch hadn't actually been that bad.

"I return her to you, safe and sound, and somewhat wiser about your shenanigans," Nora teased.

"Whatever she told you, I didn't do it." Hunter flashed them both a smile. He and Nora obviously had an easy relationship, not that that was particularly surprising. Nora did indeed come from an impeccable pedigree, but she was open and friendly, and Gina couldn't help respecting her choice to work in a legal aid office rather than a high-powered, lucrative position, even if money wasn't a concern.

"She can't possibly have made it all up," Gina said. The family actually hadn't shared much about Hunter other than subtly talking him up. Their obvious affection was quite sweet.

"I wouldn't put it past her," Hunter returned fondly.

"Why would I, when the reality is so much richer than anything I could imagine?" Hunter groaned, but Nora ignored him. "On that note," she said, "I should sneak out and change before the others arrive. We'll talk more tonight, all right?"

"It is your party," Gina reminded.

Nora glanced down at the ring sparkling on her left hand and smiled to herself. Her shoulders and eyebrows lifted simultaneously in a purely happy gesture.

"It's not too late to run away," Hunter said, also smiling.

"I've waited much too long for this to walk away now," Nora told him, before heading out toward the guest rooms.

"So," Hunter said, focusing entirely on Gina.

"So?" she echoed on autopilot. An edge of seriousness had lessened the humor that had accompanied his and Nora's easy banter. "Did you get a chance to eat?" Gina asked in the face of his well-intentioned scrutiny.

"Yeah, had that sandwich." He continued repositioning things behind the bar, putting stoppers and glasses away. "My dad even brought by some basic provisions on their way back in, so I can promise some better options tomorrow morning. That is, if you…" He trailed off, and his hands stilled.

Gina swallowed through the illogical lump that filled her throat at the implication, even though it didn't mean anything. She still had the key to the guest room, so there was no reason she had to spend the night. She could leave his place at any time, and her rental car meant she could leave the winery whenever she wanted to as well.

The silence was stretching on too long, and she didn't want to dwell on all those reasons why she should really be heading to meet up with Sabella and the guys instead of spending an intimate evening with this man and his family. She'd never been known for making smart choices, but at least this time she had a clear escape route.

"Can I help you bring those up?" she asked, nodding to the grocery bags next to him. Besides, her things were still in his apartment, and it wasn't like she would leave those behind.

Hunter couldn't keep his eyes off Gina while gathering the emptied bottles. Even in the understated black dress, she was stunning. As she danced with Greg, Tucker's best friend from back in high school, the glow of the fading sunset flirted with the fabric, and tiny beads sparkled.

She hadn't said too much about lunch, but she had seemed more comfortable around everyone during dinner. Of course, most of the focus had stayed on the happy couple, who were also dancing, as were the Wilsons. His mom and Caitria were chatting off to the side, which left Hunter's dad, walking toward him with their empty glasses.

"So this girl of yours," he said without preamble.

Hunter refilled the glasses without comment. Some part of him was curious what they all thought of her, though of course his parents wouldn't leave without telling him.

"There's no need to rush in like this, Hunter," his dad said.

"What makes you think I'm rushing in?"

"How long have you known her now, a couple of months? You've been living in different cities for all that time, and don't you even try to pretend you're not head over heels, here. Your mom and I, we both see it all over you."

"Oh, come on. You'd been with Mom less than six months when you proposed, and you both agree with me that Tuck's insane for waiting so long. And it's not like I'm about to get down on one knee."

"Your mom and I were friends for a long time before that, and yes, Tuck was dragging his heels, lord knows why. But courtship, dating, it doesn't have to be like it was for your grandparents. It normally isn't." He paused, the lines around his eyes and mouth deepening. "You've always based your idea of romance off them."

Hunter had always trusted his gut more than Tuck and their dad did, even when it came to people. Like his grandpa. The song changed, and Hunter watched Greg walk Gina over to his mom then switch partners to Caitria. Maybe something had happened at lunch that he'd missed. "Do you not like her?"

"She seems like a great girl, but you two are still barely getting to know each other." His dad sighed, seeing his words weren't having the desired effect. "There's no rush, Hunter. No need to catch up to Tucker or to prove anything."

Hunter shook his head, holding back the words he wanted to say. This had nothing to do with Tucker getting engaged. There was no point in postponing spending the rest of his life with Gina, but his all too practical father wouldn't understand. The only thing really keeping Hunter back was Gina being unprepared for a commitment, though the result was exactly what his dad wanted to hear. "Don't worry, Dad. She had a meeting in the city yesterday, and a friend of hers had already been booked to play here Thursday, so this weekend just worked out. I am planning on taking things slow."

The disbelief on his dad's face was impossible to miss.

"I promise," Hunter added for good measure. *If only for her sake.*

His father considered for a drawn-out moment, then nodded and picked up the two wine glasses, turning away. Hunter grabbed the opened bottle and followed him to the table, skirting the impromptu dance floor. Gina twisted to look up at him from her seat, a soft smile stretching through her lips. Hunter's own lips instantly mirrored the movement, and he held out his hand. A ballad was flowing from the speakers, and he led her a few steps away from the table so they'd have some room.

They swayed in an easy pattern with the other couples. "Thank you," Hunter said quietly.

Gina's gaze flew to meet his. Her eyes widened questioningly.

"For staying, meeting everyone."

"It was quite the hardship," she murmured with a smile.

At least she felt better about it in retrospect. "Oh, I know. All that food, and wine. And the questionable company." He felt her chuckle against his palm as her smile grew.

"Guess you'll just have to make it up to me."

Hunter lost count for a fraction of a second from the look in her eyes. "I have some ideas on how to do that, but if we leave now"—he paused to dip her as the song ended—"everyone will know what they are."

She laughed but took a step back.

Hunter turned slightly to see Tuck and Nora moving toward them.

"You two sure look like you're having fun," Nora said.

"My lovely fiancée is too nice to say so, but she would love to steal Hunter for a song or two."

"He's the better dancer," Nora told Gina conspiratorially.

Tuck shrugged. "Have to let him be better at something."

Hunter let that slide in honor of the occasion. "Better steal you away before Tuck gets too jealous." He looked to Gina. "If you don't mind, that is."

"By all means. It is her night."

Nora flashed Tuck one of the giggly smiles that'd been lighting up her face all day. Hunter offered her his arm as Tuck turned to Gina, saying, "I promise not to step on your feet."

"Then how could I possibly refuse?" Gina teased, then followed him to an empty spot.

When they were out of earshot, Nora said, "She is pretty wonderful, you know."

"I noticed," Hunter assured, lightly squeezing her hand before spinning her briefly away.

Twenty-Six

It's unbelievably nice of you to offer to drive Nora and Tuck to the airport tomorrow," Hunter said, taking his jacket off as they walked into his apartment.

Gina leaned against the back of the couch, shrugging delicately. "We're all going to the same place. This way your parents can spend a little more time up here, with you."

"Should I be worried about you being alone in the car with them, though?" Hunter moved closer and braced his arms on either side of her. "You won't actually believe all those terrible things they say about me, right?"

Her lips twitched. "Every word."

"Maybe I should drive them myself." Not that he actually believed they'd badmouth him.

"Maybe," she said, tilting her chin up, "you should give me something else to think about, besides their stories."

An offer no sane man would refuse. Hunter leaned closer, softly brushing her mouth until she arched gently away from the couch. His hands came to her waist, and he slipped his tongue between her lips, languidly tasting her.

Her fingers skimmed over his chest, finding the buttons of his shirt. Her gaze never left his face as she slowly undid them then slid her hands beneath the fabric. Hunter unfastened his cuffs behind her back then stripped the shirt off, tossing it somewhere. He cupped her jaw, keeping his hold gentle. The lighthearted glint faded from her expression, replaced by a penetrating sincerity. He swallowed roughly, focusing on the sensations rather than the words she wasn't ready to hear.

Understanding and maybe even reciprocation widened her eyes and parted her lips. Hunter dipped his head down, joining their mouths. They took their time, softly tasting and exploring each other. He undid the zipper at her back and peeled her dress off, relishing the shiver that ran over her body as his lips found the curve of her neck.

She stumbled a little, trying to step out of the dress. Hunter smiled against her skin, trailing kisses down her torso as he knelt to help. Out of her heels and dress, she resettled on the back of the couch, covered only in a touch of lace and the moonlight streaming in behind him.

His breath caught, but she hooked her fingers in the belt loops of his pants, tugging him closer and arching until their bodies met.

"You're so beautiful," he exhaled.

Gina froze for a heartbeat, but then a small smile curved her lips, and she stretched up toward him in a silent request Hunter was only too happy to oblige.

✧ ✧ ✧

"So how's the boyfriend?" Roger asked the next day as he pulled away from the airport curb.

"*Hunter* is just fine, thank you," Gina said, brushing off the amiably presumptive question. He was better than fine, actually, but now she'd returned to reality. The almost idyllic weekend had nothing to do with her day-to-day life.

"Thanks for picking us up, Rodge," Sabella said from the back seat, redirecting him.

"Well if I can't go on the weekend away, at least I get to play chauffeur."

"Don't pout," Gina said. "You'll get wrinkles."

Sabella smacked her shoulder lightly. "I thought you and Michel had plans this weekend?"

"We did. But he's working today."

"How are things with you guys?" Gina asked.

"You two are the ones who left, and what, I don't even get to hear about it now?"

Gina couldn't help rolling her eyes along with her smile. "You first, Sab." They themselves had had plenty of time to talk in the airport and on the flight over.

"Considering how much you hate Kane's music, I'm not sure you have a right to complain," Sabella teased Roger. "But the tour is going well, a little bigger and more hectic than last year's, of course. Spending time with them all is less stressful than it was at first, thankfully. Everyone seems almost happy to have me around, though they might be faking for Kane's sake."

"Oh, shush," Roger cut her off. "Everyone loves you, Elles."

"Well, regardless, it's been lovely, though I can't say I'm not thrilled to be off the road for a bit, have a little space."

"So they're happy to have you, but the feeling's not mutual," Gina said, glancing at Sabella over her shoulder.

"Yes. Exactly. I obviously hate them all," Sabella shot back.

"You should tell Kane that."

"Stop causing trouble," Roger chided uncharacteristically.

"What's up with you?" Gina asked.

"You first."

Something was definitely going on, but apparently he didn't want to talk about it yet. Gina shrugged. "Great sex. Good food. Lovely wine, as you remember."

Roger stopped at a light and looked over at her, pursing his lips.

"Spending time with Hunter was wonderful," she elaborated obediently. "It just all feels a little unreal, especially when we're at the winery. An escape from our actual lives that can only survive in its own little bubble."

"Aren't all relationships at first?"

Gina exchanged looks with Sabella, both surprised at Roger's insight.

"I think you're right, in a way," Sabella said finally. "Good relationships just eventually transition into a coexistence with reality. And there's no reason that couldn't happen for you and Hunter, if that's what you want, Gi."

"I think I'm okay with it staying a sexy getaway." *Probably. Maybe.* "Anyway, your turn. What is going on with you?" Gina poked Roger's shoulder for emphasis.

"Well." He pulled into a parking spot by Sabella's apartment then shifted in the seat to face both of them. "We're talking about moving in together."

"Michel and you? That's wonderful!"

"And fast," Gina added.

"I know, it is. But we've known each other longer than Sabella and Kane before she ran off on tour."

"With your encouragement," Sabella reminded Gina pointedly.

"Going on tour wasn't quite as permanent, or it wasn't supposed to be." Only Sabella could have turned a sexy summer fling with a musician into happily ever after. "But if you're sure this is what you want to do, then Sab's right, of course. It's wonderful."

"That's just it, I don't really know. It doesn't feel like it's too soon, when I'm with him. Maybe fast is how it happens, sometimes, when it's right?" He turned to Sabella, eyes wide. "Like it happened for you and Kane?"

"I think it depends on the people, whether both are ready, even if it's right between them," Sabella said. "Every relationship has its own pace."

"You know what we should do?" Gina said as an idea struck her. Both of her friends' eyebrows shot up. "We should drop our things off, go surprise Michel at work, get some manicures, and then all have dinner."

Sabella smiled tolerantly, but Roger was unappeased.

"Look," Gina said seriously, "don't overthink it. If you want to fall asleep with him, and wake up next to him, and don't mind his little homey quirks whatever those are, then living together sounds like a good next step. You're allowed to have a good, solid relationship, and it seems like Michel's been good for you."

Sabella's eyes narrowed, but Roger smiled, blushing slightly, so Gina didn't ask what was going through her mind right then.

"All right," Roger finally said then patted the seat divider excitedly. "Get your stuff out of my car so we can go have dinner with my boyfriend."

Twenty-Seven

Gina was just settling down on the couch with her latest stack of competitors' magazines when someone knocked on her door. All in all, it had been a good day, with some good movement for their next issue, an early evening with plenty of time to make a decent dinner, and even a call with Hunter set for later. Company wasn't in her plans. The sharp tapping repeated before she'd set aside her work.

"Coming!" Gina called and made her way to the door. Reflexively, she peered out the peephole, then sighed and pulled the door open for her landlord, blocking the opening with her body so he wouldn't see the illicit colors of her walls. Painting the apartment had been one of Sabella's inspired ideas last summer. "Hey, Louie," Gina said before noticing the man beside him.

"Gina," Louie acknowledged. "I'm just making the rounds, introducing everyone to your new landlord, Alistair Talbot. He'll be taking over the lease in a few days now."

Gina's fingers spasmed around the handle as a tightness filled her chest. *New landlord?*

"We simply wanted to come by, ensure everything is in order before finalizing the paperwork," Alistair said with a thin smile that couldn't hide the triumph in his eyes.

"We won't take up too much of your time," Louie added.

"Sorry, boys." Gina kept her eyes on Louie. "As you know, you need to provide twenty-four-hour notice before entering my apartment, and I, well—" She threw what hopefully came off as a coy glance into her apartment, still blocked from their view by the door and her body. "I have plans tonight."

Alistair demonstrably tugged on the already perfectly placed cuff of his jacket. "Ms. Sabatino, as your future landlord, I do believe it is in our best interest to start off on the right foot."

"And I believe the best option for a successful business relationship is when both parties adhere to the agreed-upon terms, to each other's mutual benefit."

Louie looked confused, but Alistair was almost certainly paying him an inordinate amount of money for the property. He'd never before shown any inclination to sell.

"Well, then," Alistair said, clenching his jaw.

Gina fought herself not to step back.

"Not a problem, Gina," Louie said, surprisingly. "We wouldn't want to disturb your plans." He looked up at Alistair, really pulling focus to the difference in their heights. "We can easily come by tomorrow, before signing the last few papers, right?"

"Consider this your twenty-four-hour notice," Alistair said stiffly.

"Good night, Louie," Gina said as pleasantly as possible before shutting and locking the door, slipping the chain in place for good measure. She stayed near the door, listening to their footsteps recede down the outdoor staircase. Once that paperwork was signed, the only thing that would keep Alistair from entering her apartment at will was twenty-four hours and a thinly veiled excuse—and that was only if he stuck to the lease.

Her phone buzzed in its place back on the couch, but Gina ignored it, sinking down to the floor. What the hell was she supposed to do now?

"Hey there. This is Hunter. Guess I missed you, but I'll be around whenever you have a chance to call me back. Hope you're having a great day."

He certainly wasn't. He'd been looking forward to a conversation with Gina, though maybe it'd be better if he kept his horrible mood to himself. He'd ignored things pretty well over the weekend, but whoever Gunnar Hackett was, he was doing a superb job killing Hunter's sales. Things weren't dire yet, but if he couldn't count on his regulars, buying property up in Portland would need to be postponed at best. It didn't help that the owner had conveniently received another offer, bumping up the price considerably.

Hunter could convince Tucker or their dad to invest in the satellite vineyard, but that wasn't a backward slide he wanted to take. Besides, if people continued to back out of stocking his wines, he'd need to focus all his attention on rehabilitating his numbers and revitalizing his distribution strategy.

If only he could go back a couple days and focus entirely on enjoying Gina.

"I don't know what to do," Gina said. She'd finally made it off the floor and to the phone to call the one person in Portland she could count on unconditionally.

"Pack," Sabella instructed on the other end of the line. "I'll bring over all my suitcases, and we could call Roger to help, maybe pick up some boxes. We can get everything personal out of there tonight, and you can stay with me until we figure things out."

"What about my lease?"

"We'll worry about that later. I know you love that apartment, Gi, but…"

"I know." There was no way she could stay here now, with him legally entitled to a key to her place.

"It'll be okay," Sabella said quietly, unfailingly supportive.

You don't know that, Gina thought, but what she said was, "It kind of feels like running away." The whole reason they'd painted last year was so Gina wouldn't lose the apartment she had once loved to everything that had happened with Alistair.

"Leaving a bad situation," Sabella corrected. "I'll be over soon, okay?"

Gina sighed, looking around the apartment that had almost managed to be reinvented by the facelift. Even with the new chain Kane had installed for her, she had rarely been able to get a solid night's sleep here. Maybe moving out was something she really should have done back then. Now she didn't seem to have a choice, no matter how much she loved the spacious walk-in closet connecting the bedroom and the bathroom.

Half an hour later, another knock came at her door, but this time the peephole revealed a friendly, if worried, face. Sabella had a key, but Gina always used the chain now. She opened the door to find three big suitcases flanking her friend.

"Why did I not know you had so many suitcases?" Gina asked, trying to keep the mood as light as possible. It was going to be a long night either way.

"Kane had to get his things over here somehow," Sabella said, bringing them in. "There are some duffels and carry-ons inside, too."

Gina nodded, the scope of their undertaking finally hitting her. She'd already nearly filled an entire suitcase, and she'd barely made a dent. It was unbelievable how much stuff could be accumulated over a few years.

"Hey, we can do this," Sabella said, rubbing her arm. "Actually, where's Roger? I thought he would have beat me here."

Gina shrugged. "He's probably out with Michel." Packing up the apartment was a lot of work, but she also didn't particularly want too many people involved in this impromptu move.

"I talked to him, and he said he'd be here. But meanwhile," Sabella added with forced mischievousness belied by the worry in her eyes, "should we get some brownies in the oven?"

Gina tried to smile at the obvious ploy. "Sure. Good call." Chocolate was always welcome.

By the time the doorbell rang, they had devoured half a pan of brownies and packed away most of the knickknacks and personal items spread around her combination living and dining room. Sabella popped up to answer the door as Gina layered in her DVDs.

"We come bearing boring gifts," Roger announced as he came in, followed by Michel, who lingered near the door. They set down a few more suitcases. Roger brought his hands to his hips and tilted his head, saying, "Don't tell me: you decided the paint job was too last season."

"Exactly," Gina said, walking toward the others. "And since Kane's not around to move furniture this time…" She turned to Michel. "Sorry for interrupting your evening."

"No, no, please. You are friends."

Roger threw an arm around Michel's shoulders. "That's his way of saying he'd rather spend time with you than me."

"Can you blame him?" Sabella chimed in.

Roger's jaw dropped in an overdramatic gasp, but the rest of them just laughed.

"Come on, guys," Sabella said more seriously. "Plenty to do, so we should probably get started."

"Where can we help?" Michel asked, looking around.

Gina followed his gaze to her kitchen, though most of the dishware wasn't personal enough to be a priority, and then to the glass armoire that showcased all of her more special pieces. There was also the closet in the hall, and many of its contents could be used to cushion fragile things. "How about you guys work on the pieces in the display case and armoire, and the hall closet, and I'll take care of my clothes and bedroom? You don't have to do it all, of course, anything will help."

"Why don't we start that way and see how it goes," Sabella agreed.

"You should put on some music," Roger instructed, heading to the plate of brownies still on her dining table.

By two in the morning, they'd made a pretty solid dent in the packing, and in her snacks. They'd also filled up six big suitcases and a duffle bag, and loaded most of those into her and Sabella's cars. It was almost impressive.

"You guys should go get some sleep," Gina told Michel and Roger as they took a break with some sangria.

"I thought you wanted to get everything out tonight," Roger said.

"I do, but I wouldn't want to take inordinate advantage of your help."

"Since when?" he quipped, earning reproving looks from

both Sabella and Michel. "I was kidding! Of course we're going to stay and help."

"If I may," Michel started to say, eyebrows drawn together.

Gina nodded. After all of his help, he could say pretty much whatever he wanted, not that she was expecting anything inappropriate.

"What is with the hurry?"

She could practically feel Sabella's protective gaze on her. "My ex is now my new landlord, who can legally enter my apartment almost whenever he wants," Gina said as emotionlessly as possible.

Roger sobered, his eyes narrowing. "What are you going to do about the furniture?"

"I don't know yet. I'm more worried about personal, mobile things." Furniture presented an entirely different problem, but presumably he wouldn't be doing any damage to it. Hopefully. At least not while Louie was with him.

"You could put cameras, if you're unquiet," Michel said, picking up on their tension. "We use them at night in the salon. They work on movement."

"That could be useful," Sabella said quietly.

Alistair might not find cameras a deterrent, especially if they were hidden, but at least his presence would be documented, for whatever that was worth. Gina nodded. "How do they work?"

Twenty-Eight

Hunter turned his phone over and over in his hands as he stared at last month's sales reports. Gina hadn't called him back last night, but any manner of things could have happened.

On the other hand, any manner of things could have happened.

He groaned, firmly putting the phone on his desk so he could focus. It had taken some convincing, but he'd learned the name of the person who'd placed the competing offer on the land up in Portland. Gunnar Hackett. Hunter didn't know why, but whoever this guy was, he was unquestionably targeting Hunter and Cavaliere Vineyards.

He picked up his phone again, dialing almost automatically.

"Do you miss us already?" Nora asked after a couple rings.

Hunter's lips found a tight smile. "How could I not?"

"What's wrong?"

He hadn't meant to be so transparent, but he also wasn't

quite in the mood for chitchat. "I'm sorry to bother you, but I was hoping to get your professional take on something."

"All right." He heard her move somewhere quieter. "How concerned should I be?"

"Not at all," he assured before explaining what had been happening and everything he'd been able to find out since Caitria had given him a name. It was a long shot, but perhaps there was some form of legal recourse.

Nora asked a few questions before finally saying, "It sounds like tortious interference to me."

"That sounds promising." He picked up a pen so he could scribble some notes if necessary.

"It's not my specialty, but I do think it'd be worth talking to a tort lawyer. Sometimes, a stern letter is sufficient for people to back off, but it may even be something you should take to court, collect damages. Would you like me to find you some local recommendations?"

"Don't go to any trouble. I'll talk to Dad, see if he already knows someone. Thanks, Nora."

They chatted for a couple more minutes, mostly about the incredible progress she'd already made in planning the wedding, before hanging up.

Hunter ran his hand over his face, exhaling. Since taking over the winery, he'd managed to avoid any legal battles, but perhaps they were an unavoidable part of business. At least now he had something actionable to pursue.

He glanced at his phone again, willing it to ring. Much as he wanted to avoid pressuring her, wondering why Gina hadn't called back was driving him crazy, endless terrible possibilities popping into his mind. Rather than calling again, he settled on a simple text.

```
Hi Gina. Just checking in to make
sure everything's all right.
```

Roger skirted his desk as Gina left the editors' meeting with as much composure as possible. She'd brought up the topic of domestic violence for a feature as they'd discussed, but Vivian had stonewalled every aspect of the idea, even though Heather and some of the others had seemed to find it interesting. Gina had basically been told to stick with fashion and fashion only.

"Sabella called," Roger said. He pressed the door to her office shut. "Everything's all set."

Michel and Sabella had volunteered to set up a few of the motion-sensitive cameras, so Gina could pretend to focus on work and attend that disaster of a meeting. It was understandable that Vivian wanted to do everything not to lose her job, but that was exactly why Alistair relied on his bank account as his leverage.

"Gina?" Roger said, snapping her out of the thought.

She shook her head slightly to clear it. "Thanks. And thank you, again, for helping out last night."

Roger fluttered his hand, dismissing the statement. "Bad meeting?"

"Uh, yeah. It wasn't the best." She raked her fingers through her hair then dug them into her shoulders to ease the knotted muscles. "You know what, I'm exhausted. I think I'm going to go grab some coffee." She also needed to talk to Benny about what Sabella had told her over the weekend. She had to find a way to mitigate the damage done to the people in her life as a result of her idiocy.

"Do you want me to go get it for you?" Roger asked.

"How bad do I look if you're volunteering to get my coffee?" Roger's mouth opened to answer, but Gina cut him off. "It's fine, hon. I could use the walk. Do you want one?" She scooped up her purse as Roger nodded.

"You are coming back today, right?" He smiled as he said it, but it faltered almost immediately.

"That's the plan," she assured then ushered him out of her office.

The activity at the magazine seemed lackluster as she headed toward the elevator, but maybe she was projecting. She barely registered the hand that stopped the elevator door from closing, until Alistair slipped in beside her. *Fantastic.* She should have sent Roger.

He stayed facing her, blocking the door without pressing the button for his floor. A spike of adrenaline made the coffee she wanted almost unnecessary, sending her heart hammering.

His jet eyes skimmed over her body, making her crave about a thousand cover-ups or better yet a nice, thick wall between them.

"You know there are cameras in here," she said quietly when the door shut behind him.

A chilling twist touched his lips. He'd stopped pretending around her long ago. "They don't pick up sound."

No, but maybe Benny was downstairs watching, not that there was much he could do, especially with his job at risk. "What do you want?"

"You think you're clever, don't you?"

Anything but. A smart woman would have taken up self-defense classes.

He stepped toward her, and Gina fought the instinct to back away. He wouldn't hurt her somewhere so potentially visible.

"You've humiliated me enough, don't you think?"

Not hardly.

"Whoring yourself out."

The implied mention of Hunter stole her breath for a fraction of a second. Alistair had seen them together once, but nothing about that would have seemed intimate. Had he been having her followed?

"I have dealt with him. And as you are not entirely dimwitted, I expect you have pieced together my current influence on other aspects of your life." He stepped even closer, crowding her in the otherwise empty elevator. Now Gina couldn't help a defensive step back. The perverse pleasure her reaction brought him suffused his eyes. "You did have such potential. You will learn to behave, and then you will be mine again," he half-whispered. "I am, after all, a forgiving man. But forgiveness must be earned. Your penance will be especially satisfying."

The elevator bell chimed, and he stepped slightly to the side, ever the professional at work. But that movement would give Gina a clear shot to the door once it opened, which was all she needed. "Don't hold your breath," she said as unaffectedly as possible, stepping out into the populated lobby.

She slipped her phone out to read the message from Hunter she'd ignored earlier.

> Just checking in to make sure every-
> thing's all right.

That seemed concerned, not panicked, but Alistair didn't bluff. What the hell had he done?

She hadn't pieced it together it before, but had he already known about her and Hunter before requesting their failed meeting? Had he been interfering all along?

"Miss Sabatino," a familiar voice greeted as she moved away from the elevator. "I'm glad I caught you. There's a package waiting for you."

"Thank you."

Alistair strode past both of them, heading across the lobby to the door.

"Are you all right?" Benny asked when he was out of ear-shot.

You will be mine again. Gina shuddered, shaking her head. But she'd caused Benny more than enough trouble already. "Listen, I heard about what happened, with your boss. I'm so sorry you've been drawn into this."

"Don't worry about it." A moment later he added, "You think the complaint has to do with Talbot."

"Yes. But, I'm going to fix it, okay?" She had to.

"You don't need to take care of me, Gina. I'm still here, aren't I? This'll get sorted."

She couldn't match his optimism, but then, she knew the truth. If Alistair wanted Benny fired, he could do much more than merely filing a complaint.

Benny's palm landed on her shoulder in a rare show of familiarity while they were at work. "Worst-case, I'll find another job. And either way, some guy causing problems because he can't deal with rejection isn't your fault."

Gina held his gaze for a few seconds, but all she saw was genuine concern and sympathy. Benny dropped his hand, returning to the propriety necessitated by their surroundings. Gina forced her inner turmoil from her expression, so he wouldn't worry excessively. "I'm heading out for a fix. Can I get you a coffee?"

✧ ✧ ✧

By the time Gina strode back through the magazine's doors, she'd made up her mind. Impetuous or not, she didn't see a better way. "I need you," she murmured to Roger as she passed him, carrying their coffees.

He didn't pause in his conversation with Krystiana to acknowledge the comment, but he stepped into her office moments after she had settled in her chair.

"Shut the door, please," she said, holding out his caramel-chocolate macchiato.

Roger's eyebrows shot up, but he did it anyway before taking the drink. "What's up?" he asked, plopping down into his preferred chair.

Gina took a deep breath, giving herself one more moment of doubt—or maybe sanity—before speaking. "I know that this may seem drastic or out of the blue, and I am aware that this will affect you, possibly severely, though hopefully in a positive way—"

"You're rambling," he cut off, leaning forward and ignoring the sugary, caffeinated concoction. "What is happening?"

Gina swallowed, watching him. The second she said it, it was real. Worse, he might try to talk her out of it. "I'm resigning," she finally told him. "Before the end of the day."

Roger's mouth popped open, but for once no sound followed.

"I'm trying to decide whether I should recommend you as my replacement, but I'm honestly unsure whether that would help or hurt you at this point." So much had changed, so quickly, poisoned by Alistair's insidious influence.

"Vivian never liked me, you know that."

Gina nodded. Roger had been barely more than an errand boy when she'd started here. Despite his solid eye and indisputable aptitude, Vivian had been unable to look past his flamboyant ways and outspokenness. Gina had promoted him almost as soon as she'd become editor. To be fair, though he was great at his job, he didn't always make it easy. Then again, he had matured significantly in his approach to the business, and his dramatics wouldn't be too much of a problem if he took over for her, leading his own team.

"I want you to know that how you come out of this does matter to me," Gina said. "But this decision is for the best overall, and hopefully for you as well. Too many people are being drawn into a mess they don't deserve, and my leaving the magazine is the best way I see to help that."

"What are you going to do?"

She looked around the office that had grown with her. With virtually everything computerized, she had kept the space sleek, uncluttered. Prints and some work-appropriate family mementos livened the wall beside her desk, and potted lilacs and orchids rested on the windowsill behind her, benefiting from the occasional sunlight even Portland saw. A rack of styles for an upcoming shoot sat to her right today, in front of tack boards, one with their best past spreads and the other tracking bits and pieces for upcoming issues. She hadn't thought through leaving, through packing up and not coming to *her* office again, through it becoming someone else's domain. Even Roger would and should put his own touches to it, if Vivian could see the value of his taking over.

"I don't know," she finally answered.

They sat in silence, intermittently watching each other and looking at the room, or nothing. Finally, Roger tilted the macchiato to his lips, snapping them out of the wordless contemplation. "The magazine isn't going to survive without you, you know," he said humorlessly.

Gina tried to smile at the loyalty. "I think it'll be okay. It does predate me, and fashion has a solid team now. With me gone, it may even maintain its autonomy." Was it self-centered to bet that Alistair's interest would wane with her departure?

"Vivian isn't going to go for it, is she." It wasn't a question.

"I'll fix it. If not here, then I'll find somewhere local that needs some pizzazz." Her reassuring nod turned into a head-shake. "This is to save your job, okay, not leave you in the lurch." His job, and Benny's. And her sanity. "Besides, we both know you'd do just about anything for a crack at my job," she teased in a semi-desperate attempt to lighten the mood.

Roger went for it, though, shaking off the somber tone of their conversation almost instantly, widening his eyes and tilting his head coyly. "I would be pretty great at it."

Gina smiled softly, thinking of the fidgety, somewhat insecure, and obviously overcompensating guy he'd been when they'd first met, and how different he was now. "I have no doubts."

"Do you want to go get manicures?" Gina asked the next morning, clearing off her and Sabella's breakfast dishes.

"I have a deadline, and Kane's supposed to call," she said apologetically. "Can we go this afternoon?"

"Sure, of course." Gina leaned against the counter, tapping it with her fingers. Sabella was used to working from home, spending most or even all of the day in pajamas, or other comfy clothing. Gina was a fan of lazing around by choice, but it was weird not having somewhere she was supposed to be. "I think I might go take a walk, or a drive, or something." Sure, Sabella didn't mind having her there, but the privacy for her call with Kane wouldn't be unappreciated.

"Still don't want to talk about last night?" Sabella asked quietly, her eyes narrowing.

And then there was that. "Not really." She was still recovering from the impulsivity of her decision. Sabella would either be supportive of the choice or she'd fall into pragmatic mode, pointing out that the decision itself might not be wrong, but being so rash about it hadn't been wise. Gina wasn't sure which one she wanted to hear, or which was true. She didn't want to think about it.

"Okay, well…" Sabella trailed off when Gina's phone buzzed on the island in front of her. Her eyes dropped to the screen, reading the name that Gina couldn't see. Sabella's lips twisted, but they didn't hold back from one another, so it didn't take long for her to ask, "You still haven't talked to him?"

Gina sighed. *Hunter.* "Nope." He hadn't been excessive with his calls and texts, but he kept trying to reach her. It would have been sweet, considerate, if she had any idea what to say to him.

"You should at least let him know you're okay."

Gina shrugged, watching the phone light up. The idyllic bubble she'd left behind in Sonoma had nothing to do with the real world she now had to face. Besides, the less contact Hunter had with her, the better for him.

Twenty-Nine

"Hi, Hunter."

He almost didn't believe it when the ringing clicked off to something other than Gina's answering message, but his relief was short-lived. The voice was vaguely familiar, but it wasn't Gina's. "Hi, uh…"

"It's Sabella Hartridge. Gina's fine," she rushed to add, thankfully, before Hunter's mind could revisit all the worst-case scenarios he'd tried not to consider. "But she can't talk right now."

"Is she hurt? Or sick, or something?"

"No. She just—" The tiny pause nearly drove him insane. He thought they'd left things well, but clearly something had happened. "Has a lot on her plate right now."

Hunter tried to make sense of the words themselves, of the undecipherable emotion behind them, but his mind was on overdrive, pulled in dozens of directions with no ability to get anywhere. He shook his head, exhaling, as he searched the twisting vines around him for clarity. "Did something happen with her ex?" he asked finally, unsure how trustworthy a negative answer would be. If Gina didn't want him to know, Sabella may very well lie.

"Yes," came the answer that couldn't be false yet he wished weren't true.

"What happened? Did he hurt her? Is she—"

"No," she cut off.

Hunter tried to catch his breath and unclench his jaw.

"I'm sorry, I have to go."

"Wait, please, just—" *Just what?* "Please, call me if there's anything I can do."

"Okay," he heard before the call ended.

Hunter stared at the phone in his hand without seeing it. Sabella had said the scumbag hadn't physically hurt Gina, but otherwise, Hunter didn't know what could have happened between them. Either way, he didn't want her to be dealing with it alone. Not that she was, in fact, alone.

Hunter slipped his phone in his pocket and looked at the rows of vines growing around and under him. He'd loved this land for longer than he could remember, but the warm, constant affection that had suffused the winery, even after his grandparents' passing, almost seemed to have run out without him noticing, as he'd clung to the memories. Having Gina here last weekend had driven home everything this place, his life, had been missing. It seemed cold and incomplete without her.

Without love.

Whatever she was dealing with, she had her friends, but

Hunter needed her to know she could count on him, too. That he would always be there for her, no questions asked.

The best way to show her that may be to do so, literally. Hunter had a meeting scheduled with a tort lawyer tomorrow, but after that, he was heading back to Portland.

"Did we have an appointment?" Michel asked, pausing mid-snip as Gina walked into the salon, announced by an electric chime.

"Nope." She'd gotten into her car intending to drive around awhile, until this idea had popped into her mind. "Are you all booked today?"

"You have luck." He resumed working on the redhead in the chair. "I have a break once I'm done here. But I will *not* shave your head." He threw a stern glance over his shoulder to drive the statement home.

"If I wanted to shave my head, I wouldn't need you," Gina threw back, though the guess was a little too insightful. Maybe messing with her hair right now wasn't the smartest call. Then again, smart calls were obviously not her forte, so why pretend otherwise. "I'll be back in like, twenty?"

She ignored the concern on Michel's face as he nodded. Roger would have definitely told him she'd left her job, and he knew first-hand about the unplanned exodus from her apartment. He may think she was going nuts, but she really hadn't had a decent alternative in either case, had she?

By the time Gina walked down to the coffee shop a couple blocks away and returned with a box of chouquettes and macarons, Michel's previous client had left.

"So what are you thinking?" he asked, plucking a raspberry macaron from the cardboard and settling into one of the styling chairs.

"Highlights." Gina plopped into the chair beside his, swiveling around a bit. "Electric blue, or a nice, bright green. Or both."

Michel straightened in his chair, ignoring the remaining pastry in his hand. "You have lost your mind. I am not doing that to you."

"I want something more exciting." She wanted to start over, to forget the last year had ever happened. A crazy, vibrant new color was precisely the kind of thing she would have spontaneously done a few years ago, when she'd known exactly who she was.

"You want electric blue? Have it on your nails. Or try an airbrush tattoo."

Gina could feel her lips purse, but some lingering sane part of her knew he was right. She popped a puffed chouquette in her mouth. Restlessness thrummed through her despite the sugar.

"What is happening with you?" Michel asked finally.

How could she explain? Resigning had gone fairly well. She had taken Vivian by surprise, though the older woman had barely protested, likely relieved to have the tension resolved.

The immediate resignation meant Roger had to be trusted to take over, at least temporarily. With any luck, by the time they were ready to hire a new fashion editor, he would have more than proven his suitability for the role. Although, Alistair may stand in the way out of spite.

But now, with no job and no apartment, Gina was untethered in what was hopefully the aftermath to the nightmare. "I'm just trying to reclaim my life."

Michel's dark eyes watched her with an unnerving understanding. Roger had hinted at something in his past, but Michel had always hidden the weight of those experiences, especially at work. The moment passed quickly, and he rose from the chair to come stand behind her. He ran a hand through her hair, exposing the uneven locks to his expert gaze. "We could do burgundy lowlights. Add a dark raspberry or purple in for some extra color."

"Too safe," Gina said, looking at herself in the mirror. She missed the spontaneous, radical part of her that had made split-second decisions without caring about appearances or consequences. Though Michel was right about the neon colors, and there was no point in butchering her hair.

"All right. Well, what if we make the raspberry lowlights, with some pink tips. Worst-case, we can trim them off in some weeks."

She might not be in Portland a few weeks from now, but otherwise the plan made perfect sense. A bright, summery statement, but one that was easy to get rid of as soon as she got sick of it. "Genius." She smiled at him in the mirror. "I knew I could count on you."

Gina blew gently across the purple swirls decorating her bright-blue fingernails as they waited for the timer on Sabella's nail dryer to run out.

"So what next?" Sabella asked. "Late lunch and a movie?"

She'd been entirely chipper ever since she'd come to the salon, but the supportive perkiness was rubbing Gina the wrong way. Sabella meant well, allowing her to enjoy the day together rather than focus on everything that had been going on, but the denial felt disingenuous. It even made her wonder if her best friend thought the dye job was ridiculous, though Michel had done an amazing job. But Gina wasn't exactly a reliable judge at the moment.

"Okay, out with it," she said, watching Sabella closely.

Her eyebrows lowered, instantly going from questioning to concerned. "With what?"

"We both know you have an opinion on everything that's been going on, everything I've been doing."

"No, I..." She broke eye contact, staring at the beeping dryer. "I don't know how I can help, other than being here. I do wish you'd talk to me, though."

"I am talking to you," she protested, but the words rang false immediately. "Everything's just, jumbled up, in my mind."

She shook her head. "I'd have to untangle everything to say anything."

Sabella glanced around them, at the cheery busyness of the salon. "Why don't we get out of here, go somewhere a little more private."

They didn't say much more until they slid into a corner booth at Tasty and Sons, one of their favorite lunch spots. Neither of them glanced at the menus.

"Do you think I made a mistake?" Gina found herself whispering.

Sabella placed her hand over one of Gina's, the pale-yellow polish she'd chosen an undeniable contrast to Gina's nails. "I think you've been unhappy, and that he put you in a miserable, impossible position at work. Leaving a bad situation is never the wrong choice."

Gina held Sabella's gaze for a moment, ignoring the prickling in her eyes. "Well, I was talking about my hair," she teased to lighten the mood.

"Of course you were." Sabella's lips tightened into a smile. "And I already told you I like your hair. I would never be able to pull off something that eye-catching, but it looks amazing on you."

"Thanks," she exhaled.

"What else is spinning around up there?"

"I think I have to get out of here," Gina confessed, barely believing she'd said the words. Would leaving Portland mean letting him win? Losing everything she'd built here?

"The restaurant?" Sabella asked, obviously confused.

Gina shook her head, swallowing. "I think I may go home, for a while. I don't know what my place here is anymore, or that I have one, really."

The line between Sabella's brows grew deeper with every word.

"I just feel like I came here, and I faked my way through, pretending I could do it, be independent. And I failed, epically."

"No you didn't. And you know I'm happy for you to stay with me, for as long as you need, right? This isn't—"

"No," Gina interrupted. "I know, thanks. Roger actually offered his place, too, since he won't be using it for the foreseeable future. But you have Kane now, and, you know, Roger has Michel." She sighed, tapping her fingers on the tabletop. She didn't doubt their friendships, but life did move on, as theirs were. "Plus, I miss my family." Her absolutely insane, meddlesome, overprotective, unquestioningly sup-portive family.

"Well, East or West Coast, or anywhere in between, you know you won't be able to shake me," Sabella said, prompting a smile.

"I wouldn't dream of it. And I haven't entirely made up my mind yet, either way."

Sabella nodded, smiling back briefly before licking her lips. "What are you going to do about Hunter?"

Run—far, far away so Alistair leaves him alone? Gina shook her head, then brushed away the pink-tipped strand that fell to her cheek. "Good question."

Thirty

Hunter tried to focus on the documents the lawyer had emailed him, but his mind kept drifting to Gina, as it always did lately. She'd actually responded to his text letting her know he was coming up today, and they'd agreed to meet for lunch. It had to be a good sign that she felt comfortable meeting him at the hotel. Unfortunately, now all he could do was wait until she showed up.

He brought a hand to his eyes, rubbing his thumb and middle finger in circles over his temples, before opening a new email from the tort lawyer. Nora had been right, the interference was legally actionable, and the lawyer had recommended pursuing that rather than merely sending a cease and desist letter, as the meddling had already significantly impacted Hunter's business. Since he hadn't been able to find a link between himself and Gunnar Hackett, the lawyer had recommended a direct approach, in case a third party was behind Hackett's actions.

Apparently, the notice the lawyer had sent had already been effective, and Hackett was entirely willing—eager even—

to give up the person who had hired him to destroy Hunter's winery, to avoid the financial responsibility of losing a lawsuit and owing Hunter damages. Turned out money had bought the man's services, not his loyalty.

The lawyer was asking how Hunter wanted to proceed, and whether he could think of any connections to the third party. Hunter scrolled lower then blinked, shaking his head. He read the name again, and his jaw clenched. *Unbelievable.* Though, really, it wasn't. At least he had absolutely no qualms about pursuing legal action, fighting back with all the means at his disposal.

A knock beat its way into his thoughts, and Hunter shut the laptop before going to answer. Gina stood on the other side, driving any other thought away.

"Hi," she said, unmoving.

"Hi," he breathed, taking her in. She was gorgeous as always, but tension tightened her lips and narrowed her eyes, which were underscored by faintly purple crescents, as if she hadn't been sleeping. He mentally shook himself then moved back from the door. "Please, come in. It's great to see you," he added as she stepped into the room, lingering by the door. Her lips made a faint attempt at an upturn.

"I like your hair," he said in her silence. The bright pink tips belied her serious expression, but otherwise the bit of color was fun.

Her mouth popped open, but then she shook her head and pressed it closed. "I'm sorry if you came all the way up here just…" She trailed off, and he could see her swallow.

"What's going on, Gina?"

"I think, uhm." She nodded jerkily. "I think I'm going to move back to Boston. I just wanted to come say goodbye."

Hunter ignored the tight squeeze in his chest. "What happened? What did he do?"

Gina strode further into the room, and Hunter pressed the door closed. When she turned back to face him, her arms were wrapped around her waist, her shoulders hunched. Just when he thought she wouldn't answer, she said, "He bought the magazine."

Hunter's eyes narrowed, trying to follow. It was obvious that the scumbag was trying to control her career, but that didn't quite translate to her leaving everything and moving, to *Boston*. Hunter waited quietly for her to continue, in case there was more.

"And then he bought my apartment building." She spoke slowly, almost dispassionately, but her fingers clenched into her arms, and a wet sheen appeared in her eyes. "He's also been messing with other people in my life. If you've been having problems at the winery—"

"He's behind it," Hunter finished for her. "I just learned that myself."

"I'm so sorry," she breathed, pressing her lips together strongly enough to drain them of color.

Hunter started to move toward her, drawing up short when she took a couple steps back. "It's not your fault."

She broke eye contact, looking down to the carpet. "He would never have come after you if it weren't for me. I think that's why he wanted to meet with you, too. He'd had me followed, I guess, and that's why he brought you up here."

That meeting wasn't what had brought Hunter to Portland, but that wasn't the point. Despicable as it was, it actually made sense, especially given the man's fixation on Gina even during a "business" meeting. But in a way, Talbot's twisted interference was the reason Hunter had ever had the chance to see Gina again.

"Don't worry about him targeting me," he said. "I'm taking care of it, with legal means, but that's not the point. His actions, all of the horrible things he's done, they're not your fault."

That drew her gaze back up to him, but she didn't speak. Her lips parted as her breathing grew more ragged, and tears continued to gather in her eyes, her head shaking in tiny jerks.

"Gina." Hunter could see her choking back the emotions. He couldn't stand feeling so helpless with her. "Please, let me hold you."

She rolled her lips between her teeth, her shoulders lifting, but then she nodded, and Hunter crossed to her without a second thought, wrapping her in his arms. She stood stiffly, trembling lightly against him as she struggled to control her breathing. Hunter trailed one hand up and down her back, whispering a muddled mix of, "It's all right," and, "You're okay," and, "I'm here."

He shut his eyes, focusing on the ragged puffs of her breath and wishing he could undo all of the torment she'd been through, that there was a way for him to erase that part of her life and make it better. Eventually Gina's arms unclenched, letting go of the self-imposed vise, and she wrapped them loosely around his waist, sinking into Hunter's hold. Deeper sobs ran through her until she stopped fighting the tears. Hunter brought one hand to her head, stroking through the silky strands of her hair as warm tears wet his collar and fingers dug desperately into his back.

When the frantic grip eased and her breathing slowed, Hunter turned to press his lips to her temple.

They stayed together until the rhythms of their breathing matched, then Gina lifted away from him, slipping her hands to his sides. Hunter left his arm loosely draped at her waist and dropped the hand tangled in her hair to her face. He skimmed his thumb over her cheek, brushing away a lingering droplet.

Pink tinged her eyes and deepened the shade of her full lips, but the thrumming anxiety of earlier had dissipated. Words she wasn't ready to hear pressed heavily on his chest, but Hunter swallowed them down. "How about we stay in for lunch," he said instead. "Order room service, maybe watch a movie… You could take a hot bath, relax."

He was pushing it, assuming lunch was still the plan, that she'd want to stay. Russet eyes considered him with obvious hesitation. Hunter kept his stance relaxed, sweeping his thumb over her cheekbone. Finally, lingering tension left her frame, almost imperceptibly dropping her shoulders, and she nodded.

Gina passed a hand through a mound of bubbles, dropping her head back onto the slight cushion of a folded, fluffy towel as the luxuriously hot water soothed every one of her muscles. It was easy, right in this moment, thinking about nothing and letting the world outside the luxury of The Benson slip away. All that mattered was the heated water, the fizzling crackle of the bubbles, the refreshing cucumber scent swirling in the air around her as time passed unmarked.

Maybe this was what nervous breakdowns felt like—an utter loss of control, spiraling into a floating nothingness. It was nice.

But it wasn't real.

Real was the video footage she'd had playing in the background on her laptop as she reread her lease, searching for a way to break it as she watched Alistair moving about the apartment he'd stolen from her. Real was torpedoing her career—quitting, without severance and without hope of a decent recommendation for a position elsewhere. Real was knowing that leaving her job and moving out wasn't enough.

And skimming the outer edges of real were Hunter's arms around her.

He'd said something about taking legal action, fighting the destruction Alistair's money had bought. She couldn't take a stand against that force, though if his strategy of buying her life kept up, he may eventually run out. Hunter, though, he had the resources to push back, an out that wasn't retreating.

And even with everything he'd been put through because of her, even knowing it wasn't coincidence at all that had brought them together, he wasn't backing away.

Gina sank lower in the water, letting the shifting warmth caress her.

Hunter had taken everything in stride, unquestioning, even when she'd completely lost it. And then, in his eyes, she hadn't seen a change, no shuttered backslide into disgust or pity. He saw her, past everything. That uncanny comforting effect of his had somehow withstood, anchoring her.

She flicked the water off one hand, twisting it around to look at the shimmer of the purple design on her nails. It seemed almost silly, weighing as impermanent a decision as nail color, worrying how it would impact others' perceptions of her. Maybe it really was time to go home, to surround herself with people who loved and knew her, no matter how exasperating they could sometimes be.

Hunter knocked on the door, and Gina's hand plopped back into the water as she shot up in the tub. Air chilled her exposed chest, and she settled back against the heated porcelain before calling out, "Come in."

"Hey." He leaned against the doorjamb, barefoot and holding a laminated sheet. "Do you want to take a look, let me know what you'd like for lunch?" A half smile slanted his mouth. "I figure we already know what to get for dessert."

Gina's lips found their own light curve. Shocking, considering how destroyed she'd been less than an hour ago. But that was just the effect Hunter had on her. She nodded, and he moved closer to the tub. When he'd almost reached her, she stood.

Rivulets of bathwater raced over her, teasing her skin as it reacted to the coolness of the air. Hunter froze mid-motion, and she nearly shivered under his gaze, from anything but the change in temperature.

His throat worked to swallow, and then his eyes found her face. "Did you…want a towel?" he asked.

Gina dropped her weight into one hip, lifting her shoulders in answer.

His gaze flicked down to her breasts, and he took the final step toward her, dropping the menu. "Are you sure you want—" He cut himself off, endlessly considerate.

Gina's smile deepened. "The water is getting kind of cold." And she wanted the caress of his warmth rather than the bath's, especially if this was their last time together. A final memory to take to Boston.

Hunter hesitated a second more, before his hands found her waist and his lips met hers. Gina rose into the tender kiss, balancing against his shoulders. His fingers slid in the moisture on her skin, dipping lower down her back and to her ass as his tee shirt drank the droplets on her torso. She flicked her tongue against his lips, sensitized by the bath and seeking more. His muscles clenched a moment before he lifted her from the tub, entirely and wonderfully unconcerned by the water that ran everywhere, and Gina grinned against his lips, wrapping her legs around him.

He swiveled, lips and tongue claiming hers as he walked them to the bed. Deft fingers slid lower, brushing her with torturous softness before pressing over and against and into her. She gasped, writhing against the textures of his clothes as he circled and stroked, deliberately drawing back when she arched into his hand, only to tease her again.

In the wash of sensations, she lowered one hand to his hip, slipping it below his shirt to tug the fabric up. Hunter dipped her to the bed, rubbing against her with the harsher fabric of his jeans as much as with his fingers, before rising out of her arms. He stripped the shirt off, and she lifted to her elbows to watch the rest come off, but he leaned over her instead, bracing on one arm to run his free hand over her ribcage and down, only to veer back up her abs to palm her breast.

Heated, knowing eyes watched her as his fingers found her nipple, momentarily stealing her breath. She dropped back to the bed, freeing her arms to pull him closer, and hooked one leg against the back of his thigh. She rubbed against the solid stretch of his torso, and his lips found hers once more, barely slipping together before he trailed over her jaw to her neck.

Fingers floated at the surface of her skin, touching everywhere he could reach as his tongue painted tantalizing patterns. She moaned when he found the top of her breast and nearly called out when he licked in spirals around her nipple. Hunter chuckled against her, not pausing until she could feel every thread of the bedspread against her back, and each gentle stroke of his fingers, all melding with his lips and teeth and tongue, leaving no part of her unclaimed by his caresses.

She writhed between his onslaught and the bed, and then he lifted to her mouth, sipping her moans and stretching her against the press of him behind his jeans, a last flick of his fingers the final drop drowning her in pleasure.

Hunter twisted to the side, collapsing to the bed. He snaked an arm around Gina's shoulders, pulling her close despite the sweat cooling on their bodies. His lungs strained, sucking in air and the lingering scent of the cucumber body wash as Gina hummed beside him. Her feet tangled with his, one arm across his chest, but otherwise they were still.

"Perfect" was entirely too sappy, but it was the only word that came to mind. He loved everything about being with her, about her. Standing by her as she overcame the desperate interferences of her ex wasn't even a question. Though their situation, the practical obstacles, everything was all still so complicated.

"Are you sure about moving to Boston?" he asked quietly.

"What?"

It might have been stupid, bringing this up right at that moment, but they couldn't keep ignoring the logistics, especially if she was planning to move. "There are some great magazines in California, or Seattle, right?"

She lifted onto an elbow to look at him. "Of course, but work isn't why I would move home."

"I know." He skimmed his knuckles over her arm. "And I know you're not ready for any kind of a commitment." So telling her he loved her wouldn't help his cause.

She sat up, twisting away to find the sheets they'd pushed aside and pull them to her chest.

Hunter sat up too and brought one hand to the base of her neck, brushing lightly below her hair. "I want to see this through, to be with you, regardless of where you end up living right now. But," he added when she glanced at him over her shoulder, "it would be significantly easier if we were at least on the same coast."

When she didn't say anything, Hunter moved closer, coming to sit beside her at the edge of the bed. She glanced down briefly before looking back to him.

"If you're set on moving to Boston, I would still really like to make this work. And hey, we do have modern tech on our side."

That earned a small smile.

It was true, but it wouldn't change much if she built a life thousands of miles away. What would he do then? Giving up his grandparents' winery simply wasn't an option. "All I'm asking is that you consider alternatives a bit closer, see what the possibilities are before making up your mind."

"Why? I mean." She closed her eyes, shaking her head slightly. "Everything Alistair put you through… Don't you think us continuing whatever this is would just unnecessarily complicate your life?"

"Gina." He took one of her hands in his, lacing their fingers together. "*This* is a relationship." Saying it out loud uncoiled a bit of his anxiety. He would find a way to stay with her. "And sweetheart, I'm betting on a future, a lifetime with you."

A breathless, disbelieving chuckle escaped her lips. "That's a high-risk bet right there."

He squeezed her fingers, bringing his other hand to her jaw so she wouldn't look away from the sincerity in his eyes. "Higher reward."

Gina froze for a prolonged moment, processing or panicking, though hopefully not the latter, and stilling the air in his lungs. Then her lips curved, gently rounding her cheeks and narrowing her eyes as she shook her head. "So cheesy," she murmured through the smile.

"Yeah, well." He smiled back, cupping the base of her jaw more solidly. "Get used to it."

She laughed against his hand, and Hunter ducked to kiss her, reveling in the sound.

Epilogue

Roxanna laughed, and Gina exhaled. So far, this seemed to be going well. The feelers she'd put out before her last trip to California had come through with some interesting options, including this interview. Hunter was right—it was good for her to see what was out there before making up her mind.

Her lease hadn't actually been difficult to get out of, especially with Alistair distracted by Hunter's lawsuit. With all her things safely in storage, she was free to explore and figure out what *she* wanted to do next. Much as she would miss her friends, they all seemed content, moving forward with their lives, and she could always visit, especially if she stayed relatively nearby. And staying closer to them also meant being closer to Hunter, who had been extraordinarily supportive as she figured everything out. Waking up next to him definitely hadn't hurt her mood before this interview.

"Well, everything so far sounds good," Roxanna said with a friendly smile. "I do have to ask, however, you left your last position so suddenly, and you haven't listed Vivian as a reference. What happened there?"

Gina sighed, glancing around the airy office and pushing back the edge of darkness that the question seemed to invite, though she had expected it to come up. She made eye contact with Roxanna before answering. "I know you're probably looking for an interview-appropriate vagueness, but all I can offer you is honesty."

Roxanna nodded, her smile dropping to politely detached curiosity.

"Our magazine was recently purchased, by someone with whom I had a very complicated personal history." Gina paused to take a deep breath. "I attempted to maintain a professional distance, but our past caused quite a bit of friction, which also affected others at the magazine, including my relationship with Vivian. To put it bluntly, he used his new position to harass me."

"Harass?" Roxanna exclaimed, leaning back in her chair.

"He made a concentrated effort to re-exert his previous control, over me." Gina exhaled raggedly then pressed her lips together. Alistair's actions didn't define her. "When he found that effort unsuccessful, or insufficient, I'm not sure, he purchased my apartment building."

Roxanna uncrossed her legs and sat up straighter, though her expression was unreadable.

"Long story short, I decided to step away from that situation, from the position he wanted to put me in. And I am just extraordinarily ready for a fresh start."

"That sounds like a tough situation," Roxanna murmured. "And I think it's wonderful that you extricated yourself from that."

Gina whispered a nearly inaudible *thanks* and swallowed in the resulting silence, waiting for the inevitable *but*. The facts spoke for themselves, and they weren't her fault, but who'd want to be put in the line of all that drama?

"That being said," Roxanna said after a while, "your portfolio and everything you achieved with your department speak for themselves, recommendations or no. I have no doubts you would be an asset here, if you're sure you'd like your fresh start to be in San Francisco."

Hunter stood when he saw Gina come into the café. She looked stunning as always, in a fashionable twist on a business suit, with a bright, drapey top underneath. She'd decided to keep the pink tips in her hair for the interview, but then hers wasn't even the most adventurous style in the room right now. She leaned in for a quick kiss before they both lowered to wire chairs.

"How'd it go?" Hunter asked, shutting his laptop.

She sipped the coffee he'd ordered when she'd texted that the interview was over. "Pretty well, actually. Surprisingly so."

"Not surprising to me."

Gina rolled her eyes with a small smile. "She offered me a position. Two, actually, or rather a choice."

"Wow. That's wonderful! Isn't it?" Her moving as close as San Francisco would be fantastic. The hopefully eventual transition to living together wouldn't even pose too many logistical issues.

"Maybe. She said the fashion editor position is mine if I want it, which I thought I did."

"But?" They could figure things out if she decided she wanted to move home after all, he reminded himself.

"But then she offered me a features position." Her nails drummed on the ceramic mug. "Which would mean a little more variety, a little less money at first. But a stronger effect on content, a very different focus."

"Do you have a little time to think about it?"

"At least until Monday. Beauty of a long weekend."

"Speaking of, are you ready to go?"

She hummed around the rim of her coffee mug. Hunter put his laptop away and stood to follow her out.

"Do you want to grab lunch in the city or at the airport?" he asked when they were outside.

Gina groaned with an adorable grimace. "Are you sure you don't want to back out? I won't hold it against you."

Hunter shook his head at her persistence. "Is your family really going to hate me that much?" She was still nervous about it, but nowhere near as much as she had been meeting his family. Plus he was looking forward to spending the Fourth of July weekend with her folks.

"Believe me, that is not what I'm worried about." Gina stopped by his car, and he pulled her gently around to face him.

"You don't need to worry about anything. I promise, I'll be on my best behavior. And I'm looking forward to some good Italian family fun."

She leaned back against the passenger door, crossing her arms. "I should have known, you're only in it for the home-cooked meals."

Hunter smiled, stepping closer. "Not going to lie, it's definitely a perk." He placed his hands on her waist. "Not that I need to be tempted into spending time with you."

Her feigned disbelief couldn't hold back her smile. Hunter ducked his head for a kiss. Her arms uncrossed, hands coming to his sides as their lips slipped languidly together.

"You could take a detour, visit Tucker and Nora," she coaxed after breaking the kiss. "Boston's not even all that great in July."

"Oh and New York is?"

Her shoulders lifted with insincere innocence.

Hunter laughed, unable to help himself. "I love you."

Her grin dropped along with her shoulders, though she seemed more surprised than upset. Hopefully. Hunter almost stepped back, but her hands still over his ribs tethered him in place.

She watched him pensively as the pounding of his heart echoed in his chest.

Then a soft smile reminded him to breathe. "I love you, too."

— Acknowledgments —

To Rachel: thank you for your constant support. At this point, I can't imagine publishing anything at all without getting your thoughts first.

To Kris: thank you for your invaluable feedback, and for making the time amid all the recent craziness.

To my writing group: thanks for listening to my doubts but insisting I ignore them, and for the many other ways you help.

Finally to my family and the friends who always come through: I wouldn't have gotten here without you.

Read on for an excerpt from
Forging Forever, book 1:

Mending Heartstrings

One

Kane walked out of the private back room of Nashville's Fiddle and Steel and headed straight for the bar. Every so often, he'd still try out his new material at their open mic nights. But tonight, the initially warm reception of the regulars had fizzled out as he played. They hadn't really responded to any of his three songs. He needed a beer.

A couple of the regulars greeted him, and Kane paused to exchange pleasantries. The laid-back atmosphere of the bar put everyone at ease, which was the great thing about playing there. The locals who knew him weren't intimidated by his relative fame, and he wasn't a big enough deal yet for the occasional tourist to recognize him. He relied on the reactions of this comfortable community. And they sure didn't mind telling him he had more work to do before his next tour.

When he finally reached the bar, he flagged down Cody, tearing the younger man away from a pretty brunette who was probably underage. He greeted Kane with a subtle lift of his chin.

"How's it going, man?" Kane asked.

"Just got better," Cody answered, looking over Kane's shoulder.

Kane followed his gaze to a group of women who'd just walked in but turned back after barely a moment. He definitely wouldn't mind a distraction. First, though, he really did want that beer. "Get your mind back on your work, boy," Kane scolded with a smile.

Cody's mama hadn't raised an idiot. "You just want them for yourself."

Kane grinned. "It's no competition."

"Only 'cause those three didn't hear you flame out tonight."

"Yeah, well. Some of us can rely on our good looks." Kane kept an easy smile on his face. The ribbing shouldn't have bothered him, but he was having an off night. The songs he'd played could have passed muster most anywhere else, but Nashville knew its country music. "Get me a beer, would ya?" he asked.

"Yeah, yeah." Cody slapped a coaster onto the bar in front of Kane then headed to the fridge to grab Kane's favorite.

Kane rested his forearms on the bar and bent his head down, exhaling. As always, he'd scanned the audience a few times while he played, trying to read the room's reactions. Tonight, too many people had been absorbed in their own conversations around the bar's simple wooden tables. Only one pair of eyes had met his. A striking, unwavering pair of eyes.

She'd been standing toward the back, alone. He'd felt her watching him even when he'd closed his eyes.

But she hadn't been standing there when he'd come back out. Probably just as well.

Cody set down a chilled beer in front of Kane. He tipped it toward the bartender as thanks. A couple drinks, a little bit of flirting, and there'd be no more need to think about his songs tonight.

Turning back toward the room, Kane bumped a girl he hadn't noticed seated next to him at the bar. "Ah! Sorry 'bout that," he said with a half-smile, ramping up the charm.

She twisted toward him. "I'll survive." The corners of her mouth pulled up, but Kane couldn't look away from her eyes. *Hazel*, he realized. Unlike when he'd been on stage, her gaze fell, and she started to turn back to the bar.

"Kane," he offered, shifting his beer to his left hand and offering up his right. *A handshake. Smooth.* This really was an off night.

Her eyes flicked down to his hand then laughingly back to his face. Her eyebrows drew up in a small challenge as she placed her hand in his. "Like the sugar, or the stick?"

"With a K…" He leaned back against the bar, resting on one elbow.

"So, not Abel's brother. Good to know."

Normally he'd have walked away at a line like that, but it wasn't like he'd been offering conversational gold. Maybe this would help him shake it off before he made his move on the trio Cody'd pointed out. And then there were those eyes… "Go ahead and joke. I've probably heard them all."

"Don't tempt me." Her lips curved softly. Mischief glinted in her eyes.

"And how could I do that?" Kane let himself relax, sliding back into the easy feel of the bar. Unlike his performance, this conversation didn't really matter.

"I'm sure you have a few tricks up your sleeves." She picked up the glass of white wine she'd been nursing and took a sip, without dropping her smile or taking her eyes off him.

A local girl would've been drinking beer. But then, a local girl would've known exactly who he was, which could lead to nothing more than a mildly satisfying romp in the sack. He remembered his own beer and took a swig.

"Worried?" he asked, after she set her glass back down.

That got him a bigger smile. "Please, I can take anything you throw at me."

"Maybe we should test that theory." He took another sip of beer. This was getting more and more interesting.

"By all means," she replied, not missing a beat.

He was used to women flattering him, fawning over him. His Southern charm had rarely failed him, and as a singer, he wasn't hurting for female attention, especially since country music wannabes thought he'd be a perfect springboard for their careers. But he hadn't met someone who actually intrigued him in a while. Too long.

He turned to face her, leaving his elbow resting on the bar, and set down his beer. "I didn't catch your name."

"Call me Elle," she answered, tilting her head slightly, a silent question on the change in direction. Her eyelashes didn't flutter with calculated coyness, and her direct gaze didn't falter.

Kane straightened, suddenly inspired. "Pleased to meet you, Elle. Excuse me a sec?" He grabbed the bottle he'd just set down and turned away from her. Another swig and he returned to the back room. This was nothing short of crazy, but he picked up his guitar anyway and walked back to the small stage.

Sabella had barely returned to her wine when she heard the slight strumming of a guitar as someone settled in front of the microphone. She wasn't certain what had prompted Kane to leave so abruptly, but she was definitely disappointed. Not that she was star-struck or anything. The fact that she had dressed up to venture outside her hotel room, to the Fiddle and Steel Guitar Bar, simply because she had heard that Kane Hartridge would possibly be trying out new material at their open mic night, did *not* mean she was star-struck. If anything, she was underwhelmed by his song choices tonight, and even more so by her awkward attempt at flirting. Men like Kane didn't waste their attentions on women like her.

She took another sip of the perfectly nice Riesling and silently deliberated whether she would stay past draining her glass. This bar did have a certain, inexplicably innate, country charm that she wouldn't mind exploring and observing further. After all, she had come to Nashville to learn what she could about the culture of country music.

As far as she could tell, the room around her was furnished with exactly the same style of unadorned, wooden furniture and boasted a similar smattering of booths around the perimeter as any other bar. Nothing about the décor particularly screamed "country." No posters of country stars lined the walls, and if it weren't for the distinct twang emanating from the patrons' conversations and through the speakers, she could have been back home. If she could figure out what exactly made this bar so popular among the locals, the night wouldn't have to be a complete waste. Plus, her flight the next day wasn't until the afternoon, so she could afford to stay out awhile.

"Hey, guys." Kane's voice carried through the speaker system, quieting the room. Someone shut off the recorded music that had been playing ever since he had left the small stage, his performance intended as the finale of their open mic night. Sabella twisted on her barstool to face the stage. Kane and his guitar once again occupied the unadorned chair set behind the single microphone. His beer bottle rested just behind his leg. "Don't mean to pull y'all away, but I have a friend in from out of town who is dyin', she's absolutely dyin', to sing for you. Please join me in welcomin' Elle—over by the bar, there, in the purple, that's Elle—welcomin' her to the Fiddle an' Steel stage."

Most of the patrons shifted their attention toward the bar, trying to find Kane's "friend." Sabella froze, schooling her expression. *I can take anything you throw at me*, she had said. He was clearly testing her claim. What in the world had she been thinking?

"C'mon, Elle," Kane called through the microphone. "Here's your chance." His mouth pulled into a half smile, intended to portray solicitous charm, no doubt, not the baiting nature of his challenge.

She took a deep breath, reminding herself she would likely never see any of these people again, and slid off the barstool. Apparently, her customarily rigid practicality had been dislodged the second he'd bumped into her. Not that he was giving her much choice.

The stage was closer than she would have preferred, but the walk over from the bar still gave Sabella plenty of time to admire Kane's comfortable posture. He wore jeans and a faded, black, button-down shirt, with a few buttons left unfastened and rolled-up sleeves. With his brown hair cut raggedly to slightly above his ears in front, somewhat longer in back, and his stunning green eyes, he really was more handsome than any man had a right to be. Especially one who was trying to embarrass her in front of a bar full of people.

"What exactly do you have in mind?" she murmured as she took the short step onto the stage.

He covered the microphone. "Name a country duet."

At least he wasn't going to force her to sing alone. Still, she wasn't exactly a country music savant. "The only one that comes to mind is 'Picture.'" That wasn't strictly speaking true, but she was betting he would be even less thrilled with her choice if she had named one with Kelly Clarkson.

All Kane said was, "All right." He shifted his chair so it wasn't squarely facing the microphone then started to play an intro. "Not the newest song in the book, but a guilty pleasure for some of y'all, I'm sure," he drawled, smiling at the crowd.

His voice captured her as he sang, its purity reminding her why his was the only country music to which she really listened. As she watched him, Sabella almost forgot he had manipulated her into joining him on stage—for a *duet*. She looked out over their somewhat captive audience, filled with men in worn-out jeans and flannel shirts—even a cowboy hat or two—and some amazingly beautiful women. Maybe this was actually a bizarre dream, and in reality she was sleeping in her hotel room, or even back home in her bed. If only.

When Kane finished the first chorus, he looked up at her in anticipation. Little crinkles appeared around his eyes. He didn't think she would do it.

To be fair, normally she wouldn't have. *This is simply a more active form of research,* she assured herself. Sticky sweat still gathered between her fingers and coated her palms. Sabella surreptitiously wiped her hands on her thighs and stepped marginally closer to the microphone.

She scrambled to remember the lyrics, staring at the floor as she sang. When no one booed by the end of the stanza, she risked a glance out at the room. About half of the tables had reverted to quiet conversation, but others appeared to be listening. At the end of her chorus, she looked over at Kane.

He was watching her, eyebrows drawn slightly together, as if he wasn't altogether sure what he was seeing. Maybe he was shocked she was still singing, despite the blatant difference in their abilities. She had never been one for public displays of foolery, and the remaining shreds of her rationality were appalled by the ridiculousness of her behavior. Running off the stage would be worse, though, or at the very least more memorable.

She finished their interchanging lines with her eyes on him. The last chord he strummed hung in the air until the murmuring of patrons' conversations wiped it away. Sabella backed away from Kane and the microphone, then turned to step off the stage, and wove her way toward the hallway that led to the bar's restrooms and a door with an "Employees Only" sign. She pressed her back to the wall for support and resolutely steadied her breathing. This night wasn't turning out anything like she could have expected.

✧ ✧ ✧

Kane stayed on stage through the applause that started just as Elle left. It was more applause than he'd gotten alone tonight, not that he was surprised. She sang purely, without flourish. She sure wouldn't be making a career of this, but something about her singing had captivated their audience, and him. It was so…earnest. Unassuming. Maybe that's what he had glimpsed in her eyes.

Falling back on his ingrained charm, Kane offered a smile and a "good night" to the audience. He followed Elle's route to the bar's back rooms, taking his guitar with him. Cody might whine later that he'd left the beer for the boy to pick up, but Kane didn't care.

He found her leaning against the wall that faced the ladies' room. "Waiting for a friend?"

Her head jerked toward him. She straightened from the wall and turned to face him. "Did you enjoy the show?" She wasn't smiling now.

A Southern girl would've chewed his hide for that stunt. And if she really hadn't wanted to sing, she would've found a way to bow out, or plain old told him to go to hell.

"You surprised me," he answered honestly. "You have a nice voice." *And gumption.*

"That's somewhat patronizing coming from you, don't you think?"

He smiled. "A fan, are you?" he teased, though she obviously wasn't. But that suited him just fine.

She raised her eyebrows. A second later her shoulders shrugged, and she looked down. He was pretty sure he saw a hint of a smile.

"C'mon," he said then turned toward the private room to put away his guitar. Maybe this night had potential yet.

Mending Heartstrings (Forging Forever, book 1) is available everywhere books are sold.

— About Aria —

Aria Glazki's first kiss technically came from a bear cub. Though no fairytale transformation followed, she still believes magic can happen when the right people come together—if they don't get in their own way, that is. So now Aria writes heartfelt romances about relatable people overcoming real-world obstacles to build love that lasts.

Aria Glazki

Relatable People — Remarkable Love

www.AriaGlazki.com